DESPERATE SITUATIONS

A NOVEL

BY

ABBY HOLDEN

Seventh Wave Books, LLC

Desperate Situations

Seventh Wave Books, LLC
2012

Seventh Wave Books, LLC
www.seventhwavebooks.com

First Paperback Edition: 2012

Desperate Situations: a novel/ by Abby Holden.

ISBN: 978-1938852008 (pbk)

Cover design by Jason Wilcox

Printed in the United States of America

CHAPTER 1

"Drive it until it stops!" Captain Jake McGrew barked at the driver of the Hummer as a wisp of smoke escaped from under the hood. He pressed his hands harder into the wounded, bloody leg of a young soldier writhing in agony. The gushing blood made his hands slippery.

A sharp scream ricocheted around the vehicle as a body fell against McGrew, snapping his attention in that direction. The young man, hardly more than a boy, tore at his chest, blood already soaking his desert camo jacket.

"Casey, check out Escobar. Rios, take the next right onto Halfa Street," McGrew yelled as the Hummer neared a corner. His mind worked furiously to remember the map of Baghdad, Iraq.

Shouts were hurled at the truck in Arabic from the streets. Moans came from the two wounded. Another voice in Arabic added to the confusion; the prisoner shouted insults and racial slurs at McGrew's men.

McGrew glanced up as another soldier, Stubbs, stared with wide, dilated eyes in horror at the two bloody men. "Stubbs… Stubbs!" McGrew raised his voice to grab the shocked soldier's attention. "Gag him." He pointed with his chin to the Iraqi being held by the bleeding man under him. Even in agonizing pain, Reed hadn't let go of his prisoner.

Stubbs recovered quickly and shoved material into the mouth of the Iraqi.

McGrew thought back over the last several minutes, shaking his head at the situation. It had gone to hell in a hurry.

His orders today were to interview an informant and to gather information and evidence. A lower level Iraqi official supposedly had information on an assassination three days ago of one of Saddam Hussein's head men. It was rumor and innuendo, but the General wanted the information squashed. And, he wanted proof that the CIA was once again interfering in a military action.

1

McGrew couldn't have cared less why the Iraqi official was killed or how, but orders were orders.

As McGrew and his squad of six unseasoned soldiers exited the building, they literally stumbled into Omar Ali Jamedin, the Jack of Spades in President Bush's famous deck of cards. A huge prize. Seizing the unexpected opportunity, he captured the Iraqi ex-official. Then the trouble began.

A firefight ensued.

Another cry of pain from Reed, and a contraction of muscles under his hands returned McGrew's thoughts to the immediate situation. He glanced at Casey, the lieutenant and oldest of the squad, who was checking out Escobar, the soldier hit in the chest. "How is he?" McGrew asked as he swung his head around, monitoring the rest of the squad.

Rios, dodging people and cars, drove them successfully away from the firefight. A NASCAR driver couldn't have done a better job. Hamilton, hanging out the window, gun pointed toward the rear, yelled and fired into the crowd of insurgents. Stubbs, taking the initiative, bound the prisoner's hands behind his back after a brief struggle.

Casey ripped open Escobar's shirt. He reported over his shoulder to McGrew. "Shoulder wound. Through shot. There's... There's blood everywhere, Captain." His voice was tight and pitched higher than normal.

"Pack it off. Both sides," McGrew ordered Casey then looked the wounded man in the eyes. "You're okay, Escobar. It's a clean shot."

With shaking hands, Casey fumbled as he pulled bandages from his pack.

"Hamilton!" McGrew shouted to get the excited man's attention. "Med kit."

Hamilton retreated back into the Hummer, searching for medical supplies.

"Oh man!" moaned Escobar. "I got shot! I signed up for the National Guard for extra pay. I ain't supposed to be here. Two weeks ago I was cutting grass and trimming shrubs. Shit! Oh God, it hurts!"

"Rios, slow down," McGrew ordered as the eighteen year old drove wildly down the empty street. "We got away from the fire fight, don't kill us now," he said, trying to relieve tension.

Hamilton put the med kit next to McGrew.

"Put the bandages right where my hands are. Pack'em in," McGrew instructed Hamilton. "Grab the tourniquet." McGrew swung his attention back to Stubbs and the prisoner. "Secured?"

"Yeah."

"Help Rios navigate. Head south."

As soon as Hamilton staunched the flow of blood, McGrew released the leg, wiped his bloody hands on his pants and keyed the microphone on his shoulder. "Momma Duck, this is Ugly Duckling, come in." He immediately grabbed the tourniquet from Hamilton and wrapped it around Reed's upper thigh.

"Go Ugly."

"We took fire. Two men down."

The engine sputtered and more black smoke curled out of the engine compartment.

"Transport is breaking down. Send rescue. We have the Jack of Spades in custody. Do you copy?" He secured the tourniquet, then glanced at his watch.

"Ugly, repeat that. You have the *Jack of Spades*?"

McGrew ripped open Reed's shirt, and with a fingertip dipped in Reed's blood, wrote the time on Reed's chest. He knew medical personnel needed to know when the tourniquet was applied. Jake once more grabbed the microphone. "Affirmative, Momma. Jack of Spades in custody." McGrew checked the leg to see that the blood flow had slowed.

"Good. Where you at, Ugly?"

"Stubbs, I need a GPS reading," McGrew ordered as he rechecked the tourniquet again.

Stubbs grabbed his microphone and relayed coordinates as the engine sputtered again. This time the truck died with a bellow of black smoke.

McGrew cursed softly under his breath as he panned the now deserted streets. "Momma, we're on foot. Out." He turned to his men. "Get out. Head south. Stay close to the buildings," he ordered, lifting Reed into an upright position. McGrew looked up at the stunned men. "Move it!"

Hamilton grabbed Reed's other arm as they wiggled him out of the vehicle. Casey helped Escobar, who was now moving under his own power.

"Stubbs, prisoner. He gives you any problems, shoot him. If we get in another firefight, shoot him first," McGrew ordered. "Rios, rear." With one of Reed's arms over his shoulder, he led the way down the street and turned the corner. "You're doing good, Reed," McGrew said to the moaning man.

Reed hopped along between McGrew and Hamilton as best he could with one good leg.

Stubbs hurried up next to the Captain, pulling the reluctant prisoner with him. "This looks like an abandoned part of hell," he said as they worked their way down a bombed and deserted part of Baghdad.

Shelled, half standing buildings were crumbling. People scurried into hiding. The acrid smell of smoke hung in the air. It mingled with the sickening sweet odor of decaying bodies, not yet collected, that lay in grotesque positions in the street. The buzzing of flies was louder than the background din of the city.

"We just cleared this section," McGrew said, glancing behind him to keep track of his men. "Our guys should still be in the area."

"Captain," Casey called out as he grabbed Escobar to stop his stumble.

They had jogged almost three quarters of a mile from the disabled Hummer. McGrew took stock of his men, especially the wounded. They couldn't go any farther. He swiveled his head around checking the area. They just happened to be standing near one of the few intact buildings. "Hamilton, Rios, secure that building." He moved toward it, taking all of Reed's weight as the other two men cleared the bottom floor.

McGrew entered the building and laid Reed against the wall. "Casey. Stubbs." He pointed at the windows. Each nodded and took a secure position watching for the enemy. McGrew helped Escobar to the floor next to Reed and patted Escobar on his good shoulder. He headed to check out the rest of the bottom floor.

"Ugly, this is Momma," came from the speaker at his shoulder.

"Go Momma."

"Rescue is scrambled. Estimated time enroute—ten minutes. Big Duck wants secondary confirmation. You have the *Jack of Spades* in custody?"

"Affirmative. Expedite that rescue, Momma. Out," McGrew said as he ran toward the steps.

"Captain!" Casey called out in a stage whisper.

McGrew stopped and turned to see Casey pointing out the window and down the street.

"Searching," Casey said softly, yet loud enough for the Captain to hear.

"Shit," McGrew said softly as Rios ran back into the room.

"All floors secured," Rios said.

"Good. Grab Reed and Escobar. Roof. Move," McGrew ordered, waiting until everyone was moving to the second floor before he set a small trip wire with grenade at the bottom of the stairs and another at the first landing. As he climbed the stairs, he keyed the microphone. "Momma, come in."

"Go, Ugly."

"Situation deteriorating. We're holed up in a building…" He quickly relayed GPS coordinates to command as he climbed the stairs. "We need… help now."

"Affirmative, Ugly. Big Duck has instructed you to 'cook' the Jack of Spades if you get beyond us. Do you understand?"

"Affirmative. Orders already in place. Ugly out."

***

"Listen to this," the co-pilot said. After their mission, it was habit to scan several channels including military ones.

"Sounds bad," the pilot said, glancing at the GPS radio. "We're closer than any military units."

The co-pilot nodded as he punched in Ugly's coordinates. The computer immediately showed their position and the new coordinates. "Fuel, Darlin'." His voice drawled in a southern accent as he pointed at the gage.

"We've got enough. Ugly sounds desperate."

"Yeah, but what 'bout Truman? He said he wanted us back, like yesterday."

An evil grin broke the serious curve of the pilot's eyes. "Yeah, I know. Another point in favor of doing this rescue. Heading?"

"Fly heading zero five, zero degrees," the co-pilot instructed, a conspiratorial smile formed on his face.

The pilot banked the helicopter and headed toward the new destination. "Gunner," the pilot ordered via the intercom. "Get a door gun ready. We're going in."

***

McGrew exited the stairs to find his men gathered near one of the roof vents. They were helping the two wounded down to the floor as he hurried over to them.

"We sit tight, men. Rescue's on the way. Positions." He pointed at the four walls of the square building. "No talking. Do not fire."

Rios rubbed his hands together nervously. Stubbs' eyes were wide and dilated again. Hamilton wiped his nose several times. Casey tended Reed's bleeding leg with shaking hands. Escobar closed his eyes to the pain in his shoulder.

McGrew smiled at the guys to reassure them. "We can do this. We only have to hold them for a short time. Ammo?"

Each soldier checked his supply which was diminished during the firefight. "I only got half a clip left!" Hamilton looked around with wide eyes.

Escobar grunted in pain as he retrieved a clip off his belt. "Here."

McGrew sighed. Green troops. He was stuck with unseasoned troops. Being the only person with Special Forces training and the most time in country, his gut twisted with worry at how they would hold up. Taking a deep breath to fight off his own adrenalin, he shook his head then thanked Escobar. "Auto off. One shot. One kill. Conserve your ammo. Fire on my command. Any questions?" When he saw that there were none, he motioned for the men to move into positions.

Omar Ali Jamedin grinned at him around his gag as he lay on the ground where Stubbs had thrown him.

McGrew grabbed him by the collar and dragged him over by the wounded men. He pulled the prisoner to his face and growled in Arabic, "If you make one sound, I swear to God, I'll send you to those virgins right now and with equipment missing." He jammed his muzzle into Jamedin's crotch.

Omar's eyes widened in fear momentarily as he jerked at the pressure, then resumed his arrogant attitude.

McGrew tossed him back to the rooftop. "Don't move," he ordered in Arabic. He squatted down next to the two wounded men. "Escobar."

The young Hispanic opened his eyes.

"You need to guard the prisoner." McGrew took Escobar's rifle and put a fresh clip in it. "Understand?"

"Yeah. No problem, sir." Escobar took the rifle back and glared at the prisoner. "He ain't goin' nowhere without some new holes."

McGrew patted him on his good shoulder with a nod, then turned his attention to the man sitting next to him. "Reed."

Reed focused on McGrew. The pain was excruciating, and it showed in his blue eyes. "Yeah?" The Captain checked out Reed's rifle and placed it in his hands. The implied message was that everyone needed to defend the position. "Yeah." Reed's shaky hands gripped the rifle. "I got it."

An explosion rocked the lower part of the building. McGrew keyed the microphone again as he stood. "Momma, this is Ugly. Insurgents in the building."

"Copy. Rescue moving into position. ETE five minutes."

"Five minutes," McGrew muttered as he moved to the rooftop door and secured it as best he could. He could hear shouts from the lower floors. He knew they didn't have five minutes as another small explosion rocked the building.

"Hey Ugly, ya'all see a McDonald's 'round here?" came a drawling, southern voice from the radio.

Smiles lit the soldier's faces, as the Captain grabbed the radio. "Ronald McDonald," McGrew answered back, going with the McDonald's theme since he had no idea who this was, but at least he sounded American, "this is Ugly Duckling. We need a drive through, right now."

"Affirmative, Ugly Duckling. We'll be dropping in on you like a bomb, so leave a spot open for us."

The Captain looked straight up but still didn't hear the sound of aircraft. "We've got several dissatisfied customers here, Ronald."

"Here we come, Ugly. Ya'all had better be like starvin' hogs to a slop bucket, 'cause them boys there is good shots."

McGrew motioned to Stubbs, then to the prisoner, while the others hurried to help the wounded.

By this time, the distinctive whirling sound of a helicopter could be heard. As predicted, it was coming straight down on top of them. Fast. McGrew watched as the men scrambled toward the Black Hawk. His attention returned to the roof exit.

Shouts in Arabic sounded from the streets. Bullets ricocheted and slammed into the sides of the building from below.

The door to the roof flexed inward as the insurgents tried desperately to get onto the roof. McGrew's eyes flicked to the helicopter hovering only two feet off the rooftop. The last of his men climbed on board.

The door burst open.

McGrew's barrage of automatic fire aimed at the door kept the insurgents off the rooftop long enough for him to make it to the chopper. He dove into the open door to be scooped up as the helicopter accelerated.

A crewmember of the Black Hawk swept the roof with fifty caliber bullets from the mounted door gun.

"Hold onto your nut sacks," came a yell from the cockpit.

The helicopter jerked to the side. It flew up, then jerked the other way as it continued to ascend.

The Captain's gut dumped into his boots from the helicopter's rapid movements. One bullet hit the fuselage but did no damage. Within seconds, they were out of range.

Rios and Hamilton helped McGrew to a seated position.

McGrew glanced at his watch. "Casey, loosen Reed's tourniquet half a twist or he'll lose the leg," he said as he checked Escobar's bandages. McGrew could see relief on all faces but one, their prisoner.

"Yee-haw!" came from the cockpit as the crew chief in back slammed the door on the helicopter. He smiled broadly at the soldiers as he resumed his seat.

McGrew held out his hand to the crew chief, yelling above the noise of the engines, "Out of curiosity, who just saved our butts?"

The brown-skinned man smiled broader, his jet-black hair shining in the sunlight from under his flight helmet. "We Famine." They shook hands.

"Come again?" McGrew yelled back.

"We be going by on delivery, coming back. Heard call for pick-up. We goodly at rescue." His big, toothy grin stayed in place as he plugged his helmet back in then pointed at the Captain to grab the handset in the ceiling above him.

With a puzzled look, McGrew did as instructed. *Who are these guys? They obviously aren't U.S. Military. This guy sounds Hispanic.* Then it hit him. *Mercenaries.*

"Hallo there. Ya on, Ugly?" the southern voice called out over the intercom.

"Yes. Who should I thank for saving our asses today?"

A laugh sounded over the handset. "Ya'll welcome. We work for White Pine Aviation and Security. We were headin' home when we heard your radio call to the base. Sorry for butting in, but ya sounded desperate."

"Desperate doesn't describe it. What's your name?"

"I'm Cowboy." A chuckled followed. "The pilot is the Ghost. The guy back there with you is Gunner." McGrew nodded thanks at Gunner who was listening.

"Where can we drop you boys?"

"We're out of Sierra Echo One Base. It's also the closest."

"Uh, can't do that, pardner. See, we gettin' low on fuel and that little maneuver took most of our reserve. Best we can do is meet up with your folks somewhere in the middle. Think you can arrange that?"

"Can you hook me into the right channel?"

"Shore can. Give me a minute." The radio went dead.

Suddenly a slight squawk came from the handset. McGrew could hear communications from various units moving into position for their rescue. A huge smile lit his face. "Momma Duck, this is Ugly Duckling."

"Where the hell are you, Ugly? What the hell is going on?" "Some White Pine Aviation guys flying by picked us up, but they're low on fuel and can't deposit us back in the home nest. Where is rescue support so they can drop us to them? Can you comply?"

"Affirmative, Ugly. Air support is approaching that part of the city."

"Hey Momma, this is Famine of White Pine," Cowboy interrupted, "I see another beater rapidly approaching. Hey, Tinman, that you?"

"Famine," Tinman replied from the military Black Hawk over the radio. "Are you the one needing to drop your load?"

"That's us, man. We smoking our last fumes here."

"Tinman to Momma. Permission to retrieve personnel?"

"It's in your hands, Tinman. Momma out."

"Follow us, Famine. We need to get to a more secure area."

"Lead the way, cowpoke," Cowboy intoned and began singing 'Rawhide.'

McGrew started chuckling as he relaxed still holding the handset, listening to the pilots communicate. His eyes swept over his men again, even Reed looked like he was going to make it now.

Escobar returned McGrew's smile.

It was only two minutes and the helicopter began to descend to a deserted area outside town.

"Hey Tinman, we need to be landing soon if we're making it back to home base. This looks like a good place," Cowboy called to the Black Hawk they were following.

McGrew could hear laughing from the military pilot.

"We'll be right back, Famine. We'll check out the area." The other helicopter quickly circled, then came back to where Famine landed. The camouflaged military helicopter settled close.

As the blades on the military Black Hawk began to slow, the Captain motioned for the squad to exit with the prisoner. A crewman from the Army helicopter was already moving toward them.

The pilot from each Black Hawk exited with smiles and greeted each other as the Captain approached.

With a huge grin, McGrew loosened his helmet and reached out to the tall pilot from Famine. "Thanks for your timely rescue, Cowboy. I'm Captain Jake McGrew."

8

"Shore thing. Can't let the ol' Red, White, and Blue boys down." Cowboy shook hands as he glanced at his aircraft. The others looked too.

"That was a hell of a rescue," McGrew commended as he watched the two other crewmen from Famine. Stubbs hustled the prisoner to the military Black Hawk, while Rios and Hamilton worked on getting Reed out. Casey grabbed Reed's rifle then waited to help Escobar.

"Taint me, Captain," Cowboy said with a huge grin. His head bobbed to his aircraft. "The Ghost was flying this hunk o' junk."

Captain McGrew studied the pilot in full gear, including helmet and scarf, who was helping his men out. "The Ghost?"

Tinman started laughing. "Best pilot in this sand box, Captain. Now you see the Ghost, now you don't. The insurgents hate the Ghost."

McGrew smiled with Tinman, once again the Ghost had thwarted the insurgents. His eyes swung back to the White Pine pilot. "Kind of small for a pilot," he said, almost under his breath. Something about the shape of the pilot's body intrigued him. *The pilot couldn't be over five-six.* McGrew watched the pilot of Famine walk up.

Tinman smiled even bigger catching the intense look in McGrew's eye. "Yeah, but the Ghost is still the best, Captain."

McGrew's attention riveted on the pilot standing in front of him. The White Pine pilot was short, small framed and the walk was a little odd. The flight helmet and camouflage scarf, presumably to keep out sand and other things, hid the entire face. He caught big, brown eyes staring at him.

The look in the pilot's eyes made him uncomfortable. He had only seen that kind of intense stare in bars. And there was an electrical feeling in those eyes; he could feel it in his bones. He cleared his throat after a long second of mutual intensity and stuck out his hand. "On behalf of my men and myself, thanks for the timely rescue, Ghost."

The Ghost's eyes flicked to Cowboy then a smile cracked the brown eyes. The pilot shook his hand while the other hand pulled off the camouflage material. In a swift motion, off came the helmet. "Any time, Captain." Short, brown hair framed the smiling face.

McGrew's eyes widened and his mouth dropped open. Then he narrowed his eyes as he saw the smile get bigger on Ghost's face. "A woman!"

"God, I love getting that kind of reaction out of you military guys," Ghost replied as the other two pilots cracked up.

"How the hell can White Pine put a woman in this sort of environment?" McGrew asked, his hand swinging to the surrounding area, knowing that mercenary units were usually the 'fire first, ask questions later' type.

"Didn't matter what sex I was ten minutes ago, did it GI?" The Ghost's eyes turned hard.

"Do you know what will happen to you if you get caught, Miss Smarty Pants?"

"Of course. Dry it up, Cupcake," she said. "You men are all alike." She quickly put back on her helmet and cover scarf. "Don't tell too many people that a woman saved your ass. Bad for morale." She turned to Tinman. "Thanks for the pickup. Call sometime if you feel like losing at poker again."

Tinman laughed and shook her hand. "Never. I learned my lesson." He shook Cowboy's hand and waved at Gunner who was already climbing into the Black Hawk.

Ghost jogged back to the right side of the helicopter. Within seconds, the blades began spinning faster.

Cowboy pounded Captain McGrew on the back. "Keep makin' the home front proud." With a nod at Tinman, he hurried to the cockpit and climbed in. As it lifted off, he gave a half salute to the two men.

McGrew shaded his eyes from the dust kicked up by the wind vortices then turned to Tinman. "Nose art on a helicopter?"

The warrant officer gave a belly laugh. "Only her four has them, sir."

"The Four Horsemen of the Apocalypse?"

Tinman nodded and pointed to the quickly disappearing aircraft. "That was Famine. A black horse and rider holding the scales. Her Pave Hawk has a pale horse and rider—"

"For Death?"

"Yes, sir. The Chinook that she uses has a red horse. Pestilence. And the executive one that ferries around big shots in White Pine has a small white horse with crown and a bow. War," Tinman said as they hurried to the military Black Hawk.

McGrew stopped and glanced back in the direction of the dot on the horizon.

Tinman stopped too and glanced with him.

"Is she really that good?"

"Best here in Iraq. Don't let her sex fool you. She's tougher than nails, sir." Tinman shook his head. "I wish I had half her talent."

"Why is she working for White Pine?"

"Rumor has it that she makes more in a month here than most of us in a year. Not to mention that she was military, but they wouldn't let her fly combat. Pissed her off. But that's only rumor. Personally, I think she gets off flying over here." Tinman shrugged at McGrew. "Just my thinking, sir."

McGrew nodded. "Attitude. She has attitude."

Tinman smiled at McGrew who was still looking behind them. "Yeah. That she does. And just so you know, she's also known as the Iceberg. Like ice under any pressure and..." He winked at McGrew. "No one can get her to warm up." Tinman climbed into the cockpit and watched as the Captain finally swung himself into the back.

McGrew stared off into space as the helicopter went airborne. "I like attitude."

***

"You're awfully quiet Megan."

"Why do all of those assholes have to be the same?" Megan asked as she flew back to White Pine compound. She sighed softly.

"I saw that look, Sweetheart. Did I see right? Was that a look of interest in those pretty brown eyes for a certain GI?"

"Me?"

"Yes you."

"Not me."

"Ah uh." Cowboy chuckled. "I ain't ever seen you this 'interested' before. Do I see a crack in the ol' Iceberg?"

"You know I hate that name."

Cowboy's chuckle increased almost to a laugh. "Yeah, I know. Hell must be freezin' over, Meg."

A snort was her answer.

Cowboy just laughed. "Megan, Megan, Megan. It's only natural. Hormones is hormones, girl. Chemistry happens. Love at first sight kinda…"

Megan gave another snort.

"See Megan, the boy bee…"

"Kelly, I don't need a biology lesson."

"Look, Meg, from the heart, how often do ya'all get an interest? Huh? He can't be hard to find, after all we did it once."

"Yeah right, like that'll happen. Anyway, I bet he doesn't tell too many that we saved his ass. A woman, and us being mercs. Those military guys are all alike. Hell, you *men* are all alike."

"Whoa, Girl. Don't be including Gunner and me with the rest of the male population. We're confirmed lovers of you Ghost. Ain't nobody I'd rather fly with or have at my back."

"He right, Ghost. You do goodly. Bestest in my book. *Tu eres mucho bueno*," a voice sounded in her ear over the intercom.

Megan chuckled. "Thanks, Gunner. I like you too. Okay, so I have the best of the hanging organ crowd with me."

"Meg…" Cowboy pointed at the flashing light that indicated they were running out of fuel.

"Yeah, I know." She smiled. "We should be running out of fuel… about… now…" Megan had barely gotten the words out and the engine died—then the second engine. "Here we go."

The helicopter began to auto-rotate to the ground, allowing the blades to rotate freely using only the airflow over them to slow their decent. She sited her landing place just inside the fenced compound of White Pine. Within

11

seconds she flared the blades, and Famine landed with a slightly harder than normal smack.

Megan let out a breath of relief and saw that Cowboy had the same expression. She keyed the microphone. "White Pine Tower, this is Famine."

"Famine, we have a crew already headed to tow you. The Head wants to know what you were thinking doing that rescue?"

A smirk crossed her face as she keyed the microphone. "Tell the Head, I was cooperating with the international coalition to bring about a faster end to this occupation by saving personnel vital to the effort. Also tell him, if he has a problem with my actions, he can masticate my gluteus maximus." She glanced at Cowboy as the smirk widened, then turned into a full-blown, mischievous smile. Her group was getting ready to rotate out of Iraq anyway, and she was getting real tired of Truman, the egotistical, arrogant, male chauvinist head of the White Pine base in this part of Iraq.

"There's that look that makes me want to crap my pants, Girl. Yee-haw!"

***

McGrew tossed his shower pack on the bed and sat down hard. He was tired, hot, and grimy even though he had just returned from the showers after debriefing. Running a hand over his still wet, brown hair, he looked up as a knock sounded on his door—his lieutenant. "Yeah?"

"You look beat, Jake."

"Yeah."

"I heard it was touch and go out there."

Jake nodded. "Definitely an ass-puckering mission."

A smile broke out on Ted's face as he leaned on the doorpost. "I also heard you got the Jack of Spades."

McGrew smiled. "Yep."

"Great way to end a career, man."

"It does top off a great run." He let out his breath. "There for awhile, I didn't think I'd make these last four days."

"How long do you have until you're stateside?"

"One more day. Then it's hello soft, warm bed—"

"Hello soft, warm woman?"

McGrew laughed. "Maybe. If I can find one." Both men laughed. Jake sobered up, looking at his Second Lieutenant. "I've never run into mercs before. Does White Pine use them a lot?"

"I don't know, but I know they deliver a lot of supplies."

"Yeah, I heard that too." McGrew grabbed his shower pack and tossed it onto his duffle on the floor. "Don't they also provide security for some of the higher ups in the interim government?"

"So I've heard. Why you asking?"

McGrew didn't answer for a long second. "Those mercs saved our asses."

"Ouch."

Jake chuckled. "You don't know the half of it."

Ted smiled again shaking his head. "Just think, in twenty-four hours you'll be stateside drinking whiskey, smoking a cee-gar, and making love to some lovely little thing." His hands made the curves of a female body. "Toast'em then and be happy that you're out of this hell hole."

Jake smiled as he rolled into bed. "Right now, I'm going to get some shut eye. Don't call me unless the building's on fire."

Ted chuckled as he closed McGrew's door behind him.

Jake got comfortable but couldn't fall asleep. His mind kept wandering back to the big brown eyes staring at him from under that helmet.

CHAPTER 2

Jake McGrew shook his head before entering the White Pine offices. *How in the hell did I let myself get talked into this?* He adjusted his tie again. It felt strange to be dressed as a civilian. He glanced down at his white shirt and gray pants. He had just spent over two years in Iraq, there even before the war began, and here he was being interviewed for a job with White Pine.

If the pay was as good as the headhunter, Mr. Bower, had informed him, he might consider it. And within a couple of months he could retire with more money than he dreamed. Being ex-Special Forces carried a lot of weight with independent contractor companies. Specialized soldiers were in high demand since they were trained to be the best. He would get top pay.

With a smile, he pushed open the door. Still, he had sworn to never return to the 'big sand box' across the water. However, this could be the opportunity of a lifetime. And there was something else, something pushing him to do this, something he didn't want to acknowledge. He shook his head to rid himself of such thoughts as he walked into the cooler interior.

"Ah, good afternoon, Mr. McGrew. Mr. Zingerton is waiting. Can I get you a drink or anything?" a lovely blond receptionist behind the counter asked. Talking on the phone next to her was another stunning blond.

"Uh, no. Thank you. I'm fine," Jake said, barely stopping his eyes from tracing up and down the women. Both were model material, with large breasts, thin waists, and legs that didn't stop. *Damn. Were all the women in this company beautiful?*

A huge smile flashed his way. "Very well then. Please follow me."

Jake followed, his eyes feasting on the softly swaying hips contained in the dark blue dress in front of him. He barely acknowledged the greeting of the two men that passed him in the hall.

She turned when they reached the end of the hall, and opening the door, smiled. "Mr. Zingerton, Mr. McGrew to see you."

"Thanks, Dorothy."

Jake stepped into the room, his eyes swung to the man standing up from behind a desk. The door closed quietly behind him. Jake cleared his throat silently and walked toward the man.

Zingerton smiled and extended his hand. "Hello, Mr. McGrew. Bower has already sent us your qualifications." The two men shook hands. "Please get comfortable." He swung his hand to indicate the leather, high back chairs in front of the big mahogany desk. After they got settled, he leaned back. "So, you're only two weeks out of Iraq?"

"Yes."

"How long was your tour?"

"Twenty-five months, twelve days."

Zingerton nodded. He picked up several sheets of paper. "Your jacket shows that you participated in a lot of important missions."

Jake didn't let the surprise show. Those were confidential records for military eyes only. "My jacket?"

Zingerton laughed. "We have access to a lot of, uh, 'things' that others don't. I've also checked your security clearance. Highest possible level." He looked the former Special Forces Ranger in the eyes. "Let's cut through the usual bullshit and talk money. We want you. How much will it take to have you work for us?"

Jake smiled at Zingerton's enthusiasm, knowing that he had a lot of bargaining power. "First of all, what sort of missions would my job entail?"

"Well, we deliver supplies to areas of contention. We pick up and deliver…"

"I thought we were cutting through the shit."

Zingleton chuckled. "Yes. We work in primarily four locations: Iraq, Afghanistan, Somalia and Saudi Arabia. We have a few minor bases in other places, but if you join us, you'll be sent to either Afghan or Iraq."

"And what do 'we' do?"

"We deliver supplies." Zingleton held up his hand to stop Jake's protest. "That however is sometimes used as a front to supply other things. We run security for many people in both areas. We do recon for, well, intelligence people, military and such. We provide support and protection for other divisions in our company."

"I heard that this company is also a front used by the CIA."

Zingerton shook his head. "We're an independent contractor. However, I'll not blow shit up your pants, McGrew, we do sometimes 'help' them. Joint operations with them and the military are not unusual."

Jake narrowed his eyes. *Dangerous work. But for the money needed to buy me off, it would have to be.* "My job?"

"Well, at first you'll be assigned to a regular crew, until you get your feet wet. Then we'll want you in charge. We like former military members in command, that way we know what sort of work to expect. So at first, you'll be under another crew chief." Zingerton leaned forward with a smile. "I see I have your attention. So, how much to get you?"

***

McGrew stepped into another White Pine office—this one in Germany. He was assigned to Afghanistan and was meeting his crew chief and team as they were also being transferred.

From Zingerton he had learned that this crew was considered the best in the company. They had the best record of successful missions and were 'self-contained' but had just lost a member and he was that person's replacement. This might make it hard to fit in.

"I'm looking for Cartwright's crew. I'm Jake McGrew," he said to the office manager on second floor.

This older, gray haired lady gave him a critical eye before answering. "Room four." She pointed down the hall. "Have you heard about the loss of one...?"

"Thanks. Yes, I have. Have they been together long?"

"Many months and in this line of work, that is something." She paused checking out a computer screen. "Are you fully equipped, Mr. McGrew?"

"Yes, Ma'am. When do we leave?"

"They were waiting for the replacement."

"Good. I hate hurry up and waits."

The lady finally smiled and pointed down the hall.

With a thanks nod, Jake walked in the direction indicated, stopping briefly at the door. He took a deep breath and opened it.

The room went silent at his entrance.

McGrew quickly looked the room over, typical conference room, beige table and chairs. Table littered with papers. Seven people total. Closest to him were three black men and two lighter-tanned men. His eyes narrowed at seeing Cowboy smiling at him. Then he slid his eyes to the head of the table, not surprised to see the same big, brown eyes staring at him, amused.

"Hello."

McGrew grimaced slightly. "Yeah. I'm to report to Cartwright." His eyes panned to Cowboy to see him chuckling silently. The entire room snickered. "Let me guess..." He looked back at the Ghost. "You're Cartwright."

"That's right." Megan smiled. "Can you handle it?"

"I don't have a problem taking orders from women."

"We'll see," Megan said with a hand wave to the chair at the end of the table. "Have a seat. I'll introduce you to the crew that you'll be working with. You've already met Cowboy and Gunner. Cowboy's real name is Kelly Beaton. We're the main pilots. Gunner's name is Alvaro Iniguez. He's obviously the gunner on any mission requiring extra support." Megan nodded toward the other lighter-tanned man. "Next to Gunner is Geraldo Varela, from Chili like Gunner. Fisher is usually in charge of anything computer related. These other three guys are from South Africa, Amadi Baragwanath or Tiny, Kofi Massyn or Bosser, and Sefu Yzelle or Chips. They do almost everything. We'll pick up the other two pilots when we get in country." She paused. "My name's Megan Cartwright. We get real close, real fast, especially in Afghan and Iraq. Sometimes all we have are ourselves. At the base, we use our names. In the field, we only use our designations. For safety."

McGrew nodded understanding.

"We have no ID on us for most missions. If you go missing, you can't be tracked to the company. And on some missions, they won't even verify that you work for them." She gave McGrew a hard look. "You did understand that from your contract, right?"

Jake's eyes hardened. "Of course."

"Good." Megan gave him a big smile. "Your designation for the time being…"

"Let me guess," McGrew interrupted with a disgusted look. "It's Cupcake."

The entire room burst out laughing. Megan just smiled at him. "Don't worry. When I give the bosses the thumbs up that you're trained and ready to go, you can pick your own designation."

"Beautiful," Jake said under his breath. His future, and more importantly, the pay increase commensurate with leading a crew, depended on this hard-nosed, extremely attractive female. And yet, somehow, he wasn't at all disappointed.

The biggest of the South Africans was still chuckling. "Don't worry Cupcake, my designation is Tiny. You'll get used to it."

McGrew smiled at him then turned back to Cartwright. "When do we leave?"

Megan glanced at her watch. "Right now. Is your gear here?"

"Downstairs, Chief." The name came automatically to him, since pilots of most military helos were Warrant Officers referred to always as 'Chief.'

"Chief. I like that." Megan gave Jake a bright smile. "Everyone is confined to base for a week, or until you get the obligatory lecture from the head of the base, Fahim Masood, and you learn some of the customs of the country." Megan stood. "Let's load up."

***

Two hours later, they were quickly approaching Afghanistan. The three South Africans and two South Americans were playing cards.

Jake stretched and glanced around. Cowboy was talking with the pilots and it looked like the five others were arguing over the game. Turning his head toward the back of the plane, he saw Megan sitting by herself, staring at her feet, deep in thought.

His eyes narrowed watching her. If she was as talented as he heard, this might not be too bad. He saw her swipe her nose. With a puzzled look and quick glance at the others, he stood and made his way back to the vacant seat next to her.

"Mind if I sit?"

She waved a hand to do so.

"Look, we sort of got off on the wrong foot in Iraq."

Megan's head came up.

Jake offered his hand. "Truce?"

"Sure." She shook then went back to studying her shoes.

"That's one hell of a thoughtful look."

"I'm busy. If you don't mind, I need to think. Was there anything specific you wanted?" She didn't even look at him.

"Nope. Just wanted to start fresh."

Her head rose at that, meeting his blue, searching eyes. "Don't screw up and we'll get along fine."

"I'll do my best, Chief." He smiled at her then moved off to see Cowboy watching them from the aisle near the card game. As he got alongside the other pilot, he made a motion with his head back to Megan. "Is she okay, Cowboy?"

"Yeah." Cowboy's eyes drifted back to the lady, who was once more contemplating her footwear. "Just a lot on her mind."

"She said that. Is she worried about me being in the squad?"

Cowboy gave him a big smile. "No. She'll enjoy dressing you down, 'iffan you don't live up to her standards, but don't worry 'bout that. Course, she is gonna be harder on you."

"Because I was Special Forces?"

"Nope. 'Cause you gonna be leading your own crew. She's trained four crew leaders since I've known her. She takes her responsibility in that respect real serious."

Jake turned his attention back to the lady.

"Right now she's probably still goin' over our last mission. She hates to lose a member of the crew."

"Was it bad?"

Cowboy shrugged. "Don't worry 'bout Meg, Jake. She's tough. As soon as we hit Affie, she'll be back to being social, and being a pain in your ass." He smiled at the ex-military man.

Jake chuckled and nodded at Tiny who was inviting him to join the card game. He gave one last look at Megan then sat with the group of guys.

***

Cowboy's smile faded as Jake sat down—his eyes still staring at Megan. Then he took a breath and headed straight for her. "Hey, Meg."

"Kelly."

Cowboy sat without asking. "Cheer up, Darlin'. The flight lasts just another forty minutes."

Megan snorted.

"I know you hate to be anywhere but in the driver's seat."

"Give it up, Kelly. What the hell do you want?"

"What a lovely disposition you're in. No wonder Jake thought you were on the rag."

"I'm just thinking. You know I hate to be interrupted when I'm working."

"Is that a hint, Girl?"

"Yeah, but like you'd ever take it." Megan finally looked at him with a smile.

Cowboy smiled back then it faded. "Look Meg, there was nothin' you could do. We talked 'bout this."

"I know." She sighed. "I just hope Truman can get his body back. I wanted to at least retrieve it. Damn, they swarmed all over us."

He patted her leg. "It's only because of your flying skills that all the rest of us made it out alive. That's seven for one, Girl."

Megan snorted again.

Cowboy chuckled. "Just think 'bout how you get to rag on Cupcake."

Megan chuckled too. "Did you see his file?"

"Nope."

"He's good. Damn good." She looked up at the group to see the five guys teaching Jake the card game. "He won't require much training, mostly just getting used to the way we do things."

"Bet that don't stop ya from giving him shit though."

"Ya got that right."

He winked at her with a knowing grin as he stood.

Megan made a funny face. "You know that's not going to happen. As a member of my crew, he's off limits."

"Right."

"Shut up."

"Right," Cowboy said as he walked away with a huge grin on his face.

Megan shook her head as her eyes followed him down the aisle then drifted to the group playing cards. *Why did Jake McGrew have to be so good-looking, so good at his job? And in my crew?* He had a great personality too, evident by the fact that he was already being accepted into the group after such a short time.

She studied him as he asked several questions about the South African card game. Maybe she had pegged him wrong in Iraq. It was just a normal reaction toward a Special Forces Ranger. Or maybe he was just playing nice to get his own crew and extra pay.

Jake laughed at that moment.

Megan smiled. *Damn.* His light brown hair, more a dirty blond really, and blue eyes were just the right shades of how she liked them. *And his body!* Even the fatigues and body armor he wore when she picked them up in Iraq couldn't hide the nice physique. From his file, he was also extremely intelligent. Usually that combination ripped her the wrong way, as was testament to her usual stance on specialized military soldiers. *But he was just...*

Megan quickly replaced the soft smile with a more neutral look as he turned toward her. Their eyes met across the passenger area, his blue eyes piercing hers and seemed to look deep within. It made her strangely uncomfortable, as though he could see inside and know her secrets. She broke the look first to pull out the mission folder from the briefcase at her feet—the file she was supposed to be familiar with by the time they got to the Afghanistan base.

But now her heart rate was elevated. She took several deep breaths to calm herself so she could concentrate. But she couldn't. Slowly she raised her eyes to watch the card game again.

***

"No, no. I said it needed to be refitted. This doesn't look like you did anything. Was the new part installed?" Megan asked checking out the Pave Hawk in front of her where it sat outside the hanger. She was pointing to an area right behind the engine.

"The work order said it was to be done by today. It is," said Marshall Kittering. He put his hands on his hips, disgusted. He was an American National but of Afghanistan origin. Speaking the language and having relations in the country helped him reach the position he was in as assistant head mechanic.

Megan took several deep breaths. "Fine. Is the work done on the Chinook?"

"Yes." The mechanic stuck his hands in his pockets.

"Okay. When I take this bird up, Kit, you're riding along."

"Why?"

"Because..." Megan leaned closer to him. "If we crash, I want you to be with us. Our lives depend on these machines. That means everything you do on this aircraft, including the most mundane things, affect our lives. Be ready to go in fifty minutes when I finish with the pre-flight check."

"But..."

"Yes?" Megan turned a disgusted look at him.

"Nothing. I'll be ready."

"Good," Megan said as the big, burly mechanic hurried away. Another body moved in close.

"You seem to carry a lot of weight around here." Jake had an amused tone to his voice.

"They don't realize how important it is to have things running at the highest performance." She glanced toward the hanger. "Having an absolutely smooth running machine has saved my crew's ass more than once. You think White Pine could spring for some people who understand this." She took a deep breath to calm herself.

Jake chuckled. "Stay on top of them, Chief. We don't want an incompetent screwing us up."

"Yeah. Did you need something? I thought I assigned you to help with inventory in the main stockroom."

"You did. It's done. Cowboy sent me here. He said I could help 'purtty up the steel steed.' And to tell you, he'd be out to help preflight after he 'wiggled the wiggly.' " McGrew hesitated. "As your faithful messenger, I delivered it." He gave a formal bow.

Megan chuckled. "Cupcake, there's two things you gotta learn about me. I don't take ass kissing well, but I do like a sense of humor."

"In that case Chief, care to tell me what you want me to do next?" Jake asked with a smile.

Megan reached into the Pave Hawk grabbing a flat, thin box. She pulled out a large piece of white paper. As she set the box back into Pave Hawk, she caught his puzzled look. "Have you ever put on transfers?"

"Transfers?"

Megan lifted one corner to show the reversed painting of a pale rider on a horse. She gave the ex-military man a wry smile. "I get chewed out every time I put these on the choppers, but once they're on, they're bitches to get off." She looked around the area, especially into the hanger. "Spray the nose of the cockpit with adhesive." She pointed to a spray can sitting near the box. "Let it dry, then peel away the backing and it'll stick on. You get one shot at it, Cupcake. There's Death for the Pave Hawk and Famine for the Black Hawk. One for each side." She handed it to him. "Make'em look 'purtty.' "

Jake chuckled. "Sure thing, Chief."

Megan continued with the preflight check. It took over half an hour to go over every inch of the helicopter. These hadn't been flown in eight months, so they had been mothballed, and it was a very thorough inspection. Finally, she was in the cockpit checking out dials when McGrew walked up and waited. She glanced at him.

"All 'purttied' up, Chief. What's next?"

Megan glanced out the cockpit door at the Black Hawk. The nose art was in just the right spot on the front. She also saw the other two pilots finishing with pre-flighting the Black Hawk. "Good job."

"Thanks. What else?"

Megan glanced at her watch then leaned out the cockpit toward the back of the aircraft. "Hey, Kelly. How long?"

"I'm just finishin' up. Give me two."

She turned her eyes to Jake. "We need to give the 'steel steeds' a little test flight. Take a break until we get back, assuming the others are done with their jobs. If not, help them."

With two quick taps on the side of the helicopter, Jake moved off to the nearby hanger.

Megan watched him walk away, admiring his butt and general physique. She shook her head. *He's off limits. Totally off limits. Completely and absolutely off limits.*

***

"What the hell?" Megan said, noticing the light that flashed on the collective she held in her left hand. It was the instrument with which she controlled the pitch of the blades. The light indicated there was a problem in engine number one.

"What?" Cowboy asked, swinging his head toward her.

"Light. Problem in number one." She intoned quickly and keyed the microphone to the back of the helicopter. "Kit, look out the left side and see if we're smoking… Kit?"

"Damn it." Megan glanced at Cowboy who was looking into the back of the helicopter.

"He's not plugged in."

"Do you see anything coming out?"

"No." Cowboy was straining to look around back.

"I'm going to turn." Even as she said so, she slightly turned the helicopter left to see if she was trailing smoke.

As soon as she began the maneuver, Cowboy spoke, "Yep. Smoke outta one."

Megan grimaced. "That oil line. I told him—"

"You got smoke, Death," came from the other helicopter over the radio.

"Yeah, we see it. We're shuttin' number one down and headin' back," Cowboy said. He always handled communication and navigation while they flew, leaving the pilot to fly.

"We'll follow you."

"Can we make it back?" Cowboy asked Megan.

"I'm sure as hell gonna try. You know if I put it down now, it'll be stripped before you can count to ten, not to mention if we stay with it, the locals will kill to get the parts," she cursed softly.

She shut down the engine and turned again to see if the craft was still smoking. The smoke was less but still there. In her ear, she heard Cowboy alerting White Pine Tower that they were returning with a crippled aircraft.

***

McGrew returned from the soda machine in the main office complex to join the rest of the crew when he saw several people hurrying out the door heading to the hanger. With a puzzled look, he changed directions and followed. The other members of his crew were taking a break near the patio.

There was a scramble of people coming out of the hanger too. Jake quickened his steps to join the small group standing outside the hanger entrance on the airstrip side. Worried looks were on everyone's faces.

"Problem?" Jake asked Corn, one of the mechanics.

"Yeah, the Ghost is having trouble with her Bird." He glanced back into the hanger.

McGrew followed his glance to see the two man firefighting team of mechanics quickly donning gear. Jake's face hardened. "Is it that serious?"

Corn nodded. "Could be. Any other pilot probably would have ditched it. Then the battle becomes who gets to it first, the locals or us. The parts of a helicopter go for mighty high prices on the black market. We had a crew, a year ago or so, that ditched a chopper, and it was never seen again. All we found was the fuselage. Totally stripped." Corn shook his head. "Serious shit. Cartwright hates to loose a bird."

Jake turned to see the crowd getting bigger, including the rest of his crew, as news spread across the White Pine compound.

By this time, they could hear the whirl of the two returning choppers. The Black Hawk was pacing the smoking Pave Hawk. A small black cloud trailed the crippled helicopter.

Jake's eyes still focused on the quickly approaching helicopters as he heard the two firefighting mechanics discussing possible situations.

"Looks like she's got an oil fire."

"Had. Look close. One of the engines is down."

"That means she can't hover. She'll have to land on the wheels." Both jumped into the small fire truck, and it pulled out of the hanger to stop near the runway, waiting.

Suddenly the Pave Hawk dipped and swung to the side.

Jake sucked up an involuntary breath. His heart stopped for a brief second until Megan got control of the helicopter. Quickly, it descended at a steep angle toward the end of the runway.

"Come on, Megan," Jake whispered, watching the helicopter approach more like a fixed wing aircraft.

Death touched down once, lifted slightly, then put back down as it rolled down the runway. The other engine was cut and it glided to a stop.

Jake glanced around at the still gathering crowd to see most of his crew waiting anxiously while the fire apparatus accelerated onto the runway. As Famine landed a short distance away, Jake took off running toward the disabled aircraft followed by his crew.

As soon as it was on the ground, Jake saw Kit the mechanic scramble out of the back. He moved to a safe distance and stood staring at the firefighters spraying the tail rotor area. He was breathing hard and whiter than his grease-smudged shirt.

Jake slowed as he got closer to the crippled aircraft, especially when he saw a pissed off Megan exit the cockpit.

Megan was already discussing the situation with the head mechanic and Corn when he got near. The firefighting guys were also investigating. All of them were pointing and moving from one side to the other in heavy discussion.

A curse word caught McGrew's attention as he stood nearby assessing the situation. His head snapped up to see Cartwright heading toward the still pale mechanic standing off the side of the runway. He glanced at the others, and moved on an intercept course. But Cartwright moved fast. Jake got there right as Megan grabbed the shaken mechanic.

"I told you to replace that oil line. If that had been a mission, we might all be dead, you…" Her eyes narrowed, her breathing fast as her fist rose.

Jake grabbed Megan by the arm, breaking her hold on the mechanic, and with his other hand captured her clenched fist. She struggled, but he turned and pinned her arms to her sides. "Get him away," Jake ordered Gunner who was following behind him.

Megan continued to struggle against his body, cursing softly under her breath at the quickly retreating mechanic. "Calm down," Jake said to the woman in his arms as Gunner moved Kit out of sight into the hanger.

"Let me go. Let me at him."

"Calm down!" Jake ordered. After one last struggle, he could feel her muscles relaxing. Still he held her.

"McGrew let go. Now."

"Are you calm?"

"Damn it. Let me go or…"

"Or what?" Jake asked with a smile as he released his hold on her.

Cartwright turned and glared at him. "Don't ever do that again," she whispered through clenched teeth.

Jake held up his hands in surrender.

Megan stalked over to join the head mechanic inspecting the disabled helicopter with a backward glare at him.

Jake shook his head as he watched her walk away. A chuckle sounded over his shoulder. He turned to see Cowboy standing behind him.

"That's one way to grab the bull by the horns."

A smile flashed on his face as he glanced again at the three people working on the helicopter. The firefighters were gathering up their equipment. Jake turned to the others in the crew standing there. "Hey guys, show's over. Why don't you head back to work?"

"Will do, Jake," Tiny said and motioned for the others to follow.

Jake stepped up to Cowboy's side standing near Death. "Is it fixable?"

Cowboy nodded. "Not irreparable, just dangerous." He glanced back into the hanger. "I'd hazard to say that the shit-head didn't even replace the line like he was 'posed to, probably just wiped it down."

Not knowing anything about the workings of the helicopter, McGrew was lost as to the technical terms being thrown around.

It wasn't long before Megan stepped up to the two men. "McGrew, my office. Twenty minutes." Her brown eyes were hard and threatening.

"Yes, Chief," Jake said immediately and watched her angry stride as she followed Fahim Masood, the Afghanistan head of the base, back toward the hanger. He turned to Cowboy. "Looks like I stepped in it."

Cowboy slapped him on the back with a huge grin. "Cow patty city."

***

Megan hurried down the hall to find Jake waiting outside her office. She didn't look at him as she strode past. She tossed her helmet on the couch and threw her flight gloves into the corner, then swiveled to face him standing in front of her desk. She glared, but his expression was neutral.

"You wanted to see me, Chief?"

"Don't ever do that again."

Jake didn't answer.

"Do I make myself clear?"

"Crystal."

"Good. Dismissed." But he didn't move as his blue eyes held hers. "What?"

Jake just shrugged.

She narrowed her eyes, noticing that his blue eyes were amused. "Get the hell out of here."

"Sure, Chief."

Megan watched him walk out, then flopped down into her chair. That had been too close. Both times. First with the bad oil line—that had almost been deadly. It was a good thing she had chosen to take a longer than usual test flight, because if she hadn't, she might have been caught with her pants down under fire.

Then the second close call. She'd almost lost it with the mechanic. She had had problems with Kit on her last rotation to Afghanistan. After the first incident, she had specifically left orders that he was never, ever to touch her helicopters. Now this. She made it clear to management that he needed to be dismissed. They complied only after Masood had dressed her down about coming unglued. If McGrew hadn't held her back, she might be looking for work.

Not that finding another job would be hard. She was constantly getting calls from White Pine's competition trying to lure her away. No, she would be out of work maybe ten minutes, just long enough for the competition to hear.

McGrew.

Megan sighed.

He'd been right to stop her. *But did he have to do it in front of the crew and everyone else on base? At least he wasn't smug about it. Damn him.* And he had held her so easily. She hated that most of all. Being smaller and without muscle mass, she was at a huge disadvantage. Only her flying talent and her other less known 'ability' kept her in charge. *Damn him anyway.*

She took a deep, cleansing breath.

CHAPTER 3

"Okay people," Megan began the crew meeting the next morning. "We got a simple job today. We have to ferry food and medical supplies to a small village in the mountains." She paused to check her sheet. "Since Death is down, I'll be flying Famine with Punky. Cowboy will be flying the Chinook with Stick, but that leaves us more vulnerable than I like. It'll be four days before Death'll be ready with a part cannibalized from another craft, and another week or two before the new part comes in. So until then we limp by." She looked down the table at Tiny. "This means you need to work fast and hard. The less time on the ground, the better. Got it?"

Tiny nodded. "Yes'em."

"Gunner, you're in the Chinook with Cowboy. I want the best protection for the ground crew. Guys, if he starts firing, haul ass back to the chopper. Bosser, you're with me in Famine. As usual, we'll be circling overhead providing cover. The rest of you will be the unloading crew. Keep your guns locked and loaded. You never know when al Qaeda or the Taliban will show up." Megan looked at Jake. "Tiny will instruct you about procedures for unloading and stuff. You're to follow Tiny's orders. Got it, Cupcake?"

"Got it, Chief."

Megan nodded back at him. "I don't want a repeat of Iraq. Understood?" She looked around to see everyone agreeing with her. "The helicopters are loaded. We leave in ten minutes."

The group stood as one to leave.

"McGrew stay." Megan stood, slowly gathering her paperwork. She finally looked up after the room cleared. "You were right to stop me from punching Kit. Thanks."

"Ouch." Jake smiled. "I bet that hurt to admit."

"Worse than you know." Megan smiled back. "Just don't do it again."

"Got it, Chief." Jake winked then left.

***

Jake and the others were unloading supplies as fast as possible. They had been at work for fifteen minutes, and he was not only out of breath from the high altitude but was also dripping wet. He swiped his brow and grabbed another box, this one marked 'penicillin.' After setting it on the pile, he hurried back to the Chinook. As he waited his turn to get another box from those inside, he glanced at the surroundings.

They were in a large valley. There were few trees here, although the hillsides were carpeted in green from small bushes and tough grasses. Most of the valley was covered in a rust-colored hew. At one end was the main village, a small cluster of about twenty houses. They looked crude from the air, with flat tops and looked like they were made of mud. Small corrals near each house kept goats and sheep contained.

He'd read that the major crop in the country, especially in this poor mountainous region, was poppy—from which opium and heroin were made. Hence, the rusty color of the valley floor from the poppies blooming. The only other means of industry for these people was raising sheep. Large flocks were seen on the hillsides, but this far up into the mountains, poppy was the biggest cash crop. Even though extracting poppy gum was very labor intensive, it paid better than sheep farming.

Three crew members plus ten local Afghans were unloading the helicopter, which was running with blades slowly swirling.

The men worked in silence. Jake had asked Tiny earlier what was in the boxes, but Tiny informed him not to ask such questions. Sometimes only the crew chiefs knew what was being delivered, and many times even they didn't know.

Jake was handed a huge, heavy, unmarked box. As he hurried to the pile, he glanced up to see the other helicopter circling. It was taking wide passes around the valley.

As Jake sat the box down, a mortar hit close by, sending locals diving for cover and the members of the crew running for the helicopter, which was hovering a foot off the ground.

As he climbed in the back, he mentally counted the crew. One was missing. "Where's Fisher?" Jake asked Tiny.

Tiny shrugged and began pushing boxes out with no care as to the contents. "Help me empty the back."

McGrew hesitated then glanced back toward the last place he'd seen the Chilean. Another mortar hit, closer this time. The locals were grabbing a few boxes and making for cover away from the pile and the helicopter.

"Cupcake!"

At that moment, Jake saw movement behind the boxes. With only a glance back to the South African, he un-slung his rifle and hit the ground running.

Machine gunfire swept near the chopper as he dove for cover behind the boxes.

Sure enough it was Fisher, slowly getting up.

Jake grabbed him and helped him behind the boxes. "Wait." He peeked out but heard the whine of another incoming mortar. Pushing the still stunned Fisher to the ground, he dove on top of him. The mortar landed several feet away spraying them with dirt, weeds, and rocks. Jake stayed covered for a second more then stood up, grabbed the Chilean by the back of his collar and hauled him up. Half carrying, half dragging his companion, Jake scrambled back to the helicopter now hovering two feet off the ground.

Cowboy swung it around as Gunner began firing in the direction of the incoming rounds. He didn't have a shot in hell of hitting anything; he was just providing cover for the returning crewmen.

But the firing had stopped, as had the incoming mortars.

Jake glanced behind him while others helped Fisher into the back. Famine was hovering near the ridge of the small foothills nearby, the M60 door gun firing nonstop toward the ground. With a smile at Tiny, Jake jumped into the back and Cowboy accelerated up and away. McGrew slid the door closed and breathed a sigh of relief.

Fisher rubbed his forehead.

"Are you okay, Fisher?" Jake yelled above the noise of the engines.

"Si. Gracais. Thank you." Fisher smiled still rubbing his head, a red spot forming a goose egg.

"What happened?" Tiny asked.

"One local. We collided in…" Fisher made a motion with his hands, slamming them together. "Hit head. I fell."

Jake patted him on the back.

"You have saved my life, Cupcake. Muchas gracias."

"Nah," Jake said, disarming his M-4. "Just lending a hand." He glanced over to see Tiny frown. "Did we get everything unloaded?"

"Yes. No thanks to you. It only took several shoves," Tiny said, a disgusted look on his face.

"Good," Jake said, ignoring him.

A red blinking light flashed near the handset in the back. Tiny grabbed the nearest helmet and put it on. He listened for a few seconds then yelled to Jake, "Ghost wants to see you as soon as we land." The smile didn't quite make it to his face.

Jake sighed but nodded. *What a pain.*

***

Jake finished cleaning the back of the Chinook until both helicopter crews were in the hanger. Then he walked up to the two pilots having a heavy discussion near Famine. They both looked at him. Cowboy caught his eyes, then nodded at Megan and headed off in the same direction as the rest of the crew.

"Yes, Chief?"

"What happened down there?" Megan asked. Her hands anchored firmly on her hips. A scowl on her face.

"I'm sure you already know."

"True. But I want to hear from you what happened."

"When the firing started, I headed to the aircraft as instructed. I noticed Fisher was missing. I found him. We took off."

"I heard you disobeyed orders."

Jake hesitated a fraction of a second. "Yes, I did. I felt that a man's life was worth more than some cargo. If that's going to get me in dutch, then it'll happen every time, Chief." He stared into her dark brown, almost black, hostile eyes. "You can disagree with me, but that's the way I am."

Megan turned on her heel and started walking away. Over her shoulder she called, "Five minutes—crew meeting. Briefing room."

Once more Jake sighed. *God help me and protect me from this woman.*

Twenty minutes later, after the meeting, Jake tapped on her open office door. Megan sat at her desk shuffling papers. Jake shifted his weight on his feet. "You said you wanted to see me after the crew meeting, Chief?"

Megan motioned for him to come in. "Pull up a chair, McGrew." She pointed to an empty chair near the wall next to her desk. "The worst part about being a crew chief is the paperwork. Sit. You start learning today."

Jake's eyebrows flew up. Tiny had told him it was usually a couple of weeks and at least six missions before she started paperwork training.

Megan missed the expression as she was once more concentrating on the file in front of her. "We get pre-mission information from management. These are put into the crew chief's box near the front desk. I'll show you where when we get done. Check it every morning and night, just in case the flight leaves at dawn." She hefted several sheets. "At the end of a mission, take the pre-info along with the crew chief's report, pilot's report and each person's report and file them. Each base is a little different, but the Head will acquaint you with the procedures when you first arrive." Megan paused with a glance at Jake. "God, I can't wait until they get us those promised laptops. You'd think we'd already have them."

"Why don't we?"

Megan shrugged. "Security. So I'm told. Seems stupid to me but hey, it's their money." She grabbed two sheets sitting on her desk. "This is my report and an inventory list of any items brought back with us. Tonight, the mechanics will give me a computer print out of the hours on the aircraft, a daily report, and such. That goes in here too." She paused. "Give it to the clerical, don't call them secretaries." She winked at Jake. "Or depending on the base, just fax it in and file them in the cabinet."

Jake nodded.

"Here. Read my report." She held out a sheet of paper.

Jake hesitated, slowly taking it. "Why?"

"First of all, so that you learn the sort of things they want in them and the things they don't want said. This mission was fairly straight forward but some require more, how shall I put it, more creative writing. Second, I want you to read my comments."

Jake quickly read the report. "Thanks."

"No thanks necessary. What you did was right. Tiny should have thought more of the crew than the merchandise. He's merely in this for the money."

"Aren't we all?"

Megan leaned back in her chair and relaxed. "Yes, but…"

"But?"

"I would have thought it obvious to you."

Jake leaned back too. "I don't understand."

"This is natural to you. The squad's the most important thing. Never leave a man behind. Your buddies are more important than anything. Right?"

Jake nodded.

"That just can't be instilled in some of the guys here. They're true mercenaries. Money is tops to them. They're the ones you need to look out for. Tiny was mad at you because you thought of Fisher. Sometimes, if we return with merchandise, it comes out of our pay. It depends on the mission. He's here for money only, but he knows that soon you'll be in charge of your own crew. That means more money. He's jealous. I'll never give thumbs up to him for crew chief."

"Because he wouldn't care if he left anyone behind?"

"That's right. Out here, most of the time, we're all there is. I'd get rid of him, but he's actually a good worker. Still, he'll never be in charge if I have any say." Megan looked intently at Jake. "Good people are hard to find."

Jake smiled. "Is it getting any easier?"

Megan scrunched up her face. "What?"

"The compliment. I bet that hurt to admit."

"Ha, ha. I was being serious."

"Then I'll return the compliment. You did good attacking the mortar installation. Thanks."

Megan smiled back. "Did it hurt you?"

"Only a little." Jake's smiled grew. "Seriously, it's nice to know that back up is so dedicated."

"It's getting thick in here," Megan said chuckling.

Jake joined in. "I checked you out after the Iraqi rescue and, except for some negative comments about your attitude, all I heard, especially from the pilots, were high compliments."

"Yeah, I got them hood winked." Megan leaned forward as her phone rang and picked it up. "Cartwright." She listened for a few seconds. "Okay. Why can't the Coalition pick him up?"

Jake watched as she frowned.

"Okay, we're on our way." She tossed the phone in its cradle. As she stood, grabbing her helmet and scarf from the cabinet behind her, she motioned for McGrew to follow. "Gather any of the crew you that can find. Meet me in the hanger as soon as possible. Find Cowboy."

They exited the room and she took off running down the hall.

***

Megan grimaced at the three crewmen present, Cowboy, Fisher, and Cupcake. "Where are the rest?" she asked McGrew.

"Couldn't find them."

She looked around. "Okay, then we're it. We have a medical rescue. We're picking up a military doctor, then a young victim, and taking them back to the U.S. military hospital." She motioned to Cowboy who headed out to Famine being fueled on the runway. "Fisher, you'll be in charge in back. Cupcake, you'll be with the doc and his people as protection. Both of you get your normal, hot mission equipment, with full body armor. Be back here in…" She glanced at her watch. "Five minutes."

Both men took off running to the barracks. Less than five minutes later, they were fully loaded and ready. They climbed in back and put helmets on, plugging in their headsets. Famine was already warmed up, blades twirling.

"Guys, we're heading into a hot zone, so don't spare bullets if need be," Megan said as she increased the blade speed. She glanced at Cowboy who was just finishing with the last pre-flight item. "Ready?"

"Ready, Darlin'."

Famine went airborne.

"Cupcake?"

"Yes, Ghost?"

"Here are your instructions. You're the security on this detail. The military doc and medic are top priority. Next comes the little kid. Under no circumstances is anyone allowed near my aircraft. I mean no one comes near—no mom, no dad, no crying grandparents, no village leader, no anybody. Do not accept gifts from anyone. And…" She hesitated a second. "Pat the kid down. Do a thorough inspection of his entire body. Understand?"

"What's this about, Ghost?"

"I don't have time to explain. Just follow orders. Do you understand?"

"Yes, Chief."

"Fisher, get both door guns ready. When we're landing and taking off, Cupcake will man one of them. He shouldn't have problems with anything, but help him if he needs it. Sorry to throw this at you Cupcake, but I'm sure you'll adapt."

Soon they picked up the military personnel and were heading into mountains surrounding the city.

"Fisher, Cupcake, get into position. We'll be at the pick up zone in two minutes."

The landing went off without a hitch. They were in a valley similar to the one earlier. Again poppy fields were the dominant feature, but this time the village was larger with more houses.

McGrew accompanied the two medical personnel to the gathered group of Afghan locals. It seemed that the entire village had come out to see the helicopter. And the crowd continued to get bigger as the Bird sat on the ground, blades still rotating.

Megan cursed as she watched the growing crowd. She no longer see Cupcake and the medical personnel. "What's taking them so long?" she asked no one in particular. "Cowboy?"

"My side's clear, Girl."

"Fisher?"

"Don't see none looking funny, Ghost."

Megan's eyes roamed the group trying to watch everyone and everywhere. Finally, she spotted the Americans. The two medical people were bent over working near the ground. Jake was trying to keep people away from them, so they could work. "I don't like this."

"Who's this anyway, to warrant us comin' on this little roundup?" Cowboy asked as his eyes panned the small field.

"Masood's forth cousin twice removed or something, some relative that's connected to his tribe and a family member of this area's warlord. This is a personal favor from Masood. The kid's maybe a year or so old."

"And this kid? What's the emergency?"

"I don't know. A head injury of some sort. Something about the kid fell off the roof last night. Why they don't put a fence on the roof tops when they sleep there in the summer to beat the heat, I'll never understand. The military picks up a few every year because of this." Megan saw the small group heading back to the chopper.

She watched as McGrew shook his head at an elderly woman who was pointing and crying. He kept trying to shake off her arm as she kept grabbing him. His attention was divided between her and the military personnel carrying the child. With a final headshake to the old woman, he took her hand off his arm and pointed away from the aircraft. Then he hurried to the side of the medical personnel.

Megan continued to watch the slowly departing crowd as she heard the three scrambling in the back. Most of the people backed farther away, except the father, mother, and elderly woman. She narrowed her eyes watching them.

The parents looked truly distraught but the elderly lady didn't look particularly sad anymore. Megan's left hand started to leave a slight sheen of sweat on the collective. She added more power but waited before lifting off for the 'go ahead' from Fisher.

Finally, his voice came on. "We good. Go Ghost."

As Megan lifted off, she still watched the retreating crowds. Her eyes flicked to the family members. Megan's eyes narrowed more at the way the elderly lady was smiling.

"Damn it. Cupcake?"

"He not on," Fisher replied. "He helping doctor."

"Ask him if he inspected the kid. And tell him to get the damn headset on." Megan hovered the chopper twenty feet off the ground as the elderly lady's eyes met hers.

Within seconds, Jake's voice came on the intercom. "I'm on."

"Did you inspect the kid?"

"All except the big bandaged area on the head of the baby. And he's head is strapped to- Why?"

"I told you everywhere. Do it now."

"The doc said…"

"Something isn't right. Pull those bandages off. Now!"

There was silence for several seconds. Megan saw the elderly lady get a puzzled look on her face. There was arguing over the intercom between Jake and the doctor.

"Shit. The kid has some sort of…." Jake's voice stopped.

"Get it off my ship now! Toss it out the left side away from the crowd," Megan said still hovering above the field.

"Open the door. Damn. It's stuck." McGrew's voice was heightened.

Megan cursed under her breath. Her eyes locked with the elderly lady who smiled at her, then chuckled.

The parents stopped focusing on the helicopter and turned to the old lady. There was confusion on the ground, lots of yelling at each other. The elderly lady spoke with what could only be a sneer at the father and mother. With that, the mother screamed and fell to the ground crying, with her hands held toward Famine. The father of the child hit the elderly lady. And hit her again.

"Get it out now!" Megan repeated.

"Out!" McGrew yelled.

Megan accelerated up and off to the right. The blast rocked the helicopter but with a quick adjustment to the foot pedals and some fancy maneuvering, she kept the craft under control.

Some distance above the ground, Megan hovered. She glanced at Cowboy who wiped his brow and shook his head. They glanced down at the small gathering to see the father of the child beating the old woman, probably to death.

Megan muttered a curse. "How's the kid?" she asked to no one in particular in the back of the helicopter.

Fisher answered. "Doctor is stopping blood from leaking. Bomb thing was, uh, near head. Stuck in blood and bandage. Wound is ugly."

"Yeah." Megan gave out another breath in relief. She shook her head and tried to calm her frail nerves. *Too close. Again.*

Cowboy summed up her feelings. "Crap. That was an ass burner, Girl."

***

Famine landed at the White Pine compound after dropping off the injured child and medical personnel. Megan scrambled out of the cockpit as the two crewmen in back were still securing guns and picking up the mess. "McGrew!"

Jake hopped out of the back. His face hardened. "Yeah?"

"What the hell were you thinking? I gave you specific orders for a reason." Megan jammed her hands on her hips.

"Look, the doc said…"

"I don't give a shit what the doc said. You do what I say. I told you to inspect that kid. You damn near got us killed. We've had other tours here. We know how things go. Don't do that again. When I give you an order, you follow it or you're gone. This was your one mistake."

"Can I say something?"

"No. There was no excuse for this. If Famine is damaged, so help me God, I'll drum you out of White Pine. I don't give a shit if you don't like taking orders from me." Megan strode off to the side of the chopper.

***

An hour later, Jake stood in Megan's office doorway, watching the sad expression on her face. She sat at her desk fiddling with her camouflage scarf. She was listening to the phone, not saying anything.

"I'm sorry, Fahim. Is there anything they can do?" Megan asked softly. She frowned at whatever was said on the phone. "Tell him not to worry. It didn't damage the chopper and there are crazy people everywhere. None of the crew has hard feelings toward him or his village."

Jake knocked quietly on the door frame to get her attention. Seeing her with defenses down caused a quickening of his heart and made her even more attractive.

35

Megan looked up at him and her expression changed. It became hard again. She motioned him in. "No. Thanks. When it happens, please express our condolences… Yes, thanks." Megan placed the phone in the cradle softly, all the while staring at Jake. "What?"

"Crew reports," Jake said. He hefted the three reports.

She sat back in her chair still glaring.

Jake placed them on her desk. "Look, I want to explain—"

"Look nothing." Megan sprang up, sending the chair crashing into the file cabinet behind her. "Because you didn't follow orders, we about died."

"Yes, I know, but…"

"Can you follow orders?"

Jake swallowed the apology and stiffened. "Yes."

"Then do it. Get out of my face."

Jake stood his ground for a second, then strode out of the office. He didn't stop until he entered his room and slammed the door. Slowly, he unclenched his fists and took a deep breath.

It wasn't that he didn't deserve the dressing down. It was the fact that she hadn't even wanted to listen. The least she could have done was to ask why he hadn't looked the wound area over. *But no. She just assumed I didn't want to follow her orders. Damn her.*

He flopped on the bed and laid his arm over his eyes trying to relax.

***

"Chief?" McGrew asked as he entered the briefing room the next day. There had been a note left for him to report early today in the squad room.

Megan motioned for him to sit near her. "From here on out, you'll be working with me from the beginning of every mission. The faster you're trained, the faster you'll be out of my hair. Kill your own crew."

Jake sighed softly but sat.

Megan handed him several sheets of paper. "Pre-mission for today."

Jake nodded as he looked the paper over. The work order was to provide security for a construction crew of White Pine's along with locals who were rebuilding runways that had been abandoned when the Russians pulled out. Right now Kabul International Airport only had one usable runway, the rest had been bombed during the war with the Taliban.

Before the Taliban, the Russians had merely used large concrete slabs as a runway, which meant that with every change in season the runway would buckle. Once the new runways were built, bigger cargo planes could be brought in on a regular schedule. This not only facilitated military troop movement, rotation, and associated supplies, but it also meant that people in the city and surrounding communities would again have an international airport—very important for the city and nation.

"We're support," Jake said. "Do the execs know where this 'possible attack or sabotage' might come from?"

Megan shook her head then leaned back. "You've seen the runway and area being built. Give me your opinion of where we should deploy security."

Obviously, she's testing me. Jake thought hard. "Definitely need more security at the entrance to the runway. I'd have at least a couple of guys on the actual building site with local workers watching them. If we're going to get an attack on the ground, it'll probably come from the surrounding foothills. I'd have someone watching that area too." Jake looked at Megan to see if she was satisfied with his answer.

Megan gave him a cocky smile. "It was a trick question."

"What?"

"I doubt there'll be an attack. I'll spread the two crews with the workers like you said, but the rebuilding crew is actually the safest group in the whole area. They're mostly in danger while flying with us or here at base."

"Excuse me?"

"What do the terrorists want?" She didn't wait for an answer. "Easy access to the world and their own people in charge. The only way they'll accomplish this is by letting the Coalition rebuild the airport and runways. They want this to happen as much as the U.S. military and the UN forces. Trust me."

"I guess that makes sense, but what about some crazy fanatic?"

"Won't happen. Even the fanatics are listening to their warlords, al Qaeda, or Taliban leaders. They need this. So, this is a milk run for us. Several easy days of light duty." She motioned for the pre-mission papers. "You'll be in charge on the ground. Stay alert anyway. Stranger things have happened, but I highly doubt anything will." She glanced at her watch. "Briefing with the full squad, that's our crew and another, in five minutes."

"About yesterday…"

"Concentrate on today." Megan turned her attention back to her paperwork.

Jake waited a couple of seconds then stood up and left. He knew when he was dismissed.

Chapter 4

Four days later was a celebration of Afghanistan independence from the British. The celebration lasted a couple of days with the actual Independence Day on Friday. It was a time of feasting and a chance for employees of White Pine to see the real Afghanistan people.

As predicted, the last several days had been a milk run. Not a whisper of trouble. Actually boring. Megan walked into the base office when one of the clerical walked up to her with a big smile on her face.

The secretary wore a head scarf while on base but off base wore the full chadari, sometimes mistaken as a burqa in the West. This was a full covering from head to feet of blue or white material with a mesh opening for the eyes. Even after the Taliban had been ousted, most women still wore it in public.

"Ms. Cartwright."

Megan smiled at the Afghan woman. Zarin Saikal was not only intelligent, but being the only two females on base they had naturally been drawn together. "Hello Zarin."

"Mail today." Zarin handed two envelopes to Megan.

"I got mail?" With only her brother, who she hadn't spoken to in years, and her father being her only living relatives, she never received anything that she didn't send for over the internet. "Thanks."

"You are most welcome." Zarin smiled and walked off.

Megan glanced at the outsides of the envelopes but neither had a return address. The post office mark showed them to be from her hometown, which meant they were probably from her dad, who hated to write letters. With a frown, she grabbed the work reports and headed to the briefing room. The rest of the crew was due in a few minutes to turn in reports, then they had a couple days off.

After sitting down at the head of the table, she tore open the first postmarked letter with a frown. It was short and to the point.

'Megan, I'm writing to tell you that I was taken to the emergency room four days ago after a car accident that I caused. I blacked out and they're still working on the reason why. I don't think it's serious and I considered not even writing you, but I thought that you should at least know about it. I'm home now, only a broken arm. I'll write again if they find out anything. Take care. Dad.'

The frown deepened as she read. This was not good. She tossed the first letter onto the pile of blank crew reports and tore open the second, postmarked two days after the first.

'Megan, I have a brain tumor. Cancer. I have an appointment on the sixteenth with some asshole cancer doctor. For all of the shit I went through and this is what's going to kill me. Damn Russians couldn't kill me. I retire and look what happens. I should have stayed in the Company. A bullet would have been faster and easier. Keep your head down, Kid. Love, Dad.'

Megan swallowed hard. Today was the fourteenth. She leaned her head on both of her hands and stared at the letter she had dropped on the table, her mind completely blank.

"Hey little Cowgirl, I like this kinda job. Fly and park. Fly and park. No shooting at us..." Cowboy began as he walked into the room. He stopped seeing Megan's expression. "Meg? Darlin', you okay?"

Megan swallowed back the tears threatening to come. She sniffled twice before looking up. With a quick swipe, she brushed her hand over her damp eyes.

Cowboy slid into the chair next to hers. "What's the matter?"

Megan gathered the letters up and shoved them under the crew reports. "Just news from home."

He frowned. "You never get letters from home. Must be somethin' bad."

Megan merely nodded, pulling out a form and began filling it in.

"Wanna talk about it?"

"Nope."

"Come on. Tell me."

"I said no." Megan busied herself with the report. "Did you find out if that part was sent for Death?"

"Yeah, but who knows when it'll get here. Even the pony express went faster." He tapped the table in front of his fellow pilot. "If you wanna talk..."

Megan looked up. "Yeah, I know. Thanks."

"Sure thing, Meg," Cowboy said grabbing a form. He started to work on his report, but kept glancing at Megan.

Slowly, the crew drifted in, and within five minutes all were quietly doing paperwork. Megan finished and looked around the table.

"Let me interrupt for a minute guys, before you get out of here. All of you attended the cultural lecture two days ago. Please don't forget what was said. These people are friendly, but their customs are different than ours. We must respect their ways. For the next several days, do not flaunt your nationalism, this is their time. If you go into town tonight, don't cause problems. Alcohol is against their religion and laws. Under no circumstances does it leave the base. Don't whore around. Don't even look at their women. Don't start any fights." She looked pointedly at Tiny. "It won't be tolerated under any instances. You mess up, you're gone. Got it?"

"Yes'em," Tiny replied.

"Try to stay together in at least twos and stay in the city, the nearer the base the better. The people here are more suspicious than in Iraq. The Iraqis were more used to Western thinking and attitudes. Remember, they were fighting the Taliban and then the Russians before, and many still think that they're being occupied by us. Next month, there are several planned trips as a group to different cultural places other than Kabul. Wait until then to go sight seeing. Don't damage the company's reputation with the locals. We have it good. Be back before curfew."

Three of the men were smiling, and it was obvious that they couldn't wait to get going. Megan went back to work.

Tiny turned to Fisher. "Hey, are you coming with us? Bosser, Gunner, and Chips are heading into town with me. And what about you, Jake?"

Fisher nodded yes as he wrote. "I'll go. I want to see the, uh, local customs here. Taste new food."

Tiny smiled. "Jake?"

Jake glanced up from his work. "Not tonight. Maybe tomorrow. Thanks anyway."

Tiny handed his paperwork to Megan, as did the other three. "Meet us at the front gate, Fisher."

"I'll be there in many minutes," Fisher replied.

Jake smiled at the guys and with a glance noticed that Cowboy was taking extra time with his paperwork. Usually he was the first one out of the room. His eyes swung to Megan. It was obvious she wasn't concentrating. He frowned.

Soon there was no one in the room but the three of them. He laid down his pen and glanced at the others. Suddenly he wondered if there might not be more going on. He narrowed his eyes as he watched Cowboy reach out and gently pat her arm.

Jake cleared his throat. "I got a bottle of whiskey in the mail today from an old army buddy. Care to join me in a drink? Or were the two of you heading into town together?"

Cowboy smiled. "Tonight, I got a hot date."

Megan snorted. "With what, your hand?"

"No. Do ya'll remember that restaurant we ate at the last night here 'fore we got shipped to Iraq?"

Megan nodded as she gathered the papers.

"The owner invited me back tonight for a special meal. I'm thinkin' it's part of the Independence thing. Babrack said that there'd be lots of food." He licked his lips.

"Ah, a date with food," Megan said jokingly. "Don't forget to take a gift with you, Cowboy. And watch your mouth, I'd hate to have to break you out of the pokey."

"Be a good side kick and keep an eye out for your pardner," Cowboy said as he stood.

"I'm not the cavalry."

"Not true, Darling." He winked at her. "You wanna jaw anytime, ya'll find me."

Megan looked him in the eye with a slight smile. "Don't worry, ya mother hen. Get out of here."

As Cowboy left the room, he began whistling.

"And Kelly, I don't want to have to nurse maid you through a stomachache tomorrow, don't 'date' too much." Megan raised her voice to reach him as he walked away.

Cowboy's laugh could be heard from the hallway.

Jake smiled. "So, what does our fearless leader do with her time off?"

"Relax."

"In town?"

Megan shook her head. "This isn't exactly Europe or the United States. No, I stay on base."

"Any good sights to see in town?"

"I don't know. Ask Kelly. He'll point you in the right direction, but unless you're adventuresome and have a cast iron stomach, don't listen to his advice about food." She shook her head. "That man could eat a cactus and claim it tasted like chicken."

Jake chuckled.

Megan smiled then it faded as she picked up the paperwork, her eyes falling on the letters under it. Quickly, she picked them up and shoved them under a crew report.

"Well, in that case, since you aren't headed into town, care to join me in a drink?"

"Thanks but no," Megan said and stood up after taking Jake's report. "Have a good evening, Cupcake."

Jake smiled. "You too, Chief."

But the smile faded as she left the room. Megan was in a strange mood. One he had never seen before with her. She almost seemed distraught. He shook his head. He would never understand women.

***

Jake stepped out onto the rooftop as the waning sunshine poked out from behind the mountains that surrounded the city. The colors of the sunset blended in harmony as the air cooled. There was little humidity, so once the temperature dropped, it cooled off quickly.

The foothills that faced the city were green but not from trees. Years of occupation by Russian forces had caused the timber to be harvested for various things, not the least of which was for heat and cooking. Small groves of trees were being nursed back since the Russians left, but these were still immature trees. Bushes were the tallest things on the hillsides.

The air was crisp and clean. There was no smog here even though Kabul, which the White Pine base sat on the edge of, was the biggest metropolitan city in the country. He could hear city sounds off in the distance with an occasional military helicopter or plane passing overhead.

Unlike other countries Independence Day celebrations, this one would have no dancing and music. There were no parades or large gatherings. This was a quieter affair but no less celebrated. People invited others to their homes, and food was lavished on each other as much as people could afford.

Afghanistan was below poverty level, most people barely surviving. Still, when they invited visitors in for a meal, they provided well, even if it did impoverish the family. That's why, as Westerners and rich in comparison, it was considered polite to take a gift to the family.

Here on White Pine base, meals weren't huge, but they didn't starve either. There was always enough to go around.

The rooftop was located on the main barracks building. The base was an enclosed, almost fortified city, surrounded by thick walls. The barracks the crews lived in were near the northern wall. There were three employee living barracks, each two stories high, and they were closest to the foothills. The main base building was next to the hanger, which was closest to the front gate. The other buildings on base were used for storage.

There was no air conditioning. So on hot summer nights, like tonight, the crews either hung out near the patio or on the rooftops. The patio area had a barbeque, tables, chairs, and was one of the few places that had a sheltered cover to protect from the beating sun.

Several guys had told him that rooftops were the best place to catch the slight breezes that only occasionally relieved the heat. On this particular building there was a very small retaining wall about four inches tall. Most of the older buildings had no ledge, including those lived in by the native Afghan people, especially those that lived in the mountains.

Movement onto the roof caught his attention. Meg turned to look at him. She sat near the edge, staring into the distance. Her slightly reddened eyes quickly turned away.

"They said downstairs that this was the coolest place." He wiped his brow. "They were right." He hesitated; her look indicated that he might have interrupted something. "Do you mind?"

Megan shrugged, but her expression seemed to say that she'd rather be left alone. "Chairs are over there." She pointed to a small recess by the door. Her attention returned to the mountains.

Jake hesitated then decided to follow his gut. He put his chair next to Megan's and sat down. He poured himself a drink, then sat silent. It was a long time before either spoke. The sunset was entering its last stages of brilliance.

"Pretty sunset," Jake said softly in the quiet of the rooftop.

Megan nodded.

Jake now studied her. "Sure you don't want a drink. I brought an extra glass."

Megan shook her head but continued to stare out into the distance. She sighed softly with a soft sniff.

"Is everything okay?"

Megan didn't answer.

Jake shrugged and got comfortable. Now the silence stretched out. Noises from the base and nearby town became louder. A military helicopter flew by. He watched it and as it passed, his gaze lingered on Megan.

She seemed sad. He couldn't figure her out. She seemed tougher than nails, yet the brown eyes revealed the fact that she cared deeply about things—first and foremost, the welfare of her crew.

He had been walking down the hall before the meeting when he heard her arguing with Masood about days off. Masood wanted them to work, but she stood her ground. They would do her no good if they were tired and on edge, she reasoned. If they needed to work on a mission, she knew she could rely on them for weeks, but this was a stupid reason to stretch her crew. She won in the end. Jake had been impressed. He wanted to tell her, but every time he tried to approach on a personal level, she responded with anger.

He grabbed the bottle off the roof and poured her a shot. Without asking, he handed it to her. "To living another day."

Megan glanced at him. She raised the glass and with a motion that demonstrated practice, tossed it back.

Jake hesitated, then with a smile, tossed his back.

"Good stuff," Megan whispered as the effect of the strong alcohol took her breath away.

"Yeah. My friend doesn't buy cheap." Jake poured himself another one. "Another?"

Megan hesitated. "Sure."

Once more they tossed the shots back. Jake smiled. "You're not inexperienced in drinking."

"Poker nights with military guys. I learned from the best."

Jake laughed. "We do know how to drink."

"And lose money." Megan turned her attention back to the mountains.

Without asking, he poured her another.

"Are you trying to get me drunk, McGrew?"

"Jake."

"Let's stick with Cupcake."

"Fine, Chief," Jake said, pointing with his glass toward the mountains. "A sad memory?"

"They kinda look like home." She sighed again.

"And that would be where?"

Megan glanced at him. "The United States."

"Well, that does narrow it down," Jake said with a smile.

"Idaho."

"Ah!"

"The Sawtooth Mountains. Similar in nature." She also pointed with the glass to the now darkening mountains. She tossed this drink back then handed the glass back to him. "Thanks."

"You can have more if you want. I'm not saving it for any special occasion."

"Nope. Too many drinks and I loose my inhibitions."

"Sounds like fun."

Megan snorted. Her eyes drifted once more to the mountains. A shooting star caught her eye and she glanced up.

Jake followed her glance to see the stars starting to twinkle. When he glanced back she began tearing up.

She cleared her throat quickly and stood up. "Enjoy the view, Cupcake."

Jake stood with her. "Chief—Megan, you seem sad. Want to talk about it?"

"Nope." Megan started to move away, but his hand on her arm stopped her.

"Look, I know what it's like to be alone. Being the only woman on base and in charge, well, it's got to be tough. I've been told I'm a good listener."

Megan raised her eyes to meet his. "Thanks but no."

Jake stared into her eyes. He could tell she was torn up about something. Every now and then his sisters would get the same attitude. Maybe he should try a tactic that worked with them. "Then, would a hug help?" He lifted his arms.

Her eyes softened, and tears formed in them again. "Sure." She leaned into him, putting her arms around him.

Jake encircled her with his arms and gave a slight squeeze. His eyebrows arched. She had body armor on underneath her large shirt. He could also feel her shaking as she laid her head on his chest. He held on to her, waiting until she was ready to break contact.

Megan patted his back and let go. She wiped her tears. Taking a step back, she studied the rooftop. Finally she looked up. "Thanks."

"Anytime."

With a soft smile, she headed away.

"Hey, Megan."

"Yeah?" She turned.

"Out of curiosity." He sat down, reaching for his glass. "Why do you have on body armor, off duty and on base?"

She stepped back. "Three reasons. One, it's habit. I almost feel naked without it. Two, for protection. Believe it or not, I have a lot of enemies. And three, it hides the fact that I'm a woman. I can, if I dress the right way, blend in as a man. About the only time I don't wear it is in my room."

Jake nodded in thanks.

"Have a good evening, Cupcake."

Jake winked. "You too, Chief."

After she left, his eyes turned to the darkening mountains. There was one last stray ray of sunlight peaking out from behind the foothills giving just a touch of pink to the surrounding area. He poured another glass and toasted silently the last visual scene, a smile playing on his lips. The hug had worked. This was the first time they had been on a first name basis.

***

The next afternoon Jake was walking down Chicken Street with Gunner shopping for gifts for their families. Chicken Street was the main market street near the base. They stopped twice to sample local food: very spicy, yet good. Gunner enjoyed it immensely. Jake was polite, but it just wasn't his thing.

The market was similar to those in Iraq, only the streets were more littered with trash and some of the buildings were bombed out, many having never been rebuilt after the fighting.

Traffic was mostly bicycles and foot traffic, although the occasional Toyota rambled by. Jake made a comment to Cowboy as the group left the front gate about the weird fact that there were a lot of white Toyotas in Kabul. Cowboy merely laughed in answer.

Now they were in a rug shop. Gunner was negotiating with the shop owner on a particularly stunning rug. Jake looked at a few, considering buying one for his mom but decided to wait. He might find something better later on.

He stepped out of the shop and stuck his hands in his pockets, looking around the street. Two young street urchins, boys age seven or eight, immediately accosted him wanting a handout of money. Neither looked like

45

they had eaten in weeks, but he knew once he started handing out money, he'd be swamped.

Jake held out his hands and shook his head no, then he held up one finger in the universal sign for 'wait.' Being in Iraq prepared him for this. He pulled out two Dumdum suckers and handed each kid one. Their eyes lit up and smiles adorned their faces. Although not better than money, it was a unique gift from a foreigner.

They thanked him heartily in their language. Even though Jake couldn't understand them, it was obvious that's what they were saying. Then they hurried off, their prizes stuck firmly in their pockets.

Jake smiled, watching them run off. He liked making kids happy, not to mention that kids in Afghanistan had witnessed many atrocities and anytime someone could provide them with a little pleasure it was always appreciated. He went back to watching people in the area with his hands in his pockets.

A white Toyota pulled up down the street that caught his attention. He nonchalantly watched it. Two men stepped out. One was dressed in traditional pants with a long vest garment. His hat was the round, flat type worn by most Afghans in Kabul. The other was dressed in a more traditional Muslim way. He had a full beard and turban.

Jake was puzzled. *Something isn't right.* The fully dressed man was very short and his walk familiar. Both men looked to be nervous and entered a jeweler's shop.

Jake turned to see Gunner walking out with a medium sized, rolled up rug draped over his shoulder. He smiled at the Chilean. "Haggled him down, huh?"

Gunner smiled. "I learn from bestest in Iraq."

"The Iraqis are shrewd negotiators."

Gunner nodded then hefted the rug to a more comfortable position. "However, I miscounted."

"Miscounted?" Jake asked.

"Very heavy. Cannot walk all day with rug. Must take back to base."

Jake did a silent 'Ah hah.' "You meant miscalculated."

"That too." Gunner smiled thanks to the American. He told Jake to correct his English. He wanted to be able to speak flawless English by the time his contract was up. "We go?" He thumbed back toward the White Pine compound. "We come back then."

Jake stopped Gunner with his hand. "Let's check out one more shop, then we'll head back. Okay?"

"Yes. That is okay."

Jake led the way down the street toward the jeweler's shop. After crossing the street and dodging bicycles, they came to the run down shop. Grimy, dust covered windows obscured some of the merchandise, but several beautiful pieces of jewelry could be seen. Jake was amazed at the artistry. He pointed at one and looked at Gunner.

"Most beautifly."

"Beautiful," Jake corrected. "Yes, it is. I think my oldest sister would love this piece or something like it."

"How many sisters do you have?" Gunner asked leaning closer to the glass.

"Five."

Gunner chuckled. "And other, uh, brothers?"

"None. I was the only boy. Four older sisters, one younger sister."

"I am sorry."

Jake laughed. "Yeah. Tell me about it. You? Siblings?"

"Two brothers survived. One sister. She is married and has three children. Her husband dead and she now lives with my parents. I am baby," Gunner said. "I send her rug to put on floor of her room. I wait here. Rug big for store."

"I'll be right back." Jake stepped into the store and waited for a few seconds letting his eyes adjust to the dimmer interior. It was empty except for the clerk.

CHAPTER 5

Immediately the store clerk stepped up to wait on him. He smiled broadly and waved to the display, inquiring if Jake wanted to buy something. The store was darker than Jake anticipated, and smaller, but lined with display cases overflowing with jewelry of all sorts.

"Lovely stuff," Jake said with a smile, knowing the guy probably couldn't speak English. He pointed at the piece in the window. "Can I see it?" He pointed at his eyes then the piece again.

The clerk nodded his head as he reached for the necklace. He handed Jake the item. The clerk's smile got even bigger with pride as he patted himself on the chest and pointed at the piece. Jake took it to mean that the guy probably made it. He went back to looking at the necklace.

What caught his eye in the window was the incredible deep blue of the stone and the symmetrical beads cut from it. There were dozens of round, identical blue beads each separated by a small bead of silver. At the clasp was a stone about the size of a thumb with streaks of gold flecks in it. This was encased in a bed of silver. Jake studied the clasp and noticed that it looked like the necklace could be worn with the pendant on or off, as the clasp was an integral part of both sides of the pendant.

"What is it made of?" Jake asked, holding the necklace up. "Uh…"

The clerk seemed to understand the puzzled look on Jake's face. He rattled off something then pointed at the blue beads. "Lapis Lazuli." He made motions of mining and pointed toward the north. He imitated the carving of said beads then patted himself on the chest.

Jake rubbed the smooth blue stone. He nodded approvingly. "How much?" Then he indicated money.

The clerk rattled something off, then reached into the display and pulled out a card to show the price writing in Afghanistan currency. The card had been hidden by another piece.

Jake almost gave the piece back but the look of pride in the clerk's eyes was so prominent that Jake didn't even haggle. It was still cheap for a piece of this quality, even in U.S. dollars. He reached into his pants and pulled out a roll of local currency, counting off the correct number.

As he did so, the clerk reverently wrapped the piece in a red silk cloth and tied it with gold colored string. He held it out for Jake to inspect.

Jake looked up from his counting, pausing. The wrapping itself was a work of art. Jake smiled at the guy letting him know that it was beautiful too. He handed the money over and took the necklace with a slight bow.

Again the clerk's eyes beamed with pride.

Jake waved goodbye, and as he left he said with another slight bow, "I'll be back."

The clerk gave a slight bow back.

Jake stopped outside the shop. "Gunner, look at this."

"That is… goodly wrapped. Is it the necklace from the window?"

Jake nodded. "I almost don't want to send it to my sister. I bet she won't even unwrap it." He smiled at Gunner.

At that moment, the door opened behind him and he moved off to the side so that whoever was coming out could leave. He turned to see that it was the guys who had entered the shop earlier.

Jake was momentarily puzzled. He'd been so distracted by the necklace that he forgot the main reason for going into the shop. But they had not been in the store. *They must have been in the back or somewhere.*

The regularly dressed guy looked at them then hurried toward the truck. The other, more traditionally dressed Muslim man, came out second and almost ran into Jake because he was tucking a bundle of papers into the folds of his clothes. Their eyes met and the Afghanistan quickly looked down. He mumbled something.

Jake froze. *Have I met this guy before?* Something about him looked familiar, but Jake just couldn't place it. Still the feeling that he knew this guy was instant and gut wrenching. He watched as the guy hurried to the truck, which quickly pulled away.

"Jake?"

"I…" Jake shook his head and glanced around the area out of habit. "Too weird."

"What? Is everything good?"

"Yeah." Jake glanced back to where the truck had disappeared. "Just a feeling that I know that guy, the one with the turban."

"You come here before?"

"No. That's the weird thing." Jake shook himself again, then motioned for Gunner. "Let's head back to base. After putting our stuff away, Cowboy gave me directions to a good restaurant. Are you up for an adventure?"

"Most goodly," Gunner said with a nod.

Jake smiled. "How about we see if we can't find someone else to go with us? We know that Cowboy is out. How about Megan?"

"She not come off base often."

"Yeah, I know, but she needs to get out."

"We all invited to big feast, last day of Independence. She go then. I bet she no go now," Gunner said even as they started the trek back to the base. They were two miles from the compound.

"You're probably right but..." He winked at Gunner. "All work and no play, makes the Chief an unhappy camper."

"What? I do not understand. What is 'camper'?"

Jake chuckled. "Never mind. Let's see if we can't find her anyway."

"Most goodly."

But Megan was nowhere to be found. No one knew where she could be. Jake met back with Gunner after each had searched part of the compound. He frowned as they paused at the gate.

"I wonder where she is?" Jake asked looking back toward the main hanger.

Gunner shifted his weight on his feet. "Come. We go. I get hungry. Megan be okay by herself. She goodly at doing that."

Jake nodded absentmindedly. "Yeah."

They left the compound again, and as they walked Jake couldn't shake the feeling that he had seen something of importance. For some reason, those two guys were up to something. He didn't know what, but he knew that it was something. And he also knew without a doubt that he knew the turbaned guy.

***

The next day Jake, Cowboy and Gunner were en route to a different shop on Chicken Street. It sold mostly stone statues. As they walked, they talked about their home lives.

"She loves stone carvings. Bess is such a push over," Cowboy said.

"How many years are you being married?" Gunner asked.

"Twelve." Cowboy stopped briefly to look into a shop window that sold scarves. He looked at Gunner. "No little ones. I'm gone too much for'em. This is my last year workin' with White Pine. I miss ma home."

"Me miss family, but pay is goodly," Gunner said with a huge smile.

Cowboy nodded. "Ain't that the truth." He turned to Jake as they neared the shop. "Lookin' for anything special, Jake?"

"No. I need to get something for each of my sisters, my Mom and Dad. Maybe a statue. I sent all my sisters a scarf from Iraq." He rubbed his stubbly chin. White Pine encouraged the growth of beards as it was the local custom. Jake still hadn't decided if he wanted one or not. "How long have you worked for White Pine?"

Cowboy thought for a few seconds. "Too long. Too many scary ass missions." Then he smiled. "Four years. Like I said, this is my last. After Affie here, I'ma headin' home. I know that I can always pick up a job flyin' for someone, somewhere."

"How long have you been flying with Megan?"

"All four years. She needed a co-pilot and I had just signed up. Scared the shit outta me. Thought I was gonna die the first time out with her." Cowboy started laughing. "Been an adventure since. Ain't no borin' times with Megan."

Gunner nodded in agreement. "She make working a goodly time."

They laughed, weaving their way down the street around people. In waves, the young street urchins begged. Cowboy was fond of giving coins to the kids and they were always followed by a few.

"Here 'tis, gentlemen. The guy usually has some local glassware from Herat, too." Cowboy walked into the store ahead of the others.

Jake was the last in and the owner of the shop was hurrying from the back with a huge smile on his face. He noticed that Cowboy and the owner embraced in the local greeting of kissing both cheeks. The man greeted Gunner in the same way. Jake followed suit, although more uncomfortable.

"Come. Enter." The shop owner opened his hands. Then he motioned to Cowboy to wait. He hurried into the back then came out with a small statue. "You may like, Cowboy. I save for you. Is…." The owner struggled with the English but handed the statue over.

"Wow!" Cowboy looked at the statue. It was of one of the local sheep, an ibex mother and baby, standing on a mountainside looking down, carved out of white stone. "This is beautiful."

Jake wandered around the shop looking at various items. He'd have to keep this shop in mind for gifts too. The quality was excellent. Finally, he purchased a small snow leopard carving for his Dad then exited to stand and watch people again.

As he stood there, he was again accosted by street kids and handed out suckers. His sisters always sent candy. He had mentioned once, while in Iraq, that he had given candy to local kids and the reception he had gotten. Since then, every box from home contained hard candy, bags and bags of candy.

Laughter caught his attention down the street, and he noticed a group of men smoking and drinking. The men were sipping from small glasses in front of a chai khanas or tea house.

There were seven of them, mostly in the traditional garb. Three wore longer robes and turbans. They were arguing. Two in particular were actively discussing something and pointing north.

Jake narrowed his eyes as one of the turbaned men turned to spit in the street. It was the same guy from the white Toyota. Jake stepped back into the alcove made by the stone shop and riveted his attention on the group.

The man from yesterday was not speaking but listening intently, sipping occasionally at the tea. He was not smoking. That was odd, because most everyone in the country did and tobacco was widely used by the adult population.

Jake stared. *I know this guy.* His feelings from yesterday were confirmed. As Jake stood there, he ran though his mind everyone on base, comparing them with the turbaned guy down the street. No one matched. Then he compared this guy with men from Iraq. Nothing.

Finally, some sort of agreement was reached because the discussion went back to more civil tones and gestures. The turbaned man now nodded at someone who turned to him. He pointed toward the north and whatever he said caused the group to laugh. A quick drink emptied his cup. The man stood along with one of the others and exchanged embraces.

As the two men waited at the corner, Jake stepped out of the shop to get a better look. At that moment, the turbaned guy looked down the street and their eyes met. And in that look, from two blocks away, Jake saw recognition dawn in the guy's eyes. He said something to his companion. They hurried across the street and disappeared into the crowd.

Jake stepped farther into the street but lost them amid shoppers. He swallowed nervously. *What is going on?*

Gunner stepped into the street and saw Jake frozen. He looked in the same direction. "Is everything good?"

"Yeah. I saw that same guy from yesterday."

"The man in the..." Gunner motioned at his head.

"The turban. Yeah."

"Maybe you tell Megan about it. She in charge," Gunner said with a frown.

"Maybe," Jake said, seeing Cowboy finishing up, package in hand.

Later that night, Jake found Megan in her office reading paperwork. He lightly tapped on the door frame.

"Yeah?" She looked up.

He walked in and sat down in the chair. "I've been looking for you."

"Oh yeah?" Megan relaxed back. "Why?"

Jake smiled. "We're having an impromptu basketball game and looking for another player, if you can handle a ball."

"Pass," Megan said looking Jake in the eyes. "I was never good at sports."

Jake shook his head. With her body and quickness with her hands and feet in the aircraft, he bet she was a star athlete. "I doubt that."

Megan merely chuckled.

"I also..." Jake stood, closed the door to her office, then reseated himself. "I saw something today that...I don't know. If I were in Iraq, I'd report it to my commander. So, I guess that's you."

Megan's eye turned wary. "Yeah?"

"Yesterday and today, I saw something that seemed suspicious."

"Like?"

"A guy wearing a turban was acting, I don't know, strange."

"How strange? You've got to be more specific. What did he do?" Megan asked, drumming her fingers.

Jake sighed softly. "That's just it. He did nothing specifically wrong."

"But?"

"Yeah. But, I know something is wrong. My gut's telling me something's up."

"Describe him."

Jake did and the circumstances when he saw the guy. "My instincts are telling me something's wrong."

"Cupcake, I can't go to Fahim with a gut feeling. I have to have more to go on."

"Yeah." Jake looked down at his hands. "I know."

"What else?" Megan asked.

Jake glanced up. Her brown eyes seemed to be trying to read his soul. This neutral expression was even attractive, better than her angry face, which in a weird way was sexy too. "Okay. This is going to sound weird."

"Coming from you?" Megan said with a smile to ease the tension.

"I know him."

"What?" The surprise was genuine.

"Yeah. Twice I've made eye contact with this turbaned guy and, so help me God, I know him."

"How can that be?"

Jake shrugged. "I've thought about every man on base but…"

Megan rubbed her fingers on her lips. She finally shook her head. "Just keep your eyes open. Next time you see him, point him out to someone else. Maybe if more than one of us see him, we'll be able to ID him."

Jake nodded. "So, are you coming to the game?"

"Pass. I've got work to do."

"Chief, you need to rest too."

"There's no rest for those in charge, Cupcake."

"Are you at least coming to the big feast tomorrow night at Masood's house?"

"Yeah. I've got to go to that one."

"Good." Jake paused then frowned again.

"Look Cupcake, put this guy out of your mind. I'm sure it was nothing. After all, this isn't Iraq. Not everyone is the enemy." Megan's finger played with the edge of her shirt.

Jake studied her. This was odd. Her attitude completely changed. She was almost nervous. Finally, he nodded. He would never understand women.

***

Megan stood in the living room of Masood's house talking with a pilot from another crew. It was a modest home, small and middle class compared to homes in the United States, but in Afghanistan it was considered upper class.

The meal had been spectacular. Since most crew members were new to the country, it allowed them to experience the splendid flavors of local food. Even Megan was impressed. As always, her two favorites were served. The first was mutton kebab with raw onions covered with a very spicy sauce. The second was pilau, a dish consisting of rice with raisin, carrots and lamb. It was a hard choice between the two for her.

She glanced around and saw Jake complimenting Masood on the feast. Jake met her eyes across the room then moved with a smile toward her. Megan swallowed nervously. *Damn, he's good looking.* She could just imagine how it would feel to be pulled into him and held against his naked chest. His muscles rippling as he embraced her, his hands gently stroking her arms or caressing her breasts with his strong hands. Her mind flashed back to the hug on the roof and she could feel herself warming in places she shouldn't be, especially since it was in connection with a member of her crew.

"There you are," Jake said. He nodded at the other pilot who left Megan's side in search of more food.

"Yeah. What did you need?"

Jake gave her a smirk. "Knock it off, Chief. This is a social event. Make nice."

Megan chuckled but inside she was sweating harder than ever. Whenever he stood next to her, she felt like she was having hot flashes. *What is this about?* She hadn't felt this way since her first crush at the age of eight. She looked at her watch again. It was after prayers, yet not quite dark. From prior experience, she knew it was best to be back at base long before it got dark.

"Got a date?" Jake asked with a smile.

"Funny." Megan glanced around. "I need to be heading back to base."

"Why? Masood said he'd escort us all back in about an hour. That's still way before curfew."

"For you," she said slightly annoyed. She hated this part of Afghanistan and Muslim society. "I'm a woman. Different rules."

Jake nodded in understanding. "You came with Kelly, but he's still eating—"

"Damn," Megan said softly almost under her breath. She usually had a male escort anytime off base. It was not only safer, it was Muslim law.

"I'll walk you back."

Megan didn't answer him right away, but just studied his face.

Jake held up his hands in surrender. "Seriously, I don't want you walking back alone. I figured that was policy anyway. I'm done here. Sometimes spicy food does me in."

Megan glanced again at her watch. She really didn't want to be alone with McGrew unless it was work related. It was a test she wasn't sure she could pass. "I guess."

"That was a resounding testament to my ability to keep you safe," Jake said jokingly. He moved with Megan to Masood's side.

"Fahim, I'd better be getting back."

The head of the base looked shocked then glanced at his watch. He nodded then looked around for Cowboy.

"McGrew offered to escort me. Thank your wife again for me."

"She loved the scarf you gave her, Megan. She says thank you. And the loaves of bread were much appreciated." Fahim gave her a little bow. Under their religion, it was wrong for a man to touch a woman that he was not related too. Then he turned to Jake. "The bag of candy for the children will delight them to no end. Thank you." He gave Jake an embrace.

Jake nodded after the greeting. "Tell them not to eat it all at once. It'll make their teeth rot." Both men chuckled.

Megan pulled a dark green scarf out of her back pocket and waved at Cowboy who was sitting on the toshak mats and pillows which serve as couches in many Afghanistan homes. He nodded back, his mouth full of food. With a wink, he did a little head bob to McGrew, and his grin got wider. Megan shot him a dirty look, then turned toward the door. Jake followed her. She wrapped the scarf around her head and tucked the ends over her shoulders. They walked quietly for several blocks.

"So, how do you feel wearing the head scarf?"

Megan shrugged. "I've gotten used to it." She had barely gotten the words out of her mouth when several street kids appeared from nowhere. They were almost hanging on Jake, hands outstretched, calling out to him.

Jake smiled as he patted one on the head. "You've been here before, son. You've got at least four pieces of candy."

The boy smiled even bigger having been singled out by this foreigner.

Jake reached into his pockets and brought out the ever present candy. He held it out of their reach. Their voices clamored around him. "Do you know what they're saying?" Jake asked Megan as she stood off to the side with a smile, watching all.

Megan chuckled. "Your name is Sweet Candy Man. You're getting quite a reputation."

Jake chuckled as he handed candy to the kids. One piece per kid. They begged for more. Jake shook his head with a smile. "No more." He held out his hand in an obvious way that he was not dispensing more candy.

Megan lowered her voice and spoke softly to the kids. Quickly the kids scattered just as fast as they appeared. Several threw words over their shoulders to Jake. It was obvious they were thanking him.

Jake looked at Megan and saw the sexy smile she was giving him, which was quickly wiped off her face. "I didn't know you spoke the language. Which one was that?"

"Pashtu."

"Do you speak the other one too?"

"You mean Dari?" Megan watched as Jake nodded. "A little."

"So, how many times has our illustrious Chief been here in Afghanistan?"

"This is my forth rotation."

"And Iraq?"

"Why?"

He shrugged. "Conversation."

"Five in Iraq."

"Which do you like better?"

"Why the twenty questions, Cupcake?"

Again Jake shrugged. "I like to know the people I work with."

Megan brooded for a few seconds thinking about both countries. "Neither."

"Then…"

"Why do I come here?" Megan answered with a smile. She glanced around and saw several men walking toward them. She lowered her head, pulled her scarf closer, and wiped the smile off her face, all at the same time.

The men gave rude glances at the two, especially Megan, but they said nothing. Both glared at Jake and their conversation halted until they were a couple steps past the two foreigners. Then one spoke over his shoulder.

Jake glanced behind then turned an angry, puzzled look at Megan. "Do you know what he just said? If I had to guess, I'd say it was an insult."

Megan quickly glanced up to see who was around. "Yeah. He insulted me. Something about a daughter of a foreign pig, and a few other nasty things."

Jake's face got even darker and he turned to look back at them, now over a block away.

"Ignore them. They're fundamentalists. It's better to take the insult and get away, than the beating. Luckily, it's still light." Megan gave a slight grin. Megan could hear him take a deep breath to release anger that was visible on his face.

"The voice of experience?"

Megan hesitated then nodded. "On my first rotation here. I, uh, I spoke too loudly in the market. A man belonging to the same group was there. Before I could even think, I'd been hit many times." Megan shuddered but stopped speaking.

"So, you were saying? Before they interrupted us."

"Why do I come here? The money."

"But what if you crash in the mountains and... I can only imagine how backwards the mountain people are. Okay, backward isn't really the word I meant, but you know what I mean."

"It's the risk I take." She shrugged. "Why did you join up with White Pine?"

Jake seemed to be thinking hard. He stuck his hands in his pockets as he walked. "I guess the same reason. Money. A couple of years doing this and I can retire to do whatever I want, not just a job." The question bothered him. *Why did I sign up?* Something was nagging at him as he thought about it.

They walked in silence for a few minutes. Finally, they could see the compound ahead. Megan slowed. It was nice to walk with him when she wasn't his boss or needing to establish authority over him.

"What's wrong?" Jake asked, instinctively slowing with her. Out of habit, he glanced around the area for intruders or anything amiss.

"I don't get off the base much, except on missions when I'm flying. This is nice." Her voice was softer than normal.

Jake smiled and stopped. He waited until she stopped and looked at him. "Me too."

"Me too what?"

"I enjoyed the walk."

Megan made a funny face at his wry smile. "Shut up."

"Seriously, Chief. I had a good time." He motioned her through the main gate and they both greeted the security guard, then walked toward the crew's barracks.

A man dressed in khaki shorts and shirt stepped out of the main office building across the compound area. He stood looking at them. It was enough to get their attention.

Megan paused as she swept the headscarf back down onto her shoulders. "Damn."

"What?" Jake asked as he followed her gaze. "Who is he?"

"Someone I need to see. We probably have a new mission first thing in the morning. See you bright and early. Seven o'clock. Post a note for the rest of the crew." She looked Jake in the eyes. A small smile curved her lips. "Thanks for the escort." With that, she walked with a quick stride to the man.

As she entered the building behind the mysterious man, Megan glanced back. Jake was still watching her, his hair highlighted by the beginning of the sunset. *Damn, he looked good.*

***

The next morning, the entire crew was gathered in the briefing room, except Megan. As with most missions, she was first in and last out. She definitely worked harder than the guys.

Cowboy leaned back, laughing with Gunner about the day before. The others had been invited to join a 'football' game with the locals. It had been a good game of soccer with the local team trouncing White Pine. And even though they knew they were going to be beat, it fostered good relations, so it was 'strongly suggested' that everyone play.

Jake glanced at his watch again. Fisher was retelling the way Jake surprised the locals with his footwork and how he had stolen the ball from their best player, only to have it re-stolen from him and the Afghan scored a point. He smiled at Fisher's rendition of the action.

Glancing at the doorway again, Jake caught Cowboy's glance too. "Kelly, where's the Chief?" Lately, Megan had been meeting him five minutes before the crew meetings to 'teach him' and let him see the pre-mission paperwork. But today there'd been a note in the crew chief box to just show up with the rest of the crew. *Odd.*

Cowboy gave him a slight smile. "Just wait."

Sure enough she showed up within a few minutes. The room settled into silence as she slid into her chair. She was dressed in her flight suit, which meant the mission would begin immediately.

"Okay. We got a split job today. Cowboy, Gunner and Cupcake are with me. Everyone else will be in the Chinook with Punk and Stick as pilots. Tiny, you're in charge in back in Pestilence. Your job is merely a drop. You aren't even landing. When you get over the area, Stick'll tell you to drop and you guys push the crate out of the back of the Chinook. Back to base and your day is over. Any questions?"

The room stayed silent.

"Good. Gunner and Cupcake stay here for a minute. The rest of you head out. Cowboy, could you start the preflight? I've got a few more things to do then I'll be out. Should be in about ten."

"Sure thang, Darlin'." He left the room right behind the other group of men.

Megan turned to the other two. "If you don't have body armor on, get it when we're done. This is a hot mission. You'll be manning both guns, so make sure that they're good to go and you have enough ammo. We might not be back until after dark. It depends on a lot of things."

"And our mission?" Jake asked, still leaning back in his chair.

"Just do as I say. Don't ask questions. Get going," Megan ordered.

Gunner immediately stood and left. Jake stood.

"I thought I was being shown everything so I can learn? I'd like to know what the hell I'm walking into."

"Afterwards," Megan said also standing up.

Jake frowned.

"I could replace you. I picked you because you have a level head and don't panic. Was I in error? Can you follow orders, Cupcake?"

"I can and I will. But I think Gunner and I deserve to know what's going on."

"Gunner's already guessed," Megan said putting her hands on her hips. "I don't have time for this. Are you in my crew or not?"

"I'm in, but we'll talk when we get back." He stalked out of the room.

"Just great," she said softly to the empty room. She should replace him, but there was no one in the group that she trusted except Gunner and Cowboy. *No. He'll do fine.*

Megan dropped off an envelope at the front desk. "Zarin, mail this for me, please. And try that number again. If you don't get an answer, try the second number. Ask for Todd. He's my brother. Ask him if he's talked to my dad and if he knows anything. Thanks."

When she got to the Black Hawk, Cowboy was half done with the safety check. She helped with the walk around then both of them moved up to the cockpit. Cowboy started the helicopter. The Chinook was already warming up with both pilots settling in. The pilot saluted to let her know they were ready.

She was still standing outside Famine. Glancing in, she saw the two men buckled and ready. With a quick nod to herself, she raised her arm to signal the main hanger building.

Seconds later, a man ran out. The camouflage, floppy hat mostly hid his black hair, but he looked normal and could have blended in anywhere. He was clothed in full camouflage gear. All of his pockets were bursting at the seams with stuff.

Megan met him a few feet from the helicopter. They spoke quickly then she motioned to the back of the Black Hawk. "This is Gunner and Cupcake. Cupcake's a former Special Forces Ranger. Get head gear on, but this is a silent trip." Her eyes glued to Cupcake. She knew that Gunner understood what was going on.

Jake narrowed his eyes with a glance at the mysterious man, but nodded at her as he plugged the helmet into the intercom system.

Megan shut the big door and headed to the cockpit. Minutes later, they were airborne behind the larger Chinook.

***

They traveled northeast for forty minutes. Then the Chinook turned right and the Black Hawk banked left. Up to this point, there had been nothing spoken. "Okay Rover, we drop you in five minutes."

"Thanks, Ghost."

After another couple of minutes, they circled back to where they had split from the other helicopter.

Jake looked out his side and saw what looked like the Chinook heading away from them in the direction of the base. He frowned with a look at the guy who was checking his pockets.

The guy glanced up and smiled.

Jake nodded back, then it hit him. This guy was probably CIA and this was a covert mission. Whatever was in the delivered crate was for this guy.

Sure enough they were quickly descending near an opening in the terrain. The clearing was empty, but as he searched for anyone suspicious, he saw the crate upright off to the side in trees. It looked like it had knocked a couple trees down as it fell.

"Rover, the object is about twenty yards at two o'clock from our position." Megan's voice sounded over the intercom.

"Got it."

The Black Hawk didn't fully land but hovered inches from the ground. The man hopped off and ran for the area of the crate. When he got there, he gave a slight wave. They accelerated up and away.

They traveled several more minutes, then quickly descended to a small area in a different valley cut out of the heavily forested area.

Gunner smiled at him as the helicopter shutdown. Jake looked at him then back toward the cockpit. *What was going on?*

"We wait," Gunner said softly.

"Yeah." Megan's voice came over the headsets. "But keep your eyes peeled. This isn't a safe area. Cowboy and I will take the first break. Then we'll rotate one on each side watching at all times. Assuming nobody comes across us, we might be here until dark. Keep quiet as much as possible."

Silence settled over the aircraft.

***

The sun was setting in the valley. All day the four of them switched between watching and taking breaks. Gunner had come back to the Black Hawk from taking a leak when a static crackle sounded over the headset.

"Ready, Famine."

Megan nodded at Cowboy as she moved to the cockpit to begin warming up the helicopter.

"Give us fifteen minutes, pardner," Cowboy replied. "Bark if ya'll see anyone."

"Got it." The static died.

Megan started the engines and let the chopper warm up. "Positions, guys."

Jake glanced at Gunner as both got behind their guns, ready for action.

As the aircraft lifted, Megan spoke, "Keep sharp. The bad guys like to shoot us down, something I hate happening."

Gunner chuckled and Jake smiled.

Minutes later they were nearing the drop off area.

"Ruff. Ruff." Came a static filled sound.

"Rover?" Cowboy intoned into the radio.

"I got company coming down the hill. Looks like a small squad, maybe ten."

"Damn," Megan said softly over the intercom. "Guys?"

Jake scanned his side. "Got'em. They're about three quarters of the way down. More like twelve."

"Distance?" Megan asked.

"Coming into rifle range."

"Rover, this is Famine. Scoop and run. Be ready," Cowboy said. "Cupcake, you're in the hot seat. Fire at will."

Jake took a deep breath and cocked the door gun.

"Here we go," Megan said as the chopper swooped down at full speed and appeared like it would crash. At the last minute, she leveled it and hovered inches from the ground with Jake's side facing the enemy's position.

Bullets were already ricocheting off the helicopter. Jake fired as fast as the gun would allow, sweeping the area with no specific target in mind. The aircraft was down less than thirty seconds when it lifted off again. Jake kept firing at the enemy's position even as Megan tilted the helicopter to allow the best angle for firing. At the same time, she was accelerating up and out of the area. And fast.

Jake finally stopped firing when they were out of range and released his tight grip on the gun. He wiped the sweat off his hands and relaxed into his seat.

The mysterious man laid his head back and was obviously relieved to be in the air.

"Good job, Cupcake," Megan said, a smile in her voice. "Everyone okay?"

"We all good," Gunner said smiling at the other two.

"Rover, which drop off? One or two?"

"Two. Appreciate the pick up, Ghost."

"That's our job. Relax. You got twenty minutes 'til we reach your rendezvous."

***

"What was that about?" Jake asked after Gunner and Cowboy finished their paperwork. They weren't in the usual meeting room but in Megan's office.

Megan pushed her paperwork across the corner of the desk to him. "Joint operation."

"I figured that out," Jake muttered, still disgusted. He quickly read the post paperwork. "This is completely different from what happened."

Megan nodded with a smile. "This was one of those missions that required creative writing. Read Gunner's report. Basically copy his." Megan tore up Jake's report and pushed a new copy to him.

Jake read Gunner's two sentence report. It said they dropped a crate in the mountainous region and flew back to base, total hours for the mission two, which included pre and post mission. His head came up to look at Megan.

"For all covert operations we get more pay. I file the appropriate total hours on this form. The extra time is listed as maintenance on the aircraft." She showed him the last form. "This is one of those instances that's mentioned in your contract about selective memory."

Jake frowned. "How did you get the assignment? I checked the box late last night and again this morning for pre-paperwork."

Megan at first didn't reply. "They let you know. In this instance, it was the guy last night, remember? Sometimes it's a call, other times a written note. It depends on the base, the local CIA agent in charge and how sensitive the mission." She paused. "Last night the 'cargo' arrived. I instructed the ground crew what was needed. A quick call to Rupert, the head mechanic or Corn if Rupert's not available, is all it takes. No one asks questions. You just do the work and collect your pay."

"Do you know what this was about?" Jake said as he filled in his paperwork with the same information as Gunner only using different words.

"I'm only informed of things that I need to know." She smiled as Jake's head snapped up. "I can guess a whole lot more."

"Then guess."

Megan shrugged. "Since we were near the Pakistan boarder... That area is possibly one of Osama bin Laden's training camps. My guess is that Rover was confirming the camp's location. Maybe confirming other information and getting a count."

"A count?"

"A count of how many men are in the camp."

"What was in the box?"

"I didn't ask."

"Guess."

"I know when to stop guessing."

"So, this was to get bin Laden?"

Megan immediately shook her head no. "The U.S. Military and other agencies know where he is, generally. Between satellites and other intelligence, besides drops like this, I would guess they pretty much know his location."

"So why don't they go get him?"

"Why?" Megan asked. "He's contained in the mountains."

"But..."

"Have you heard of his successor, his top lieutenant, Ayman al-Zawahiri?"
Jake shook his head handing her his paperwork.

"If bin Laden is killed, he becomes a martyr. And that would bring in more recruits than anything. Al-Zawahiri is ten times worse. Bin Laden is smart. This other guy..." Megan shrugged. "Besides, do you know the force it would take to ferret bin Laden out of his various holes in the mountains?"

"Yes, I realize that but..."

"He'd slip from one hole to another." Megan interrupted. "The Russians couldn't ferret out the rebels from those mountains in ten years." Megan shook her head. "For once, the military and the White House are actually being smart about this."

CHAPTER 6

Megan's voice sounded around the corner from Jake as he walked in the hallway. He slowed, perking up his ears.

"Zarin, did you reach anyone?"

"There was no answer at your father's number, Megan. All day it just rang. I tried the other number. A woman answered. She would not answer my questions. She was rather rude I'm sorry to say."

"Did you ask for Todd? Why didn't you ask for him?" Megan's tone took on an urgent note.

Jake backtracked to the corner, listened, then with a lot of trepidation, he peeked.

"He was not at home according to the lady. And she said to tell you that if it was important to you, you would be here with him," Zarin said softly. "I am sorry, Megan." She stood behind the counter with Megan in front, one hand tapping on the grey top.

Megan sighed. "Yeah." She glanced at her watch. "Can you try my brother's number one more time? Maybe if I let him yell at me, he'll at least tell me about Dad."

Zarin dialed the number and handed the phone over. At White Pine there was only one reliable satellite phone for long distance calls.

Jake leaned on the wall and crossed his arms as he listened, glancing around the corner occasionally.

"Marsha, is Todd there?" Megan asked. "No, I just got back from a job and..." She leaned on the counter as she listened.

Zarin tried to appear busy and not eavesdropping. She turned around shuffling papers and filing.

"Can you just... I know that... Can you just tell me how it went with my dad at the doctor's?... Think what you will Marsha... Yes, I would like to talk to him... Todd, how's Dad?"

Jake frowned, pulling his head back around the corner.

"I got the letter, but he said he had an appointment with a..." Megan sighed again. "Look, let's not get into this old issue. Neither of us has changed. Yeah, right. Just tell me, is the diagnosis correct?"

Jake peeked around the corner to see Megan frowning. She was facing away from Zarin, her eyes focused into space as she listened.

"So, make him tell you." There was silence for a few seconds. "Damn it. Can you at least call and leave me a message when you find out more?... Why not?... If you call the number I gave you, the message will get to me. You don't have to call where I am... I can't tell you that... Damn it, it's my job!... Dad would understand."

"Fine. Tell Dad to call me... Whatever." Megan reached over the desk and hung up the phone. "Thanks, Zarin. If I get a cable or message, find me right away." Megan stalked off down the hall.

Jake jumped back, then after hearing her footsteps fade, he stuck his head around the corner. He walked up to the counter. "That sounded serious."

Zarin nodded. "Her dad has a serious medical condition. He went in for tests. Ms. Cartwright was trying to find out the results."

Jake glanced down the hall where Megan disappeared. "Did I understand right that her family won't talk to her?"

"Yes. The, I think you say, sister-in-law was quite rude. Cursed at me and told me to tell Megan something very rude. Megan is a nice person; she does not need to hear such things." Zarin mumbled something in her language.

Jake almost smiled. He just bet it was a curse at Megan's sister-in-law. With a soft tap on the counter, he headed down the same hall toward the outside door.

Megan was nowhere.

After stopping in his room to retrieve whiskey, he noticed that her door was open, which meant she was not in. Megan always closed her door. With a determined look, he headed for the roof. There was no one there in the dark. Jake frowned. He stood thinking for a few seconds then headed to the hanger.

Dead quiet. There were very few people out this late at night. With a puzzled look, he headed back to the crew quarters area. Jake would check her room one more time then head to bed.

This time Megan's door was closed. He knocked softly.

"Yeah?"

Jake swallowed before speaking. He was treading on unfamiliar ground. "Hey Chief, I got a question." He heard her sigh through the door.

"Can it wait until morning, McGrew?"

"Nope." There was no answer. "May I come in?"

"Yeah," Megan said softly. She swung her legs over the bedside and got comfortable. She was dressed in a pair of khaki pants and black T-shirt.

Jake walked in and closed the door. He glanced at himself as she looked him up and down. He was still dressed in camouflage pants but had gotten rid of the rest of his outfit and was also dressed in a black T-shirt. He saw her questioning look as she took in the whiskey bottle and glasses. Their eyes met.

He gave her a soft smile. "I kind of overheard your phone conversation in the hall. Thought you might like a little company." He hefted the bottle.

"Nice thought, but I have to fly tomorrow, so there's no getting drunk."

"I know, I just thought…" Jake stopped and stared at Megan. "Look, I didn't mean to overhear the conversation." He opened the bottle and poured two glasses. He handed one to her.

Reluctantly she took it, staring at him.

Jake grabbed the body armor off the chair and tossed it on the bed next to Megan. He sat down, knees close but not touching hers.

All of the rooms were alike, one twin bed, one dresser, one closet, one chair. Everyone shared the bathrooms and showers on a floor, including Megan. Most of the men, the base was 99.9 percent men, decorated their rooms somewhat. The decorating had to be tasteful, given where they were. Her room was austere. The only colorful thing was a multicolor, geodesic designed, old quilt.

He held up the glass in a toast. "To living another day."

"Yeah. To another day," Megan said but didn't drink with him. She merely held the glass between her hands staring into the amber liquid.

"A toast is supposed to be shared, Chief."

Megan absentmindedly tossed it back then handed him the glass.

He refused to take it. "Another?"

"Nope. I said I gotta fly."

"Dedicated."

Megan snorted as she studied her pant legs.

"Trouble at home?"

"Yep."

"Wanna talk about it?"

"Nope."

"It might help."

Megan looked up at him, gazing into his blue eyes. "Amateur psychiatrist?"

"It was almost my major in college."

"Really?" Megan scooted back on the bed to lean on the wall. She relaxed one leg straight while the other was bent. She absentmindedly played with the shot glass.

"But I hate sick people." He faked a shudder.

Megan smiled then it faded. "Sick people?"

"I take it your Dad's sick?"

"Yeah. He won't answer his phone. Todd, my spineless, mealy-mouthed brother, can't or won't go over to make dad tell him how the doctor's appointment went." Her voice took on a whiny tone. "'Dad'll tell us when he's good and ready.'" She sighed. "Dad's a stubborn, pigheaded bastard. Won't answer the phone. He doesn't trust them. Thinks they're all bugged. I got to admit, I understand where's he's coming from, but this is a little different. Won't write me. 'Don't ever trust the mail, Meg.' He once told me." Megan sighed again.

Jake said nothing.

"I'm surprised he wrote the two letters I got. And if it turns out bad, what the hell will he do? Will he trust the doctor or be his usual self and do what he wants anyway? If they can help him, will he let them, or will he think someone's out to get him. Paranoid old man. Worse, if it's curable, will he even want to?" Megan looked up at the ceiling, tears flowing freely down her face. "I only have four months left on this contract. Why couldn't this have waited? What's going on back there?"

Still Jake said nothing. He knew she was just vocalizing to come to a decision.

"Ornery, bullheaded, opinionated old coot," she said with a gentle tone.

"Sounds like his daughter." Jake spoke softly, not wanting to break her mood.

Megan's gaze came back to the room. She quickly wiped her eyes and cleared her throat.

"It's okay to cry."

"Amateur psychiatrist strikes again."

Jake smiled.

Megan moved to the edge of the bed. "Thanks, Jake."

"I didn't do that much, just a drink between friends."

Megan stared into his eyes. Her own began to fill with tears again.

"What's this?" Jake asked as she started crying again.

"I thought you said it was okay."

Jake set the bottle on the floor, stood up and brought her into a hug. He held on tight as she cried. While she let it out, he gently patted her back. Without the body armor on, she was just like any other woman. Soft. Soft in all the right places. She wasn't crying hysterically, but he could feel her small breasts crushed against him. *Nice.*

Megan sniffed twice and pulled back a few inches. She looked up at Jake, her eyes a deepening brown. There was no longer a sad look in her eyes. More of a 'doe in heat' kind of look. She slowly pushed up with her legs and their lips brushed.

Jake hesitated. This was not a good time to start anything, not with her in turmoil. He pushed her away and looked deeply into her eyes. He saw the same eyes that he saw between a helmet and her camouflage scarf in Iraq— eyes that showed desire.

With a gentle but fast move, he pulled her back to him and crushed her lips against his.

***

She felt a thrill that she hadn't in a long time. His lips were causing her to get warm all over. Heat coursed through her veins and settled in all the right places. *Damn, he can kiss.*

Megan gave back as good as she got. They moved closer as the kiss lengthened, their bodies pressing against each other, passion increasing. His lips and tongue explored her mouth and hers were doing the same for his.

This is a member of the crew!

Megan gave one last ferocious kiss then pulled away from the warm, honey lips. She looked into his eyes as she took a heart slowing breath.

He was breathing just as hard, and his eyes showed his desire.

"We can't," Megan whispered.

"I know." Jake took a deep breath as he moved a step back from her. "I know."

Megan licked her lips anyway, their eyes still locked in a passionate embrace. "I uh…"

"I need to head," Jake said softly as he broke the look between them. He grabbed the whiskey and his glass off the floor.

When he stood, she picked up the shot glass off the bed and held it out to him. He slowly reached for the glass, his fingers gently wrapping around hers.

Megan didn't let go. His fingers were warm. Gentle. *What would it feel like to have them wrapped around me? To touch me in all the right places?* She slowly released the glass. A tear formed in her eye.

Jake reached out and gently swept his fingertips over her cheeks. It was a light touch but the sparks were there.

"Eight sharp, Cupcake. Don't be late for the meeting."

"Yes, Ma'am," Jake said with a slight grin as his hand dropped away from her face. He winked at her as he took the offered shot glass and turned to leave. As he was turning the knob, her voice stopped him.

"Jake."

He turned.

"Thanks."

"Anytime, Megan. Anytime."

Megan watched as he closed the door behind him. *Where'd my brain go? How could I have let that happen?* She picked up her pillow and tossed it against the wall. Now her hormones were in turmoil. It would take a long time to sleep tonight, and on top of the problem of her Dad's disease, now this.

She rubbed her hands together absentmindedly. Her fingertips were still tingling from the touch. His chest had felt so tantalizing through his shirt as she touched it during the kiss. *I bet his muscles would…Stop! This was not conducive to getting a good night's sleep. Damn, he can kiss though. He wasn't taught that in the military.* She smiled, picking up her pillow.

***

Jake pulled the door closed behind him as he took a deep breath. *That was great.* He took one step, then noticed someone watching from down the hall. Jake smiled as Cowboy leaned on the wall, arms crossed, waiting. He hefted the whiskey bottle at him then moved down the hall.

"Jake."

McGrew stopped and waited for Cowboy to catch up with him. The pilot had a concerned look on his face. Jake swallowed. This was not good, him seen coming out of Megan's room late at night.

"Is she okay?" he asked Jake in a whisper.

Jake nodded and responded as quietly. "I overheard a conversation between her and her brother. I thought she might want to talk about it." Cowboy's eyes took on a 'yeah right' look. "Her Dad has been diagnosed with some disease. She didn't go into details."

Cowboy glanced both ways down the hall and stepped closer to the ex-soldier. His voice dropped even lower. "Tread lightly."

"I don't understand."

"Meg has a heart of gold, and I don't like to see her in pain. Don't break her heart, pardner."

"I think you misunderstand what I was…"

"I know exactly what you're doing. And I know Meg. Don't screw with her brain. She needs her head on straight in this business. So do you. Don't put us in jeopardy. Just a warnin', pardner." He walked away.

Jake stood staring at Cowboy's back. He continued to stand there after Cowboy disappeared into his room.

What was that about?

***

Eight o'clock sharp Megan looked up from paperwork to see McGrew walk into the room. She avoided his gaze and busied herself.

Jake cleared his throat. "Eight o'clock."

"Yep." Megan pushed the file to him. "Standard job today. Protect the crew rebuilding the runway. You'll be in charge on the ground like last time. You'll also run the crew meeting."

There was a long pause—she could feel his stare. Megan still didn't look up. Tension increased as the file lay untouched. Finally, she raised her head. "You got a problem with that, Cupcake?"

Jake's blue eyes delved into hers. He shook his head. "Not at all, Chief. If that's how you want to play it, then that's how we'll do it."

Megan nodded. "Good."

Jake grabbed the file and began reading.

Masood stuck his head in the doorway. "Megan, I need to see you."

"Sure thing." Megan stood and followed him out. By the time she returned, the rest of the crew had assembled. It was eight-thirty and the room quieted as she entered.

"Okay people, I don't know if Cupcake informed you of our job today..." She paused looking around to see that he already had. "Well, that just got changed. The military needs our help. Stick and Punk will fly Tiny and Bosser to the runway with the other full crew. Tiny's in charge on the ground doing security like last week. The rest will be with me in Pestilence. We're helping move some large containers to a village nearby, then deliver Red Cross packages and food to several other villages."

"Our job?" Jake asked.

"When we're delivering the large containers with the military, you'll be security on my aircraft. Gunner, Fisher and Chips will help unload. When we're on the ground, no one and I mean no one, approaches us. If they aren't U.S. Military, they stay away from us."

"And that would be why?"

"Look Cupcake..."

"It doesn't make much sense. You seem adamant about it. If it's this important, I want to know," Jake said, locking eyes with Megan.

Megan blinked. *He was right, he ought to know. And why am I being so pissy with him? I'm the one that instigated the kiss last night. And besides, Jake should know the reason for my policy.* "Other crew chiefs don't feel the same way, but we've had several close calls with fanatics trying to blow us up, like with the kid in the mountains. I just want to keep my people and aircraft safe. Is that enough?"

"Yeah. Thanks."

"We leave in forty minutes."

The military part of the operation went off without a hitch. The White Pine and military Chinooks carried large containers slung under. One was going to be used as grain storage for the village. The other was going to be used by locals as a school. Along with that, they delivered several tons of grain. The villagers were ecstatic with both.

They headed back into Kabul and picked up a helicopter full of supplies from the Red Cross and Red Crescent Societies. White Pine's contract with them stipulated that they deliver to several villages, as this was easier and faster in helicopters than in small vans and buses. Also one village was so far away, because of winding dirt roads, that it would take a vehicle over twelve hours one way to get to it.

At each stop, the helicopter shut down while the group unloaded supplies. And at each village, the entire population came to gawk, since many didn't see helicopters often.

Locals helped the crew unload bags of grain at each village. Some of the grain was for food; the other bags would be used for crops for the following growing season. The drought had lasted a long time and many of the villages were using their seed to eat. The Red Cross and Red Crescent Societies were trying to refill the stores and, at the same time, allow the villages to be self-sufficient—thereby not dependent on poppy trade for opium.

At the last stop, the farthest from Kabul, the helicopter crew and guests stayed to see the kids receiving supplies. It was a special treat to see them getting school chests donated from American kids.

The delighted kid's faces made it a great show. Each chest contained spiral notebooks, pencils, pens, rulers, chalk, and safety compasses. But the biggest winners were the jump ropes and soccer balls. Smiles lit the kid's faces as they held them up. The crew and guests from the Societies received lots of hugs and cheers.

The only one not out of the helicopter was Megan. She stayed in the cockpit in full disguise, but with a smile on her face. These were her favorite runs. These kids may not know where their next meal was coming from, but for the moment they were happy, all else forgotten.

Jake kicked a soccer ball back and forth with one of the young boys. As with all of the other White Pine crew, his M4 was strapped to him, but the kids didn't even notice. Guns were a natural part of their world. He laughed as they played. Soccer was a universal language.

He stopped the ball, rolled it onto the top of his foot and kicked it straight up. Then quickly taking off his helmet, he head butted it several times, before bouncing it off his knee, then off the inside of his foot. Finally he 'caught' it with his foot, and with a smile gave it a kick to the kid.

The boy clapped in appreciation and caught the ball with his hands. His smile was from ear to ear.

Jake laughed as he put his helmet back on. He patted the kid on the head, who ran off, calling to his friends. Jake looked around for a security check.

As he settled his strap back in place, he saw relief workers conversing with the village leader. Cowboy was holding onto one end of two jump ropes tied together and twirling for some little girls. Gunner and Fisher were playing an improvised game of soccer with a group of kids. His eyes panned past the Chinook to the other side of the field, but there was no one. He looked at the Chinook to see Megan relaxed, watching all. He walked up to the cockpit.

Megan opened the window.

"Did you see that kid?"

"Yeah. Let's hope they remember that we aren't the bad guys when they get older," Megan said softly.

Jake nodded. His smile was genuine as he leaned on the side of the helicopter. "Sorry you can't get out, Chief."

Megan shrugged, then glanced at her watch. They would need to be heading back soon. Still this provided great relations between Afghans and Americans. Perhaps there was bridge building going on that might last a lifetime.

Jake stood up and chuckled. "Look at Cowboy."

Megan started laughing.

Cowboy was jumping rope. He looked silly bent over trying to miss the rope as it went over his head. Within seconds, he fell. He lay there laughing as the aid workers hurried to help him. The little girls and boys were laughing too. Cowboy got to his feet and brushed himself off, then bowed to the kids. They laughed and clapped at his antics.

When Megan looked back at Jake, he was smiling at her. "What?"

Jake glanced around but no one was near. "You're so beautiful when you laugh."

Megan's smile fled from her face. "Cupcake, I told you this can't happen."

"I know. Still doesn't stop the fact that you're gorgeous."

A blush crept into her cheeks.

Jake laughed. "Even more beautiful." With a wink, he started to move off.

"Hey, Cupcake."

Jake stopped and turned.

"Round them up, Handsome."

"Handsome. Much better than Cupcake."

Megan shook her head. "You're stuck with Cupcake. It fits."

Jake chuckled, tapped on the side of the chopper twice and headed for Cowboy. Once the helicopter was warming up, the others would know it was time to go.

***

As Megan shut down the helicopter at the White Pine base, she glanced around. Cowboy was staring at her. She frowned. "What?"

Cowboy turned around to see that the crew had already vacated the back and were heading into the hanger. He returned his look. "Watch yourself, Darlin'."

"Excuse me?"

"McGrew. Don't be losing your head over this one."

"I have no idea what you're talking about."

"Right. Late night meeting? Darlin', try to be more discrete. There are much better places for a liaison than your quarters." Cowboy winked at her conspiratorially as he exited the cockpit.

Megan caught up with him and grabbed his arm. "What do you mean?"

"I saw Jake coming out of your room last night."

A blush spread over her face. "It's not what you're thinking, Kelly. He overheard a conversation I had with my spineless brother. Jake was concerned."

"Jake was fishing," he said looking down at Megan. "But did he catch or was he caught, is the question."

"There was nothing like that at all."

"Sure. Okay," Cowboy said as he continued walking into the hanger, Megan at his side. "Then what 'bout that little smile exchange in the village today. Luckily, I think I was the only one that saw it. Be careful, Darlin'."

Megan stopped walking and sighed. It did look bad, Jake in her room even if they hadn't kissed. And the village exchange, although it warmed her heart, was very dangerous. *That can never happen again. I can't be alone with Jake again, unless it's work related. Damn it.*

She jammed her fists into her pockets.

***

The next three days Megan's crew was on security rotation at the runway. It was their turn to watch and guard, and as always, it was a milk run. When they returned to the base on the third night, Megan informed them that they had two days off, with tomorrow night being the Annual Executive Cookout near the patio.

The executives, including the three crew chiefs, were cooking for the staff, giving the cooks a night off. Everyone would be at the picnic since they were serving traditional American food, hamburgers and hot dogs.

Megan sighed after filing reports in the cabinet behind the main front desk. "Any news for me, Zarin?"

The Afghan shook her head. "Sorry, no word."

Megan nodded; she actually didn't expect to hear anything. Her dad would never call, maybe write. And her brother was even less dependable. She'd wait another week then try calling again. "Thanks anyway, Zarin." Megan started to step away then moved back to the high desk. "Are you staying for the picnic tomorrow?"

Zarin shook her head. "I do not think it wise. My husband would not approve. It is bad enough I must work, but to socialize with other men, no." Zarin shook her head emphatically.

"Why can't he come too? There'll be plenty of food. Bring everyone that lives in your house. That's your parents, your sisters and brothers and all their kids. I'm sure no one will care."

"I think not. But thank you for the generous offer." Zarin gave her a slight smile.

"Okay. How about I save you some of the food then? You can eat it the next day or take it home with you. What about that?" Megan asked, shifting on her feet. She knew that White Pine paid Zarin a pretty good sum according to Afghanistan standards, but it was way low by U.S. standards. And she also knew that Zarin's wages fed all of the people in her house. Megan had never found out what her husband did for a living, but she guessed that he had recently been fired.

"That would be fine. I believe my family would like that. Thank you, Megan."

"Sure," she said with a smile and headed to her room. She grabbed a paperback, heading to the roof. She got settled into a chair near the edge and soon was lost in the mystery.

Occasionally, she heard laughter from the basketball court, where it sounded like some of the guys were playing ball. The compound slowly quieted. Off in the distance, she could hear the call for the faithful to prayers as evening began to assert itself. Finally, she didn't feel like reading anymore and just sat looking at the mountains.

As the sun set, she headed downstairs intending to go to bed, but decided she had better check the crew chief box in the main office building, just in case. She hurried over, heading through the hanger to peak at the choppers. It was weird, but she occasionally liked to spot check them. Nothing was amiss, so she headed into the office. There were no papers in her box, so she slowly walked back to the barracks.

As she passed the patio area, which was enclosed by the three barracks, she noticed that the guys were still playing basketball. In the waning sunlight, they were trying to finish.

Megan paused with a smile. Her crew was playing another crew and it looked like they were winning. She stopped near one of the picnic tables and sat down, putting her feet on the seat with her butt on the table.

The team was Cowboy, Gunner, Tiny, Fisher, and Jake. Bosser and Chips were seated on the ground nearby cheering them on. The guys were going all out, but the score had just become tied. The five met near the hoop to discuss strategy.

Megan smiled, watching them. She rested her chin on her hand. As she panned her eyes back to her guys, she noticed Jake looking at her. He gave her a wink, then headed with the rest of them back to finish the game.

It was half-court basketball. The other team brought the ball back into play, but her crew played very defensively. The other crew shot but missed. The ball was recovered by Tiny, who passed it to Gunner, who took it out at half court. Now it was her crew's turn to play offensively.

Megan's eyes involuntarily followed Jake. He was sweating profusely through his t-shirt, but on him it looked sexy. His sweat-soaked, khaki shorts allowed her to watch his thigh muscles flex, his calves taut. Cowboy threw him the ball. Jake bent over trying to fake out a guy, giving Megan a good ass shot.

Megan took full advantage of the view and sighed softly when he executed the fake, went for a lay up, but instead, as he jumped for the hoop, passed it to Fisher who was in the corner, unguarded. Fisher paused after catching it, and shot at the basket. It missed and was recovered by the other team.

Within minutes, the other crew scored a point and won the game. Despite the competitive nature of the crews, everyone shook hands. Tiny and Fisher sat down on the court to catch their breath, while Cowboy headed to Megan to sit at the table. Jake followed.

Cowboy collapsed on the bench in front of Megan breathing hard. He laid the length of the seat. "Damn."

"Having fun?" Megan asked with a teasing smile.

Jake moved to sit next to her on the table, pushing at Cowboy's legs so he could put his feet on the seat. Then, as though totally exhausted, he collapsed to lie on the table. Megan's eyes flashed to his sweaty shorts again but quickly pulled her eyes back to study Cowboy, who didn't answer.

"When was the last time you played ball, Kelly?" Megan asked leaning down to look at him, desperately trying to keep her eyes off Jake.

"High school. I should never 'ave agreed to this. Damn, I hurt."

Jake laughed. He sat up, wiping his brow. He smiled at Megan who hardly looked at him.

Megan tried not to be obvious that the man sitting next to her was making her heart race. He even smelled good, the sweat enhancing his normal odor. It turned her on more than she wanted to admit. She wouldn't be able to sit here much longer.

Within a few seconds, Gunner showed up, followed by Tiny and Fisher. The whole crew slowly cooled down near the table.

Megan stood with a smile. "You did good guys. Congratulations."

"We lost," Jake said, matching her smile.

Megan shrugged trying not to meet his gaze. She tingled in all the right places. *Get away now!* "You'll get them next time."

Gunner patted her on the shoulder. "Nextest time we need the secretive weapon."

"Secret weapon?" Jake asked, again wiping the sweat from his head. Everyone laughed.

Gunner pointed at Megan. "In Iraq we learned that she was star on the basketball field. We play several other....Uh..." He looked for help from the others.

"They beat the tar outta a couple of military teams," Cowboy informed Jake, looking up at him from his supine position. He gave the ex-military guy a huge grin. "Smoked'em good, they did."

Megan chuckled.

"Really, Chief?" Jake asked, amusement in his blue eyes.

"They over exaggerate my contribution. I distracted the guys in Iraq. Most of them had been there over a year, and to see a woman in shorts and a T-shirt... Well, let's just say it was more than a distraction." She winked at Jake. "I didn't wear my body armor."

Jake cracked up.

Megan congratulated them again and headed to her room. She needed to cool down. That man did things to her, things that she hadn't felt in a long time. Things that she didn't want. Things she tried to ignore but failed. Miserably.

***

It was nearing eleven o'clock and Megan still wasn't asleep, tossing and turning in bed. Her mind kept returning to the basketball game and the sweaty man driving her insane. She sat up in bed and sighed, turning on the light. She tried to read, but she couldn't. She wiggled a little from a full bladder and decided she'd better use the bathroom.

The halls were quiet. Somewhere down the hall, she could hear a radio playing a soft tune, but for the most part it seemed like the men were turned in for the night or at least in their rooms. There was a breeze blowing in the hall since most of the guys left their doors open.

As she passed the rooms, she tried not to look in. Being the only woman in the barracks, she kept her door closed, but most of the guys were not shy about what they did or wore most of the time. She found it better to be in her room by curfew and stay there, to avoid embarrassing situations.

When she reached the bathroom door, which also housed four showers, she knocked. It was policy that the last person out was to leave the door open or, as was the case tonight, the sign on the door was switched to the male stick person, so she would know that there was a guy in there. They would know if she was taking a shower if the female stick person was on the door.

There was no answer.

She opened the door a crack and heard a shower running. With a sigh, she closed the door. It was a good thing she wasn't critical. It wasn't long and the shower shut off.

Megan opened the door a crack and called out. "I need to pee. So don't dawdle."

No one answered as she closed the door again. Even if she stuck her head all the way in, she wouldn't be able to see the showers. They were farther inside the room, which was shaped like an L. The stalls were on this end of the bathroom, with a quickly constructed wall hiding the urinals. The changing area and showers were around the bend.

She leaned on the wall waiting.

CHAPTER 7

The door opened. Jake walked out of the bathroom with a smile on his face and a towel wrapped low around his hips, still dripping water. "Sorry, Chief."

Megan didn't answer. Jake saw her looking him up and down. He hurried after hearing her and hadn't even dried off. With a wry grin, he shook his head, flinging water on her.

That drew her out of her reverie. She blushed. "Not a problem."

Jake didn't move. He blocked her entry with his body. His shower stuff was in one hand, while his other hand held the door open.

"You're dripping," Megan said with a grin.

"I didn't want you to wait." His smile got bigger.

"Can I get in, or is someone else in there?"

Jake could see her desperately trying to keep her eyes front and center, off his cut chest and washboard abs. His smile was now from ear to ear. "Nope. Just me." He could tell she was having a hard time controlling herself.

"Do you mind? I need to pee." She motioned with her hands for him to move.

"Sure, Chief." Jake moved fast, brushing up against her.

She jumped to the side as though she had been singed by a flame. She narrowed her eyes.

"Sorry again." But his smile stayed in place. "Have a nice night, Chief." He slowly walked away, his smile getting bigger. He could tell she was still watching him; he could feel her eyes on his back. Right as he got to his door, he wiggled his butt at her.

A snort sounded as the door to the bathroom closed.

Jake laughed, walking into his room. It was fun putting her on the spot. And he knew the reaction he was causing. *As soon as I'm out of her crew, I'll have her. So help me God.*

***

Megan checked the cooler again to see if the sodas needed replacing. The other crew chiefs were actually cooking on the barbeque grill. The executives were dishing out potato salad and coleslaw. Her job was to keep the refreshments stocked and play gofer for the others. That was fine with her. She hated cooking. Whenever she tried to cook, it turned out either raw or burnt.

"I'll take one." Jake's voice sounded behind her.

Megan jumped.

"Sorry, Chief. Didn't mean to scare you."

With narrowed eyes, she turned to face him. Through clenched teeth she whispered, "Would you stop that."

"Stop what?" Jake asked, his smile getting bigger. In his hand was a plate full of standard American grub: hamburger with fixings, chips, and assorted salads.

"You know what," Megan said still whispering as she glanced around. The guys were busy eating and when these guys ate, they ate. The world could explode around them, but don't interrupt their hot dogs and hamburgers.

"I just wanted a soda," Jake said, his smile fading but the amused look still in his eyes. "That's your job, right? Refreshments?"

Megan almost growled.

"Lighten up, Chief." He gave her a cocky grin.

"You know what I meant."

"Yeah, I did," Jake said, holding out his hand for a soda. "But I still want a soda, Ma'am."

Megan reached into the cooler and grabbed one. She held it out to him. As he took it, he looked deeply into her eyes. It caused a pulsing in her loins and a tingling in other parts of her body.

"Stop it, Jake." Her teeth were still clenched.

Jake chuckled. "You want me bad," he whispered to her as he passed.

Megan snorted.

"You know you do." He walked off nonchalantly.

Megan bent down fiddling with the ice and sodas in the cooler again. When she stood up, she took a piece of ice and ran it across her forehead. *Cool down, idiot. He's just a guy. A reckless, good-looking guy, but off limits.* She checked out the food table, but everything was still full. No need for refilling yet. She glanced around the food area and as she rubbed ice on her forehead she caught Jake's eyes who sat down next to Gunner. She immediately dropped the ice cube to the ground.

Jake's smile widened.

Megan kept her face neutral even as her eyes narrowed, but then and there she vowed to get even. *Oh, this is war, Jake. You'll get yours for making me hot and teasing me. Payback. Some how. Just wait.*

Two hours later she was watching her crew playing basketball again. This time they were losing. Another crew chief sat down next to her.

"Hey Megan, your crew looks like heart attack city."

"Gee Bob, yours doesn't look much better. Is Tippy having a stroke or what?" Megan asked pointing at the oldest guy on the court. His face was red and he was huffing like an old, worn out bellow.

Bob chuckled. "Probably."

"Why aren't you playing?" Megan asked him as she applauded her crew getting another point.

"Bad back." He placed a hand on his lower back with a smile. "You?"

"Didn't want to get the guys too worked up." She winked at Bob. They both laughed. Megan glanced at her crew then at Bob, a plan springing into her head. *Oh yeah. This will work. Pay back time, Jake.* "Besides, my crew doesn't need the help. They're just playing around."

"Oh yeah?"

Megan nodded.

"Damn, that requires you to put money on the table."

She smiled. "Name it."

"Five hundred."

"Done." They shook hands. "And I might even pay for the hospitalization for your guys."

Bob laughed. "I'm still gonna win, Megan."

"I'm not even worried."

At that moment, both teams called a time out to get drinks and rest. Megan walked over to her crew as they gathered around one of the picnic tables. Everyone was breathing hard and sweating, again.

"Okay guys," Megan began as she walked up. "Here's the deal. You win, you get an extremely easy work week. You lose, and I take it out by working you extra hard."

Cowboy groaned loudly. Everyone else looked stunned. With a grunt, Cowboy sat up. "Who the hell did you bet with? Bob?"

Megan smiled.

"Shit, Girl. Would you fuckin' stop that! You'll kill us yet." Cowboy tossed an empty soda can at her.

Megan caught it with a grin.

"What's the bet, Chief?" Jake asked.

"Five bills."

Cowboy cursed as he lay back down on the table.

"Suck it up, old boy," Megan said nudging him. "This is for the honor of the crew."

"Bullshit, Meg. This is, you can't stand to lose." Cowboy said with a disgusted look. "Iffan you want this so bad, you play."

Megan shook her head. "This isn't co-ed."

Cowboy cursed under his breath again. "Just a fun game. It was just a fun fuckin' game."

Jake chuckled. "I've got a counter offer, Chief."

Megan narrowed her eyes, looking at him.

"If we win for you, you have to play one of us in one-on-one. We choose who you play."

There was no immediate answer from Megan.

Cowboy smiled. "Oh Lordie, I love this. Yeah. Come on, Darlin'. Put your ass where your money is." He sat up.

Her eyes flicked to Cowboy and back to Jake. They narrowed again.

"Or not," Jake said.

"Damn."

The whole crew burst out laughing. They knew that Jake had her. She was extremely competitive and Jake had pushed one of her buttons.

"Well?" Jake asked, the picture of innocence.

"Just win the damn game." She stalked away from the table with a smile on her face. *Perfect. Everything is going according to plan.* She slightly chuckled. *Revenge is best served on a basketball court, on my terms.*

Her crew behind her laughed.

And the game continued. Both sides were playing harder than ever. Bob sat down next to Megan, again with a smile on his face. "Wanna up the bet?"

"Come on! Watch the base line!" she yelled at her guys, and then she turned to Bob. "I'm always up for taking money from you. What's the new bet?"

He chuckled. "My team is two points ahead. Let's say for every difference in points, we tack on another five hundred."

Megan considered. "So you're saying that if my team wins, twenty to nineteen, you'll pay me a grand. But if they win twenty to eighteen, you'll pay me fifteen hundred? I kind of like that." She smiled.

Bob assented to the new bet. "But my team's gonna win."

"Ha." Megan stood up and cupped her hands around her mouth to get her crew's attention. "Hey guys…" They were just switching sides again, her crew going on the offensive. "I just increased the bet. Stop playing with these jerks and beat the snot out of them by as many points as possible." She sat back down to the dirty looks of her crew. Megan laughed.

Bob chuckled and pointed at his team too.

The other crew chief and executives, plus most of those courtside began placing bets. Anything like this spread like wildfire around the base, and soon the entire compound was cheering on one of the teams.

Megan applauded, but was no longer yelling at her guys. There were plenty of people doing that for her. She just watched and contemplated. She knew that they would pick either Tiny or Jake to play her. Everyone knew she could whip up on the others, particularly Cowboy. Tiny was a challenge because if he pushed his weight around, she'd be at a huge disadvantage. But she knew they'd pick Jake. She knew that he had challenged her to the contest knowing that they'd pick him too. She smiled even bigger at that. *Yes, this would be great.*

Bob started sweating when the score tied at seventeen. Each time his crew went on the offensive, Megan's crew became a blockade. Nothing got in the hoop. But when her crew got the ball, they passed and worked it until they made a basket. So slowly the count ticked in Megan's favor. Eighteen, seventeen. Nineteen, seventeen. Finally twenty, seventeen.

She smiled sweetly at Bob. "That's two thousand dollars, Bob, my man."

"What the hell did you give those guys? Uppers?"

She shook her head.

"They're animals," Bob said as he paid off a couple smaller bets from the money in his pocket. "I'll get you a check tomorrow. Okay?"

"Sure."

Bob chuckled. "What are they doing now?" He pointed at her crew.

They were huddled together under the basket, drinking and having a serious discussion. All nine guys were in on the conversation.

Megan followed Bob's glance then smiled at him. "Deciding who gets to play me in one-on-one."

"No shit? That was the reason they played so hard, so they could throw a loss in your face?" Bob asked. "Damn, I wish you'd have told me that. I'd never have agreed to the extra bet." He noticed her stand up. "When?"

"Right now." She glanced back at them. "I need to change into my tennis shoes and shorts. Tell them I'll be right back."

Bob nodded and began making bets with more people about the outcome of the next game.

***

Megan exited the barracks to find that the entire base was still hanging out at the basketball court waiting. Her smile widened as she stepped from the door. Almost all heads turned her way.

She nonchalantly walked toward the court with a towel over her shoulder. Her running shoes were laced tight and her long basketball shorts were on. Normally, she didn't own shorts while in country. A woman showing her bare legs was against the law. However, since the Iraqi basketball game, where they trounced the military teams, she now carried a pair mostly to remind herself of her own feminism.

As she reached the court, the crowd parted. Her eyes panned the area and she saw her crew sitting together at the picnic table still talking. She stopped as the crowd quieted. With a smile, and with all of the guys from her crew looking at her, she asked, "Which of you suckers got stuck playing me?"

Cowboy laughed so hard he fell off the table.

Jake stood, his eyes panning her body. He smiled back broadly. "Me."

Megan nodded. "Are you sure you want to do this now? I mean, you just played a hard game. I'd hate to take advantage of you."

The crowd jeered and cheered. Jake narrowed his eyes. Megan smiled even broader. She knew there was no way he was backing down.

"Bring it on, Lady."

"Oh, one thing Cupcake," Megan said, walking past Jake. "Here, hold my towel, Kelly." She tossed him her towel as she turned to Jake. "There's something else you need to learn about me. When I'm playing basketball, I'm no lady." With a wink, she walked over to the ball lying on the court. She picked it up and bounced it a couple of times.

The crowd snickered and the betting resumed.

Cowboy grabbed a water bottle and walked onto the court. He chuckled as he handed it to her. "Here, drink up. Ya'all need to stay hydrated."

Megan took the bottle and chugged. Then she handed it back with a smile.

"Smooth, Darlin'. You definitely smoothed your way into this one," he whispered. With a wink, he left, shaking his head at Jake who was just heading out onto the court. "Jake, a word of warning… She's fast."

Jake didn't answer but his smile broadened. "I guess you're not my Chief for the next twenty minutes or so, uh Megan?"

"No way, Jake. It's one-on-one. That means looking out for number one. And I'm best at that."

Jake's smile grew.

"Rules," Megan said.

Jake nodded at her and took a drink from his water bottle.

"Half court rules apply. Every possession has to be cleared past the line." She pointed at the half court line.

Jake nodded.

"Where do you want the two point line to be?"

Jake looked at the court then at Megan. "Line across the top of the key."

Megan nodded. "Loser outs?"

"Fine."

"Fouls?"

Jake shrugged.

"Either can call?"

"Sounds good to me." Jake took another drink. "What are we playing to, and how do we score it?"

"Every basket is one point. Anything beyond the key is a two-er. Do you want to do seven, fifteen, or twenty-one?"

Jake narrowed his eyes.

"Maybe we'd better do a game to seven. After all, you just played…"

"Fifteen."

Megan chuckled softly. "I think seven will be plenty. And win has to be by two. Okay?"

"Whatever."

"Anything else?"

"Nope."

"Who gets first out?"

"Ladies first."

"I told you I'm no lady, but…" She winked. "Okay." She bounced the ball to the clear line then put it on the ground.

The court cleared fast.

Megan stretched her shoulders then looked at her co-pilot. "What's the odds, Kelly?"

Cowboy snorted in laughter. "Even."

"Good. Take some bets for me. I'll cover anything." She smiled even bigger at Cowboy who was converged upon. She watched him while she grabbed her ankle and pulled her right leg behind her, stretching the front of her thigh, and then did the same with the other foot.

Jake tossed his water bottle to Gunner, walked up to her, wiped his brow with his hand and waited.

Megan squatted down, stretched one way and then the other. She did a couple of twists and jumped up and down a couple of times. Finally, she smiled at Jake who was merely watching. "Kelly?"

"Yeah?"

"Last call."

Cowboy covered bets left and right.

"Done?" she asked.

"Done, Darlin'."

"Give me some incentive." She smiled even broader at Jake.

"Let's see." Cowboy quickly added in his head. "What you won from Bob won't even scratch the surface of the bets, Darlin'."

Megan chuckled. "Incentive," she said softly to Jake. Jake chuckled. She held out her hand. "Good luck."

Jake hesitated but shook her hand. "Yeah, good luck."

Megan picked up the basketball. "Play ball." She tossed the ball hard at Jake who caught it in his gut with a woof of expelled air. She stood beyond the clear line.

Jake narrowed his eyes but gave her a slight bow. Gently he tossed the ball at her, putting the ball into play. He backed up several steps.

Megan bounced the ball once as she stepped onto the court. She stopped, jumped and fired at the hoop.

Swoosh.

"That's two." She smiled at Jake.

"Damn," he said softly, his eyes narrowing.

Megan turned, catching the ball one of the guys tossed. When she turned back, Jake still looked stunned. She made a motion for him to take it out. "Loser's out."

"Damn," he said with a smile.

Megan chuckled. When he was ready, she tossed him the ball, then bent slightly, resting on the balls of her feet. With a bounce she waited, eyes on his blue eyes.

Jake came at her full force. She blocked his advance and he rolled left. She moved to block. Now with his back to her, he tried working one way then the other, slowly advancing, pushing his way down court. Megan stuck with him like syrup on pancakes. With a hand on his back, she felt his muscles moving under his shirt. She rubbed gently, lightly massaging. She could feel his reaction—the muscle twitching ever so slightly. A reach in with her hand brushed his stomach, her hand lingering just a little longer than necessary. Finally, she pushed him into the corner, and he made his move along the base line, muscled past her with a hard push and laid the ball in the basket.

"That's one."

She smiled. "You've got a good base line move. Won't happen again."

Cowboy started laughing. "Hey Meg, I've got more suckers."

"Take'em," Megan said, bouncing the ball as she headed back down court. She tossed the ball to Jake and waited for the pass in.

He smiled, tossed her the ball but this time didn't move back. Now he got in the ready position.

She moved onto the court, bouncing the ball with her right hand, eyes and head up. She did a stutter step to the right and just a slight head bob in that direction. Jake made a hesitating move in the indicated direction. Megan pounced to the left, swept by Jake and laid one up as he followed her to the edge.

Megan took a deep breath. "Three, one."

"Good fake. Won't happen again."

A smile crept onto her face. She was again handed the ball by one of the guys. This time she waited for Jake at the end of the court.

A stage whisper came from the Cartwright crew table. Cowboy's voice. "She's fast."

Megan chuckled.

"Under exaggerated your contribution in Iraq? Distracted them, huh?" Jake asked standing at the clear line, very amused.

Megan shrugged. "Ready?"

"Bring in on, Lady."

Megan passed him the ball. This time he made a fast beeline for the basket. Megan hugged him hard keeping him from having a straight line like he wanted. They bumped bodies. Her hands were everywhere: his back, his shoulders, a light massage on his butt. He rammed her hard in the gut with his elbow, then with his other hand, looped the ball in.

Jake turned with an expectant but devious look on his face. Megan rubbed her stomach. She relaxed her eyes, knowing that he had jabbed her on purpose. She smiled. *So this is how he wants to play.* The crowd was groaning and yelling for her to call the foul. She ignored them and let Jake bring the ball down the court this time. "Three, two."

Jake nodded back and passed the ball to her. She came at him just as hard. Then she turned and put her back to him, pushing him down the court. He put his hand on her lower back but his eyes were on her head. She moved right, then left, then right. Jake stayed with her. One hand defending high, the other, on her back, ready to defend low. His hands gently brushed her body giving a warm embrace with sparks, looking as though to keep her in check. She began another hard drive, then in a fast move, spun on him. His fingertips traced her back and side. In the blink of an eye, she was past him and laid in another basket.

As she walked past him, breathing a little harder too, he said low so only she could hear, "Damn."

"Damn back at you," she whispered. With a quick glance around, she saw that no one was interpreting the real touching going on between them. Megan turned a smile on him and spoke in a normal tone, "Four, two."

She tossed him the ball, and he drove for the base line again. This time she blocked his drive to the basket, and he had to come up court to get any free space. With another hard shove, he pushed her, then leaned into her. His hard body came into contact with the full length of the front of her body. She gave just a little rub. He rubbed back as he looped the ball into the basket.

"Four, three," he intoned trying to catch his breath.

"Hmm," Megan said once more rubbing where he had pushed her hard.

He tossed the ball to her, and she came like hell on wheels at him. Within seconds, she had him pushed to the base line. His hands were everywhere. Touching. Massaging. Groping. This time she elbowed him, swept under his arm and under the basket. She did a jump and put one in the opposite side.

"Five, three," she said as she passed him. "And watch the hands." The tone in her voice sounded hard, but the sparkle in her eye belied her words.

Jake smiled. "Nice elbow, Lady."

"You started it."

Jake laughed and tossed her the ball to pass back to him. "Let's do it."

Megan smiled with a wink and tossed him the ball.

He drove again. This time Megan kept her hands on him, in his face and all over his body. This time she gave his butt a quick cup and grope. As he turned around to face her, she brushed his crotch area. His eyes met hers as he again muscled his way to the bottom of the basket then leaned on her with a rub and bump, and made another point, height and muscle giving him the advantage. He seemed to know that too.

"Five, four," he said out of breath.

"Yeah." She was out of breath too.

"Time out!" Cowboy yelled from the sidelines. He carried Megan's water to her, as Gunner walked Jake's to him. The two combatants stood staring at each other while they drank, eyes locked. After wiping away sweat with the towels, play resumed.

This time when Megan pressed, Jake let her gain ground quickly. She faked a move, but as she passed him, he twirled the other way, stuck his hand out and stuffed the ball. She recovered it and once again backed into him. His hands were again all over, touching her lower back, brushing the side of her body and with a very quick move swatted her butt gently. One hand slid slightly down her outer thigh rounding to the inside. She faked a move toward the basket. He moved with her, but she took a quick step out and pulled up to a jump shot. He snagged the ball down out of the air.

With a cocky grin he spoke, "Still five, four. My out."

Megan narrowed her eyes. "Could've been goal tending."

"So call it."

Megan smiled, tossing the ball hard at him out of the clear line. "Play."

Jake chuckled. He again pressed her hard as they smashed their bodies together. He pushed toward the basket. He stepped between her legs as he leaned in and tensed his muscle hard as he pushed off with his other foot. She felt the pressure on her crotch. Once more he used his height and muscle to get the basket. Again, they both paused momentarily to catch their breaths.

"Tied. Five all," Jake said still bent over.

Megan stood up straight from her bent position as she tried to suck in more air. "Yep."

Jake tossed her the ball. She drove hard, seeming to head for the base line. He blocked hard to the outside, his hand massaging her side all the way down. She stutter stepped again to the base line and he stepped in that direction. With a twist and a turn, she headed back out. He was a half second behind her and she stopped. Jumped and shot. Swoosh.

Jake shook his head.

"Seven. I win," Megan said with a huge smile.

"No. Look at your feet. You're inside the key. One point only."

Megan looked down. Sure enough, she hadn't stepped out far enough. She grimaced. *Gotta end this soon.* It was getting hard to control her hormones.

Pretty soon she'd just lay him out and make love to him. "Damn. Okay. Six, five."

Jake took possession and did his usual drive. This time she kept her hands under control. When he was almost to the place he usually leaned into her, he tripped and fell.

Megan caught him, breaking his fall. He looked up at her with narrowed eyes. She shrugged looking down at him, his shirt still bunched in her hands. "Call it, if you think I did something wrong."

Jake narrowed his eyes more.

Again the crowd was calling for a foul.

Megan released his shirt, then offered him a hand up. She smiled a cocky grin at him, both of them knowing that she had tripped him on purpose. They were still holding hands as their eyes stayed locked for several seconds—the tingling mingled with the pulse of the other's heart rate.

Jake finally grinned and released her hand. He spoke to the crowd. "My feet must be getting tired."

The crowd jeered and cheered at the same time.

Megan took possession of the ball. She faced him this time, pushing him down court, keeping the ball off to the right of her. Also no hand-play this time. She paused as though to catch her breath, sliding her hand to the side of the ball. With a quick, intense snap of her wrist and fingers whipping, she bounced the ball across to the other side of her body and scooped the ball in a low position off the court. At the same time, she moved in a fast, short, chopping direction around Jake. His hand brushed her breast as she flew passed him. Swoosh.

The crowd went wild in applause.

Megan stood under the basket, bent and breathing very hard.

Jake stood, then bent at the waist, in almost the exact position where she had left him with the quick crossover. He was smiling though. At her.

She smiled back.

He winked.

She winked back. Then they both stood up and received the crowd's congratulations as the two made their way over to the same table where the rest of the Cartwright crew was collecting on bets. Megan sat down on the table, taking the towel that Gunner handed her.

Jake sat next to her picking up his towel. Both were smiling and nodding at people, trying to catch their breaths, as men either paid or collected their bets. Within minutes, the crush ended and the crowd thinned out.

Megan hung her head almost between her knees with the towel over it. She was totally exhausted, and not only from the game. That had been highly erotic too. His hands brushing her body. Bodies bumping. Groping. *So sexy.*

Jake was leaning back on his arms, dripping sweat, head laid back, still mouth breathing. The towel lay nonchalantly across his lap.

Cowboy laughed at them. He looked around, but only Gunner was near. He spoke in a low voice. "Cigarettes anyone?"

Jake smiled.

Megan laughed softly. "How'd I do?"

"Let's see. Just from this game alone, you brought in thirty-five and some change."

Jake lifted his head. "No kidding? Thirty-five hundred dollars?"

"Yep. I made almost as much myself." Cowboy winked at Jake. "Never, ever bet against Meg. She's like a she-devil. Trust me."

Jake shook his head as he sat up and looked at Megan. "Damn woman, you play better than most guys."

"You weren't so bad yourself, Cupcake." Her voice muffled by the towel.

Cowboy laughed again. He walked away shaking his head.

Megan sat up, pulling off the towel. "Thanks, Jake."

"No, thank you. You planned that, didn't you?"

"Revenge for teasing me. When did you figure it out?"

"When you jumped the first shot."

Megan chuckled. She stood up and walked away, heading toward the barracks. "I crack myself up."

His laughter followed her all the way.

***

Jake leaned on the wall outside the showers, waiting. The female stick figure was facing out and he could hear the shower suddenly shut off. Not long after, he watched as Megan exited the room, hair still very wet and only slightly messed up. Her cotton terry robe was looped closed; she had a towel over her shoulder and her sweating clothes in a bundle.

She adjusted the bundle and her shower bag. Stopping just inside the doorway like he had before, she gave him a grin. "Jake."

Jake chuckled. "That was some game. You've got good hands." His smile was wide.

"Yeah. I am good."

Jake pushed off the wall and glanced both ways down the hall. Then he moved closer to her, leaned in and whispered, "Yes, you are. We'll have to have a rematch."

Megan shook her head. "Not happening."

Jake narrowed his eyes. "Why not?"

"I already told you it wasn't happening." She walked away.

Jake followed her several steps. "I won't give up, you know. I will get revenge."

Megan laughed without turning. "Sure."

Jake watched her walk away, hips swinging slightly. When she got to her room, she kissed her hand and waved at him over her shoulder. Jake chuckled out loud so she could hear, then headed quickly into the shower room. He needed to get out of the hall before some one saw his reaction to her. He'd barely controlled himself on the court. Only the towel had saved him while he was sitting next to her on the table. This would have been way too obvious.

He started laughing as the water hit him. *Damn, she's a great tease.*

CHAPTER 8

The next week was another security week for Megan's crew. And as always, it was easy work. On their last day off, an earthquake hit in the south mountains, and the next three days were spent transporting rescue teams, food, medical supplies, and other necessary stuff to the afflicted areas. It was hard work, but not dangerous.

The next morning Jake walked into the meeting room to find a note posted from Megan that the crew had the morning off. They were to meet back in the room at two o'clock.

He frowned but headed back to his room to finish a letter to his sister. After he mailed it, he went looking for Megan. She was nowhere to be found, nor were Gunner and Cowboy. No one had seen them since the night before. Puzzled, Jake checked out the hanger. Famine was gone. Putting his hands on his hips, he thought about that. *Odd.*

"Hey, Corn," Jake called to the passing mechanic.

"Yeah? Oh hi, Jake. What can I do for you?" Corn wiped his hands with a rag. His fingertips were perpetually black from working on helicopters and other vehicles.

"I'm looking for Megan or Kelly." Jake gestured back toward where the helicopters were kept. "I see Famine's gone."

The mechanic looked. "Yeah. We got a prep order late last night. They took Famine out before daybreak."

Jake frowned. "Do you know where they were headed?"

"Nope. I don't ask such things." Corn shook his head. "I just do as ordered."

"I wonder where she flew to."

"Oh, she wasn't flying this time. Cowboy was in the right seat. Megan was on the left hand side." Corn waved at his boss who was calling for him. "Anything else, Jake?"

"Cargo?"

Corn shook his head no.

"Thanks." Jake watched him hurry away then looked back to the empty place where Famine always sat. *Why had Megan not been flying? She always flew. She hated it when someone else flew 'her' choppers. What is going on?*

At two, he entered the meeting room to find Cowboy in Megan's chair. He sat with a puzzled look. Within minutes, the entire crew was assembled.

Cowboy smiled at them. "Megan asked me to lead this here meetin'. It'll be a short one. Today, your job is to restock all of the supplies. Should take ya'all about two hours, then you're done for the day. And tomorrow you may or may not have another easy day. I'll be lettin' you know in the morning. Tiny, make sure we have enough ammo on board Famine. And Fisher check out the medical supplies on each aircraft. That's all, guys."

The crew left with smiling faces at the unexpected easy workday—all except Jake. He waited, still staring at Cowboy.

"Yeah?"

"Megan said I would be involved with each mission."

He nodded. "This was a last minute kinda thing. Late last night. She didn't feel the need to wake ya'all."

"Where are they?"

Cowboy gathered up some papers.

"Is this a covert thing?"

"Just leave it go, Jake. You need to learn when to be lookin' the other way. Follow orders."

Jake stood. "Is she in danger?"

Cowboy smiled. "She said that ya'd bitch about this."

Jake made a noise in his throat. "When are they due back?"

"Leave it go." Cowboy left the room.

"I don't like it," Jake said to the empty room.

The next evening Jake was sitting on the roof at sundown when he noticed a helicopter returning to base. He took a drink, watching it get closer. Sure enough, it was Famine. He waited until it landed then headed to the edge of the roof. Jake watched as the helicopter shut down. Still no one exited the aircraft.

His frown deepened.

Finally Cowboy jumped out of the cockpit, from the right side, Megan exited the left side. The back door opened and out jumped Gunner. All were dressed for a hot mission. Gunner and Megan each grabbed a large duffle bag from the back and after shouldering them, the three walked into the hanger.

Jake stared at Famine for another minute then moved back to the chair. He sat with a puzzled look on his face, rubbing his chin. Tomorrow he'd ask Megan about it, but he knew better than to think that she'd give him an answer.

He took a deep breath and sighed. *Why can't I get involved with a normal woman?* His last three 'adventures' were with woman who any normal man would have shied away from.

A senator. For God's sake what was I thinking? Then the General's wife! Thank God, I found out about that before actually doing anything with her. That would have been a career-ender. And lastly, Tisha. I really liked Tisha. That was until he found out that her line of work was hard on her feet. *A stripper on vacation.* That two-week romance fizzled out fast. *Now here I am getting all bent over a woman who hates men, who loves to one up them, and worst of all, probably can on most days.*

Jake smiled. For all he knew, she was a spy. That would be all he needed, to be in love with a CIA agent. Jake laughed at that as he poured himself another drink. *No, Megan is a good pilot. Strike that. She's the best pilot I've ever seen, but she's too opinionated and stubborn to be a spy.*

Damn, she can kiss though. And the way her hands brushed my... Damn. He shook his head. Too much more of this thinking and he'd have another hard on. And he definitely didn't need another of those right now.

***

At eight sharp the next morning, Megan was doing paperwork as Jake walked into the conference room. She glanced at him but said nothing. The tension mounted as he stared at her. "Yes?" she asked looking up.

Jake didn't answer.

"Today's job." She pushed the file at him and went back to paperwork. Again she noticed he didn't move, just stared at her. "You got a problem, Cupcake?"

"Nope."

"Then look at the file."

Jake reached out but didn't open it. His eyes were locked with hers. "I thought I was to be in on every mission so I could learn the routine. The faster I learn, the faster I'm out of your hair. Kill my own crew. Wasn't that what you said?"

"I did."

Jake's finger tapped the file folder.

Megan glanced down at her paperwork. "Sometimes Cupcake, it's better to be ignorant."

"And this is one of those times, Chief?"

She met his eyes again. "Learn."

"Look Megan—"

"No you look, Cupcake. Do what I tell you, and I guarantee that you'll get the nod from me soon. Hell, you'd think with your training and all your military stuff, you'd have learned when to keep your mouth shut."

"Consider it shut, Chief," Jake said and opened the file folder.

Megan huffed once and went back to her paperwork. The tension in the room could be the new storm moving into the area, it was so cloudy.

"Easy task. Ride shot gun with a military unit," Jake said looking at her. "Deliver food to the villages. Act and look military."

Megan nodded.

"What is our illustrious Chief doing during this?"

"Flying high support. Is that okay with you, Cupcake?"

"Whatever you want, Chief."

Masood stuck his head in, then walked in and sat down with a thunk.

"What's wrong, Fahim?" Megan asked.

"My third cousin Emmer was killed yesterday. Shot."

Megan leaned closer. "Is this the same area where we picked up the child?"

Masood was already nodding. "He was the warlord in the area. The child was his grandson. Tragedy visited too many times on my tribe. First the Russians. The Taliban. The child. Now Emmer."

"Who did it?" Jake asked.

Masood shrugged. "No one knows, but I can guess." When no one spoke, he continued, "Emmer was negotiating with the U.S. government. He was opening the area up to better ways for my tribe. He was angering some of the…" Masood took a breath and rubbed his face. "I know it was bin Laden. I know he arranged the killing."

"What happened?" Jake asked sitting back, glancing at Megan. She seemed to be very sad. Her eyes had a look that he couldn't identify.

"No one knows. Emmer was gardening, as he does every day before the midday meal. He slumped over. A bullet in the chest. No one heard anything. Nothing. No one saw anything. One minute alive, one minute dead."

"What's going to happen, Fahim?" Megan asked.

"Emmer's brother will take over. Hammed will continue. The tribe wants revenge. We have long memories. We will get bin Laden. We will." He looked up at the two with a determined look. "It may take years, but he will pay for my tribe's sorrow." With that, he stood up and left the room.

Cowboy passed him as he entered. He turned a puzzled look back to the empty door then toward the two sitting there looking his way. "What's up with Fahim?"

"The warlord of his tribe was assassinated yesterday," Megan said.

Jake watched as she stared at the open doorway. The two pilots exchanged a look; some sort of nonverbal communication passed. Megan immediately glanced down and shuffled papers.

"Not good," Cowboy said sitting down, still staring at Megan.

Jake shook his head. *What is going on now? And what was that look?* "Such a volatile area. Will it ever settle down?"

"I doubt it. Damn, I hate this," Megan said softly as she went back to work. She shook her head. "Kelly, we have a fairly easy day today." She motioned to the file still in front of Jake. "Fly cover."

Cowboy nodded, taking the file from Jake. "Sounds good, Darlin'. Are we goin' in Famine or Death?"

Megan's head came up with a snap. "The part made it?"

"Yep," Cowboy said with a smile. "I made sure that Corn finished it yesterday. Rush rush, just for ya. I even took her up for a quick flight."

A bright smile flashed on her face.

"Even pre-flighted it for you this day break. Thought you might want to give the little filly a quick flight to check her out before work t'day." He winked at Megan.

Jake hid his smile.

Megan shuffled her paperwork into a pile. She turned the bright smile on Jake. "Earn your pay today, Cupcake. Run the pre-mission meeting. You organize the crew. We'll be back in an hour to pick you up for the short trip to the military base."

***

Three hours later Megan and Kelly were flying lead in the convoy, checking out the road in front. Both were silent as they flew. It was a nice silence.

"So, Meg," Cowboy smiled. "When are you givin' the nod to Cupcake?"

"He was ready when he got here. Management wanted him tested." She shrugged. Letting go of the collective, she flexed her hand briefly before gripping it again, her eyes never leaving the ground in front of them as she flew. Instinctively, she knew Cowboy was doing the same on his side and watching the other instruments.

"That didn't answer my question, Darlin'."

"They said at least one month, so anytime. In actuality, they'll say when I'm to give him the nod."

"And the other people?"

"Don't know. Don't ask. Don't tell."

"Same old policy." Cowboy sighed. "Sure would be nice to know the players. Well, well. What have we got here? Three o'clock on the road." Cowboy pointed to a small group of white Toyotas. The trucks looked beat up and abandoned. Of course, most of the vehicles in Afghanistan looked like that, even the ones being used.

Megan banked Death to get a better look. "Interesting." She looked at Cowboy. "Let them know."

Cowboy switched to the pre-arranged channel. "Razorback, this is Death," Cowboy called to the military helicopter flying with the convoy.

"Go ahead, Death."

"We got ourselves a little welcoming committee up ahead. Come on up for a look-see," he said as she banked again swinging in a much bigger arch to search for anyone in the area. It seemed that the whole place was deserted, especially along the stretch of road with the trucks. The road just happened to narrow where the trucks were 'parked.'

"Meg, Razorback coming up hard." Cowboy's head was cocked back to look in the direction of the oncoming convoy.

"Got him."

He hit the channel button. "Razorback, see the parking lot of Toys near the road. Looks mighty suspicious." They hovered farther away watching the other helicopter swing in for a closer look.

"Could be an old accident, Death," the pilot said back.

"Do you want to take that chance?" Cowboy asked.

"What do you suggest, Death?"

Cowboy looked at Megan.

"Blow it."

Cowboy nodded and relayed the reply.

"Can't determine if there are any civilians. Negative," Razorback responded.

"And what happens if it's a welcoming bang for them boys back there?" Cowboy countered.

There was silence for a few seconds. Both pilots knew that they were too far for radio communications with the military base.

"I can't fire on a nonbelligerent target," Razorback finally said.

"And?" Cowboy asked back turning to look at Megan.

"That's all I'm saying, Death. I need to return to the convoy. I'll advise them of the situation. Razorback out." The military Black Hawk flew off.

Megan glanced at Cowboy. "Well?"

"Got me, Darlin'."

"Damn." Megan chewed her lip. She hated these split second decisions. Once more she looked at Cowboy. "I hate this."

"What to do?" he asked, already arming a missile. If they fired one of these babies, there'd be a lot of paperwork. They were extremely expensive.

"Fly by." She tilted the rotors and in a flash flew close enough to almost read the serial numbers off the dashboards.

"Easy, Meg. Too close," he said softly.

"Take a couple pictures Kelly—I don't see any bodies."

Cowboy grabbed a digital camera and quickly snapped several pictures as she hovered.

"See the cover over something in back. Could be boxes of explosives."

"Could be," Cowboy said still snapping pictures.

"Eyes," Megan said as she flew the area again.

"Nuthin' and nobody."

"Me either." She backed the helicopter away then glanced at him. "Fireworks, Cowboy."

"Yee-haw," Cowboy said as he hit the button.

From under the aircraft a Stinger missile released. Within seconds, the four trucks were no more. The explosion sent a shock wave that buffeted the helicopter. The blast was too large for just the four vehicles.

Megan smiled broadly. "Jackpot."

"I love my job," he said with an equally huge smile.

"Some days, me too."

Cowboy hit the channel button. "Razorback, this is Death."

"Go head, Death."

"We have determined that there is no longer a threat to the site." He glanced at Megan to see her eyes dancing bright.

A chuckle came back on the radio. "Affirmative, Death. And thank you."

"Ya'all welcome," Cowboy said.

"Have Cupcake investigate from the ground," Megan ordered.

"Death to Cupcake."

There was static on the channel for a second, then background noise of wind and road. "Go ahead, Death."

"In about five miles, ya'll come across a big scorched area where the road narrows. It's still smoking, so ya can't miss it. Check it out. Quickly. Get a ground eyes look-see. We'll cover ya'all from the air."

"Affirmative. Out."

Megan smiled. "Some days it just all comes together."

Within minutes, the convoy passed the burned out remains of the trucks. One Hummer swung to the side of the road and Megan watched as Jake jumped out, followed by Tiny. He and Tiny quickly eyeballed the sight. Both of them bent over a couple of times then hurried back to the running vehicle. Fisher was standing on the hood of the truck, gun out, scanning the area.

A wave from Jake to the helicopter as he entered the Hummer sent both of them flying back to the convoy. Within seconds of it pulling away, the radio crackled to life.

"Death, this is Cupcake."

"Yeah, Cupcake?" Cowboy replied back.

"Toast. Not much left of it. I picked up a couple of pieces of metal. Looks like there might have been a trip wire across the roadway. Looks similar to things I saw in Iraq. What did you hit them with?"

Cowboy chuckled in her ear.

Megan glanced at him, smiling.

"Just a little ol' match, Cupcake."

"Well…" There was a smile in his voice. "That was one hell of a match."

***

The next day they were returning from another supply run to a small village in the mountains. They had been delivering boxes. Unmarked boxes.

Cowboy nudged Megan and pointed down.

Megan glanced over his arm then frowned. She swung the helicopter around to take another look. Two vehicles were smoking on the road, and from their angle, it was a major accident. One had apparently run headlong into the other. There were three bodies lying in and around two brightly colored trucks. One man stumbled out of the truck and fell several feet away.

She hovered watching. There was no other movement along the deserted road or in the immediate area. Her eyes flicked to Cowboy. "What do you think?"

"Who are they?"

The intercom buzzed. "Looks like they need help down there, Ghost," Jake's voice called out.

Megan's frown deepened. She glanced at the fuel gauge then back to the road.

"Gotta be soon, Darlin'," Cowboy said, also eyeballing the fuel gauge.

"Yeah." Megan tilted her head, thinking fast.

"Ghost, people are dying down there," Jake's voice insisted.

"Do you see any indication of what tribe they are from?" Megan asked as both strained to see anything to ID the people, colors or maybe a turban wrapped a certain way. She moved the aircraft into a different position.

"Nope."

"Ghost?" Jake's voice asked. "What're we waiting for?"

Megan scowled as she hit the intercom button. "ID Cupcake. This could be a trap."

"How would they have known that we were…?"

"I've seen it before," she growled at him.

"At least two are dead," Jake informed her. "The two near the burning truck. One's neck is at an odd angle. The other looks like he hit that huge boulder near by and bounced."

Megan moved the helicopter for a different look.

"The other guy is still moving. The one near him may or may not be dead. I think we should get them."

"When I want your opinion, I'll promote you to co-pilot, Cupcake."

"It's just that they are…"

"This is not a democracy, Cupcake. Do not speak again. That's an order." Megan clicked off the intercom.

"That one guy is moving," Cowboy agreed.

Megan was already turning the helicopter around 360 degrees for a total view of the area. "Something's not right. I feel it in my bones."

"Or it could get us in good with the local warlord," he suggested.

Megan nodded. She bit her lip. With an angry swat of her thumb, the intercom came on. "Listen up. We don't have the fuel for this but... Two guys, Cupcake and someone else. Not Gunner, you get a gun ready. I'll settle close to the ground. Hop out. Check those guys fast. Guns at the ready. This could be a trap. We'll cover you from here. Be ready to run. Leave the wounded. Ready?" She didn't wait for an answer but dropped the chopper.

As soon as Gunner called clear, she pulled up and hovered several hundred feet above the area. Both pilots scanned nearby hills and valleys.

"Tiny, report on below," Megan ordered. Her eyes panned to Cupcake and Fisher who were moving fast, checking out the four bodies.

"I think two are dead. Cupcake is... the moving guy is alive. So is the one near him."

"Damn, we got company," Megan called out even as she lowered the chopper.

Cowboy glanced in the direction she was looking. Sure enough, four white trucks were quickly approaching on the road. "We got seconds, Girl."

"Damn it." Megan's eyes panned to the two crew members struggling to carry the hurt men back to the hovering aircraft.

Two more of the crew hopped out to help. Before the four and wounded were near the aircraft, Gunner began firing in the direction of the approaching trucks.

A couple shots ricocheted off the side and two plunked into the windshield, one right near Megan's head. Famine jerked a couple inches but still the helicopter hovered.

"Shit. Come on," Megan whispered.

Almost immediately, Tiny's voice sounded, "Go."

The helicopter shot straight up and away. Megan glanced back to see that the four trucks had emptied of men, all of which were firing at them. A couple more bullets hit the helicopter but appeared to do no damage.

Cowboy finally let out his breath. "Gray hair. I'm gonna leave this place with fuckin' gray hair." He smiled at Megan then it faded. "Meg?"

"Fly," she said softly. Her face contorted in pain.

"Got it." Cowboy took control of the aircraft. "How bad?"

Megan let go of the controls with both hands and moved her feet back from the foot pedals as she felt him take control. She grimaced as her left hand grabbed her right upper arm. She pulled her hand away to see blood on it. Moaning, she flexed her right arm.

"Meg?"

Megan shook her head. "Painful, but I've had worse."

"Shoulder?"

"No, arm I think." She turned her arm as best she could with the pain. "Yeah. Damn it hurts." She closed her eyes and leaned her head back.

"You gonna make it, Meg?"

"Yeah. Just don't break my bird."

Cowboy chuckled nervously.

Megan flicked on the intercom. "Okay, talk to me boys."

Gunner's voice came on. "Two men. Badly bleeding. One is awake. One is… not awake. Man say he with Tashir village."

Cowboy let out his breath. "Thank God."

Megan nodded. "Do first aid."

"Doing it."

"Gunner, will they make it?"

There was a pause before he answered. "Don't know."

"How bad?"

Jake's voice came on. "The unconscious one has head injuries. Pretty severe head injuries, I say. The other one has lots of cuts and bruises, maybe internal injuries. He's fighting us and keeps repeating something." Jake must have leaned forward toward the injured man because the man's weak voice sounded over the intercom speaking Dari.

Megan grimaced again before speaking, her hand pressing hard into her arm, blood beginning to leak around her fingers. "Cupcake, repeat these words to him as best you can…." She spoke slowly and deliberately. Megan heard Jake repeating them over the intercom right after her. "It means we're friends."

There was another pause on the intercom. "Thanks. That seemed to settle him down."

"Do the best you can, Cupcake." She clicked off the radio. "Oh God!" She bent over in pain. "Damn, this hurts."

Cowboy flashed a look her way.

"I'll make it. One lousy, little bullet isn't sending this Ghost to heaven." She tried a smile for him.

"Heaven? Woman, you're going to hell for sure. In two days, you'll be running the joint."

Megan chuckled and grimaced at the same time. "Well, I'll save a spot up front for you."

"Do that, Darlin'. Just hold on. We'll be at the military hospital lickety-split."

"Yee-haw," Megan said softly.

***

Megan worried as she waited in the emergency room of the military base. Right before they landed, Famine began acting up, which meant that another of the bullets had hit something vital. Cowboy had gotten on the runway with only minor cursing, but she had no idea what the problem was.

The three injured had been transferred to a waiting vehicle, which immediately headed to the hospital. With only one doctor on duty, she had to wait, since the two guys were in far worse shape than her. A male nurse checked her out and proclaimed her 'not likely to die.' His attempt at humor. In reality, it was a minor wound. And now that she had taken painkillers, she was only worried about her aircraft.

A knock sounded on the door. Jake stuck his head in. "Hi."

Megan scowled.

"Okay, so you're still mad." He walked in and stood just inside the door. "I came to give you a report on Famine."

"Yeah?"

"Bullet nicked one of the linkages. It'll be stranded here for a day until Corn can make it over to repair it. Cowboy said to tell you not to worry, there was no other damage."

Megan let out her breath. "Good."

Jake smiled. "You look good."

Her flight suit was off down to the waist, her body armor sitting next to her on the bed, and her T-shirt, which was partially blood-soaked on the right side, cut off at the shoulder. She glanced at her bandaged wound and grimaced. "Flesh wound, I believe is the Hollywood way to describe this."

"Does it hurt?" His blue eyes betrayed concern.

"Not any more." Megan smiled. Painkillers had dulled the pain.

Jake glanced down at the floor then shifted on his feet. "About what happened, I know I was out of line, I just hate to see people…"

"Special Forces hero," Megan interrupted him. "We'll talk about it tomorrow when the painkillers are out of my system and I can be the bitch I need to be. You caught a break, Cupcake."

Jake chuckled. "Have you heard how they are?"

"Yeah. The conscious one, Abdul Jameel Daud, has multiple contusions and a slight concussion. The other is in critical condition. As you said, he has multiple head wounds. They're not very hopeful in his case." She looked Jake in the eye. "The village and his whole tribe are now indebted to White Pine."

"Really?" Jake crossed his arms and cocked his hip in a more comfortable position. "How's that?"

"Abdul is the son of the local warlord. He was the target of the 'accident,' according to my sources. The guys in the other vehicles were chasing them trying to kidnap him. My contact is not sure why, probably to get control over his father to influence him into agreeing to concessions. The other injured guy is his cousin. Abdul's father has expressed his tribe's thanks and many prayers. So over all, it's a good thing we stopped the kidnapping."

Jake merely nodded. "And you?"

"What?"

He pointed at the wound. "How long will you be out of commission?"

Megan shrugged her good shoulder. "It depends on a lot of things. The flight surgeon on base will have to certify me. Not that big a deal. The paperwork on this and the, uh, match lighting will take a good deal of my time. I was wondering how I was going to squeeze them in."

"What about the crew?"

"Well, you'll be leading them under Cowboy on the actual missions. I'll still be in command. I might even ride shotgun if necessary. Think you can handle the pressure?"

Jake made a face.

Megan laughed.

Jake glanced at his watch. "Cowboy wants me back with a status report on you. Guess I'd better get going." He looked Megan in the eyes. "Glad you're still with us, Chief." He gently massaged her good shoulder.

"You say that now. Just wait until tomorrow when I ream you a new one," Megan replied as Jake exited the room chuckling.

Megan shook her head with a smile. She stared at the door for a minute longer then rubbed her lips, remembering the kiss and more importantly, the basketball game. A heat settled in her loins again. *As soon as he gets a nod from the executives, I'm doing some nodding myself.* The smile broadened. *Yes, I'll have my way with him. For one night.*

***

A week and a half later, Jake absentmindedly shuffled the crew reports as he walked down the hallway. They had been playing security guards on the runway again and these were the boring reports that reported how boring it was. Right before he got to Megan's office he heard her voice. Pausing he frowned. She sounded upset.

"Yes, I know. But I already told you that I think he's a mistake… Look, if you want my opinion, and you did just ask for it, I think that he's wrong for the… I didn't say that… Damn it Bill, you asked, so listen… I did as you asked. I evaluated him. In my opinion, I think it's a mistake to offer him the position… Yes, I know I'm not always right, but in this case I think I know more than…"

Jake knocked lightly on the door frame and stood in the doorway. Megan cursed slightly at the person on the phone. Her eyes racked over him. *Damn, she's so beautiful.*

"Yes, Bill. When?" Megan motioned for Jake to sit down. "Is the link back up from the damage done on that last attack?"

Two days before there had been a successful attempt to take out White Pine's satellite uplink. At the same time, someone had sent several rounds of mortars into the military encampment and did damage to their links too. So

101

far the only thing affected was weather reports and some communications. Nothing extremely serious. More aggravating than anything.

Megan frowned. "By ourselves? Isn't that a bit unusual?"

Jake laid the papers on her desk and got comfortable, his eyes studying her as she spoke on the phone.

"When do they want this done by?" She grimaced then made a mocking face at Jake, mimicking the speaker talking on the phone. Her eyes suddenly flew to the calendar hanging on the wall. "So, it's at my discretion?"

Jake crossed his arms.

"Why?" She made a face. "And the reason for that would be?... Because I have the right to know. If they can wait, I can do it myself..." She sighed softly. "Fine. A test for him. Got it. Right. Before then. It'll be done..." She shook her head. "I said it'll be done." With a mad look, she threw the phone into the cradle.

"Problem, Chief?"

"No." She rubbed her face as her phone rang again. "Cartwright... Good. Yeah, I can be there tomorrow. Ten o'clock. Thanks." She made a note of the appointment as she settled the phone back into the cradle.

Jake looked over the desk and saw her write 'doctor' next to the time and date. He raised his eyebrows.

"Check up with Doctor Himbert on the military base. Hopefully he'll re-certify me to fly." She rubbed at the still sore shoulder.

"Are you ready?" Jake asked, his eyes taking in her painful expression.

"This?" Megan smiled indicating her arm. "I've just sat too long." She frowned, looking at the phone. "Close the door." She waited until he complied. "We just picked up a new mission. To be executed within the next several days. The sooner, the better."

"The phone call?"

Megan nodded. She turned and pulled open a drawer on the cabinet behind her. After grabbing several sheets of folded paper, she turned to the desk and quickly cleared off the papers that Jake brought in. She laid the new ones on the desk. "Reconnaissance. Usually we do this with either the military or a *customer*." She looked up at Jake.

He nodded back, getting the implied message that usually it was a CIA agent. She spread out maps of the mountainous area near the Pakistan/Afghanistan border. Megan pointed to one particular area.

"This is the target area. The *customer* wants us to look into both of these areas." She pointed at a small ridge that separated the biggest parts of the valley. "He wants us to visually check out the entire area. If we see anything suspicious, we're to get GPS coordinates and a count of how many people we see."

"Is this another camp of bin Laden's?" Jake asked scooting to the edge of the chair so as to get a better look at the maps.

Megan shrugged. "He didn't say. He just said to see if anyone is staying in the area." She frowned. "The big problem comes in the fact that with the main satellite uplinks down, I can't get good information about approaching storms and the weather is weird this year."

Jake was still studying the maps. When he looked up, Megan was staring at him. "Our job?"

"You'll be in command on the ground on this one. So be thinking about who and where you want to deploy. Take the maps with you tonight if you want to study them. But this is a covert mission, so..."

"Silence."

Megan laid her finger on her nose. "I'll call another White Pine office to see if I can get at least a verbal report on the long range weather systems. Meet me back here at oh-six-thirty tomorrow, and we'll discuss times to do this mission and everything else."

Jake nodded gathering the maps.

"Now you're in the hot seat, Cupcake."

Jake shook his head. "I'm trained for this. I've done these kinds of things before. Remember?"

Megan chuckled. "Yeah, but eyes on are you. More eyes than you can possibly know." She picked up her phone and dialed Fahim's extension.

***

Three days later, Megan stood in the hanger watching approaching storm clouds. A grimace broke on her face as her mood became just as cloudy.

"This ain't good, Darlin'," Cowboy spoke next to her. He stuck his hands in pockets as he watched the rolling, dark clouds.

"They'll be high and dry, so to speak."

"Not much we can do about the weather, Meg."

"Yeah, but if we had accurate weather forecasting, I wouldn't have sent them out on this mission. It could have waited a day or two longer. And who would have imagined this kind of weather system during... It never rains this much this time of the year." Megan cursed softly. She absentmindedly rubbed her still sore arm.

"I've been meaning to ask. How did ya'all get Dr. Himbert to certify you so soon?"

"I sucked up the pain when he examined me." Megan smiled. "He was going to wait another three days, but since I had full rotation and regained strength..."

Cowboy shook his head. He knew she wasn't to full strength. "What else?"

"A case of ten year old brandy."

"How in the hell did you get that here?"

"Contacts." Megan smiled even bigger.

"The big question is, are you ready?" Cowboy asked seriously. She had flown this morning to deliver the rest of the crew to the drop off point for the mission, and he had been judging her. She seemed back to par.

"It's a little sore but I've flown with worse."

"Yeah, but you had no choice then, Darlin'. You were the only pilot on that little shindig and extremely lucky that the bullet to your stomach hit nuthin' vital."

"Lucky. That's me."

"Just take it slow. I can fly the majority of the time until ya'll are one hundred percent."

Megan nodded, glancing once again at the clouds. "Think they'll pass over or hang on?"

"Before the satellite image glitched again, it showed a huge mass behind it by 'bout an hour. If we get lucky..." He made a face at Megan. "We can scoot in and pick'em up between the two. Either way, it's gonna to be a hell of a ride."

"That's why we get the big bucks, pardner." She adopted a twang to her voice.

CHAPTER 9

Jake squatted down behind a huge boulder, taking a breather. As the others joined him in close proximity, he glanced at the sky. *This is not good. The cloud bank is stuck to the side of this valley like a pancake to the wall in a food fight. Damn it. Why hadn't weather reports predicted this?*

Both Megan and he went over the reports three times before calling the meeting the night before. This weather system was not supposed to have moved in this fast. He rubbed his chin. *Will Megan try it?* He almost smiled. *She's an adrenalin junkie. Of course, she'll do it. Probably gets off on doing things like this.*

The other two with him were alert. They were deep in the mountains on a scouting mission. The group they were looking for was supposed to be in this valley but so far there was no sign of them. Jake had split the team up. Tiny was leading the other two guys.

Jake glanced at his watch again. They should be at the rendezvous anytime. The buildings they investigated were long abandoned, and the only wooded area was deserted, which would be the most likely place for a training camp.

Gunner clucked softly, getting Jake's attention. He pointed to the left.

Jake's attention centered on three approaching men. He swung his commando M-16 from the folds of his clothes and took up a ready position. Prepared.

The group was dressed in traditional herder's clothes, long outer coats, turbans and baggie pants. From a distance they would pass as natives, but up close anyone would recognize them as foreigners.

Jake tensed as the three drew close—his finger on the trigger. Every step that the newcomers took tightened the spring inside his gut. Finally, they were close enough that he recognized Tiny's black hands on his gun, since their faces were down concentrating on walking.

Jake gave a hand signal to his two men and they relaxed as the approaching men hurried to join the group. "Well?"

Tiny smiled. "Jackpot. Over the ridge." He pointed in the general direction. "There's a camp. Four tents. Lots of training. We got pictures and GPS readings."

Jake smiled back.

"But the weather." Tiny shook his head. "There's this group of clouds, then a break, then a massive front moving in behind it." Tiny frowned as he caught his breath. "No way Ghost is making it in."

Jake frowned and looked toward the mountainside and clouds. "How far out is the second weather formation?"

Tiny shrugged. "It's moving slower than this one, but it's huge. The choppers won't make it until tomorrow earliest. And then there are flash floods with that kind of rain."

Jake understood. The rains helped local farmers and herders in the spring, but for his squad, it was the kiss of death. The pick up was in the next valley, over the ridge behind them. They had two hours to make it.

Tiny glanced at the others who were watching them. "Down this valley is a road. The military sends patrols on that road. I say we head there."

Jake didn't answer. He looked up at the clouds again. *Megan will try. I know she will. I just know.* Otherwise they could be stranded for at least a day. Or they might be stranded for a lot longer if they had to walk out of the valley. That would require maneuvering to miss locals that might be associated with the al Qaeda training camp nearby.

Tiny turned to the others. "We head down to the road."

"No," Jake spoke softly and motioned for the men to gather. *She's not only the most dependable pilot I've seen, but I know she's dedicated to her crew. She'll be here and on schedule.*

Tiny scowled. "You may be in charge, but I've got more time under my belt in Afghanistan, Cupcake. This is my second rotation."

"Ghost will be at the rendezvous. She'll be there even with the storm approaching. We have time to hit the pick up early. If we hoof it now…" Jake said noticing that Gunner was agreeing with him. "We're going to stay on schedule."

"There is no way the helicopters are making it in. The time between the two storms is going to be minutes, especially the way storms stall in the mountains." Tiny's face darkened. "That means we'll be deserted for days. There's no food or water here that isn't controlled by the al Qaeda or a hostile warlord. We'd have to walk seventy miles out of our way to hit that road again, assuming we can bypass all that." He shook his head in anger. "We need to head down. Now."

Jake shifted his weight on his feet, still in a squat. "We head to the rendezvous."

"Not me. I'm going down," Tiny said. "Who's with me?" He looked each man in the eye.

Gunner spoke first. "I wait for Ghost. She not let us down. I go with Cupcake."

The other Chilean pointed at Jake. Both Tiny and Jake's eyes swung to the South Africans. Fisher pointed at Jake. Bosser kept meeting Tiny's eyes then looking at the ground.

"Bosser?" Tiny asked.

"Ghost has never failed before. In Iraq, she saved us when you said there was no way she would risk the chopper. She brought us back alive, sacrificing the chopper. Ghost. I go with Cupcake," Bosser said, his eyes apologizing to Tiny.

Jake swung his gun under the outer cloak. "Let's move. No rest stops." He stood and led the way up the hill.

A glance back revealed that everyone was following, Tiny bringing up the rear. If he wasn't pushing himself and the team, he might have smiled, but there wasn't time or energy for that.

Two hours later the six men were waiting in a grove of small trees watching clouds that seemed to be piling on top of each other. The front had stalled right over top of them. They were also listening for the familiar, welcome sounds of Death. The first bank of clouds hung on tight to the mountainside while they watched the second bank rapidly approaching. Lightening flashed in the second bank and thunderclaps rang out in the valley.

Jake clutched his gun tighter anticipating rain. Once it hit, they were goners. The lightening dashed his last hope that Ghost would make it into the mountain valley. Tiny squirmed under a nearby tree, giving Jake an 'I told you so' look. Jake merely looked away, not giving him the satisfaction. He glanced at his watch as the last sunlight dipped under the first cloud bank. He sighed. Time to prepare for night.

The only thing he was worried about was the threat of lightening or flash floods. The area they were currently in looked like it might be susceptible to both as in the first valley. He needed to get his men to higher ground and away from the trees. His eyes panned up the hill. A good place to settle down looked to be among the rocky area on the upper side of the valley and wait out the storm. His training prepared him for this, but he doubted that Tiny, Fisher, Chips and Bosser enjoyed this sort of adventure. Gunner, on the other hand, looked to be an old hat at it. With a motion, he gathered the men.

"Okay. It's fairly obvious that Ghost can't make the pick up. We'll try again tomorrow. For now, we need to take shelter on the topside of that rock formation—on the topside, in case of a landslide. The rain will be hitting soon and we need to be down and ready."

A loud thunderclap sounded, drowning out his last words.

Jake paused as the sound echoed and then continued, "Stay low to the ground. Do not stand up for any reason. That would make you the highest object and most susceptible to lightning strike. Do you understand?"

Another thunderclap rang out to punctuate his words.

"Good. Now…"

"Cupcake," Gunner interrupted. His head was cocked, listening.

Jake looked at him then also cocked his head. *Was that the sound of a helicopter? Surely not.* He listened hard as thunder continued to echo in the valley. It was difficult to make out anything.

Gunner suddenly pointed at the ridge line. "Death."

Jake smiled at the quickly approaching helicopter. It was mere inches off the ground as it topped the ridge. "Get out of the woods so she sees that we're still here. Not too far, in case anyone else is in the valley."

"Who would be out in this kind of storm but us nutcases," Tiny said with a wry grin.

Jake grinned back. "We aren't out of here yet."

Tiny nodded even as they moved to the opening, waving their arms.

The helicopter seemed to hesitate after it cleared the ridge. Suddenly it zoomed toward them. It came to an almost screeching halt as men ran for the aircraft like the grim reaper was after them.

***

"Meg?" Cowboy intoned, watching the crew scramble on board.

"We're in a shit load of trouble, Kelly. The lighting's hitting hard on this side, wind on the other," Megan said as she fought to hold the helicopter still.

"Flip a coin, Darlin'," Cowboy said, his head still bent toward the back. "Go."

Megan swallowed. "May God help the foolish."

"Amen," Cowboy agreed, his knuckles tightening on the seat.

Megan put the helicopter in motion—forward motion. She needed to gain air speed in order to get lift. A grunt escaped her as she fought for control. They were slowly rising, but not fast enough to get out of the valley. Lightening struck nearby causing their hair to rise.

"Meg?"

But Megan was concentrating on bushes near the top of the ridge. She was watching them blow back and forth as she approached. Her eyes narrowed as she continued to fly forward. With a gut wrenching jerk, the helicopter rose as the bushes bent outward in the harsh wind, as though straining to get out of the valley too. Death rode a cushion of air up the side of the ridge. "Come on," Megan whispered.

Cowboy held on to his seat. The strain of each linkage vibrated through his hands, almost as if Death was groaning.

"Come on. Hold on, one more second…" Megan pleaded.

As though riding a carnival roller coaster, the helicopter shot up and over the ridge, then plummeted toward the sheer drop on the other side.

"Shit!" Megan shouted over the thunderclap that followed them over the edge.

Cowboy blew out his breath at the maneuver, his hands welded to his seat.

Megan grimaced as she pulled back on the stick, then with another gut wrenching maneuver brought the helicopter into a more level flight. Still the Pave Hawk was buffeted by winds, swaying like a drunk, but they were now flying forward toward the other side of the valley.

"Tail wind, Darlin'," Cowboy reminded her.

"Yeah, it's making the tail rotor effect worse," Megan said as the helicopter zoomed toward the next ridge. "Come on, Baby."

Cowboy adjusted his white-knuckled grip.

Megan took a deep breath. "Up and over, Cowboy."

"Like a buckin' bronco," Cowboy said as they did another roller coaster maneuver over the small ridge top. He sucked in a sharp breath as the helicopter flew just feet over the ground.

This valley was much larger than the previous two. They couldn't see the other side of it due to rain sheeting the area. Cowboy turned his attention to the storm scope which allowed them to see where the storm was lightest in strength. He pointed at the scope. "Meg, you'd better use it."

"Yeah, I see it." She thumbed on the intercom. "If you think that was fun…" She flicked it off.

"Satan's lover. I swear that's what you are, Meg," Cowboy said.

Megan grinned. Her concentration was complete as she pushed the Pave Hawk harder, flying toward the lighter area. The clouds didn't seem so dark there. Lightening flashed close by as they flew.

"Comin' up on it," Cowboy told her.

Megan didn't acknowledge him as she steadied the chopper through the buffeting winds. The seatbelts dug into their shoulders. The feeling of having your innards mixing in a big mess was disconcerting. Then they popped into lighter air. Winds smoothed out, the oppressive feeling was all but wiped away and visibility improved.

Megan let out her breath. For a second, the pilots remained stunned into silence as she flew the area. The storm scope showed that briefly they would be out of the worst of it. She shook her head. "Cowboy, fly a minute."

He expelled a huge guff of air and started chuckling. He flicked on the intercom and let out a 'yee-haw' that sounded louder than a thunderclap. As he turned it off, he glanced at Megan, taking control of the aircraft.

She closed her eyes and laid her head back.

"You okay, Darlin'?"

"I think I messed my pants."

Laughter tumbled out of them as they flew smoothly back to base.

***

With a moment's hesitation, Megan knocked on Jake's door. It was mid-afternoon on the crew's day off after the harrowing mission the day before. Everyone was gone from base housing when they received a medical transport call. She hurried to find someone, anyone, to fly in back as crew chief. Cowboy was already pre-flighting Famine. Death's linkages were being repaired from the valley escapade.

"Yeah? Come in," came sleepily from inside the room.

Megan swallowed as she opened the door.

The room was darkened with a blanket over the window but it wasn't completely black. There was enough light to see Jake push up on his elbow, rubbing his eyes. Due to the heat, he was sleeping without sheets and only in his boxers. His stomach muscles were six-packs—lean and tight. Tanned.

Megan's eyes automatically panned the length of his body. *Damn. Yummy.* The heat rose throughout her body as her eyes stopped on Jake's obvious reaction to being awakened from a deep sleep. Her lips parted ever so slightly. Her tongue tip just showing itself.

Jake chuckled slightly. "And what's the occasion of this unexpected visit, Chief?"

Megan blushed at having been caught admiring his body. "Uh, yeah." She swallowed. "We got a medical transport call. I need someone as crew chief. Everyone else is gone."

Jake swung his legs over and sat up. "What's up?"

"Two kids were playing on the outskirts of town in an area just cleared by the dogs of landmines. They missed one." Her eyes met Jake's as he grabbed his pants. "Uh, we'll be waiting in the hanger."

Jake stood swiftly and grabbed Megan before she could leave. He gave her a breath stopping kiss, both hands holding her head still, tongue gently touching hers, then let go. "Thanks for the great ending to a delicious dream."

"What?" Megan asked catching her breath.

Jake spoke as he dressed. "You ended my dream in exactly the way I wanted it. Thanks." He grabbed his black T-shirt. His words were muffled by the shirt as he asked, "Do I need hot mission gear?"

"What?"

"Chief, hot mission gear?"

"Uh, what? Uh, no. It's right outside of town. Won't take us but a couple of minutes, an hour at the outside."

Jake leaned over and gave her a peck on the cheek. "Let's get going, Chief."

"Uh, yeah," Megan said with another blush as she hurried out the door. *What a fucking bubblehead. Stupid. Like a fucking school girl. Get a grip, you idiot.*

A chuckle followed her down the hall as he was gathering the rest of his equipment.

***

Waves washed over him as he rolled onto his back, drawing a naked Megan on top of him. Her lips warm and succulent as her hands played at his chest, rubbing and massaging his chest and stomach muscles. She lowered herself onto him...

A turbulent air pocket caused Jake to return to reality and the fact that he was in a helicopter. He chuckled as he adjusted his once more hard member to a more comfortable position in his pants. *What a delicious dream!*

Jake smiled again at the thought of Megan standing in his room looking at him. He had been dreaming of her in a seaside cove. The temperature in the dream was just right as was the water tickling their legs in the surf. Jake almost sighed. It had been a long time since he'd had an erotic dream that gave him a reaction that lasted so long.

The flight had been uneventful. They picked up the hurt kid and flew him to the army base hospital. Jake was pretty sure that the ten year old would loose his leg. There was not much holding the leg at the knee, several slivers of muscle and some flesh but not much else. Part of the foot was missing and it looked to Jake like the tibia was broken too. The other kid was dead.

Megan explained on the trip over that this was not unusual. Every year White Pine did at least eight or nine of these transports. The military did more. Even after the land was cleaned by machines, bomb experts and lastly, and most effectively, the canines, there would occasionally be a landmine left. This sort of accident usually happened during spring with frost heave. Worse, since the mines were getting old and corroded by weather, they were more sensitive.

Many people died each year due to Russian landmines. They had done a thorough job of it, too. Whole areas that could be used for agriculture and buildings had to be left empty because of the threat of mines. Military and civilian contractors were working around the clock to find and disarm mines. Megan said that even with that big of a resource concentrated in just the areas near the city, it would be another couple of years before they could be used.

Jake had asked about the red rocks that they occasionally saw near roads. Megan informed him that there were mines in that area, but they hadn't been cleared yet. Also, the schools gave classes to every kid about land mines. The Afghanistan government even paid adults to take classes to learn about mines. Still, many people died each year or were maimed. Everywhere there were people walking without limbs.

As they neared the White Pine base, Jake turned on the intercom. "Hey Ghost, there's lots of blood back here. Where's the disinfectant we use to wash it out? The usual bottle is empty. Where's the main supply?"

"Inside the hanger, near the fire apparatus," Megan replied. "Is it bad?"

"Shouldn't take long. I can handle it," Jake said with a smile.

"Good thing, Cupcake. 'Cause that's why we fly. No clean up duty."

Jake chuckled. He could tell that Megan was smiling from the tone of her voice. That almost got another rise out of him. *Damn, she's driving me insane.*

It wasn't long and the helicopter landed. Jake jumped out, opened both doors to air it out, and hurried toward the hangar. As he bent over to dump the disinfectant into the smaller bottle, he noticed a stranger heading toward Famine.

This guy was older, maybe late fifties. His gray hair was speckled with black and he wore black sunglasses. Not unusual in Afghanistan, almost everyone wore sunglasses. The thing that caught Jake's attention was his bearing and single-mindedness in heading to the chopper.

Jake stopped what he was doing and headed back toward the hanger doors. *What is going on? And who is this guy?*

Cowboy entered the big open doors and stopped Jake at the entrance. "Clean up the bird later."

Jake's gaze came back to him. "Who is that?"

Cowboy turned to look out the hanger doors. "An old friend of her family, according to Megan. Come on." He took Jake by the arm.

With a quick move, Jake broke the hold on his arm. "What's going on?" Jake thumbed toward Famine.

Megan was staring at the approaching man. The look on her face was neutral, yet she had turned pale. Gently, she placed her helmet inside the back of Famine. She jammed her hands into the pockets of the flight suit as she waited for the guy striding toward her.

"Who is that guy?" Jake asked again.

"I don't know his name," Cowboy said lowering his voice. He looked around quickly, noticing that Jake did the same, then looked back with Jake to the two on the runway. "But I'm thinkin' he useta work with Megan's Dad."

"Doing?"

"With The Company."

"Company? White Pine?"

"The CIA."

The scene by the helicopter stopped their conversation. The man took her by the arm and the two of them slowly walked farther down the runway away from the hanger. Seconds later, Megan squatted down, one knee touching the runway. Head bowed.

The man stood there looking down at her, a frown on his face. Then he looked in all directions. Finally, his gaze came back to Megan. He squatted next to her and laid a hand on her shoulder.

Jake glanced at Cowboy, who shrugged. "Bad news," Jake guessed.

"Probably."

"Her dad?"

"That would be my guess, pardner."

The two men stood in the hanger entrance but neither of the people in the bright sunshine moved for a couple minutes. Finally, Megan nodded at the man and stood with him. She walked back to the helicopter with her head bowed then sat in the open door of Famine, her back to the hanger. The man spoke to her for a few seconds, then with a brisk step headed toward the main office building.

Jake took a step out of the hanger.

Cowboy grabbed his arm. "Leave her 'lone, Jake."

Jake looked at the hand on his arm then back at Cowboy. "She needs a friend right now."

"Ya don't know what was said."

"It doesn't matter. She needs a… Let go of the arm, Kelly."

"Look pardner…"

"Let go of my arm before this turns ugly."

Cowboy dropped his hand.

Jake started walking toward Famine.

"Jake."

He half turned to look at him.

"Don't take advantage of her."

"I would never do that," Jake said, then walked with a quick stride toward the helicopter. As he neared Famine, he slowed down. *What the hell am I doing? I'm not good at this sort of thing.* Despite his gut twisting, he knew he had to do this.

Jake stopped several feet from the helicopter to see Megan crying. Not sobbing, just tears flowing down her face. She held her helmet in her lap, tapping her fingers in a steady rhythm.

Megan's eyes rose to meet his, then lowered just as fast.

Jake hesitated, then slowly walked up to Famine. He sat down next to her and looked out over the runway, watching the birds fly in the distance. He folded his hands on his lap and waited. He didn't know what to say but maybe just his presence would comfort her. If not, he was sure she would tell him to leave. He didn't know how long it was before she spoke, her fingers were still beating a tempo on her helmet.

"Dad shot himself."

Jake said nothing.

She choked on the next word then cleared her throat and tried again. "He… He shot himself in the head. Didn't want to face brain cancer."

Jake nodded with a glance.

Tears flowed unchecked down her face. Her eyes followed the birds as they swooped down and up in air currents. The heat was oppressive, but neither of them felt it.

Jake reached into the back of Famine and grabbed a water bottle from the small cooler. He knew the water wasn't cold but was better than nothing. He opened the bottle and handed it to her.

Megan took it with a shaky hand. After taking a drink, she poured some of it over her head, then handed it back.

Jake poured the rest over his head.

"Guess he found his own answer."

"I'm sorry, Megan."

"Stubborn, old coot."

Jake reached out and patted her leg. He left his hand resting on her thigh and gave a slight squeeze. Megan's hand covered his and curled around his fingers. They sat for a long time, sweating and watching the birds.

***

The next night Jake found Megan sitting alone on the roof sipping from a water bottle. Grabbing a chair, he sat next to her. "Hey."

Megan grunted.

"Everyone else is in town."

Megan's brown eyes flicked to him then back to the setting sun.

"I was a little worried that you were nowhere to be found," Jake said with a smile. He got comfortable in the chair. The temperature was already starting to drop.

"I wanted to be alone."

"Do you want me to leave?"

Megan turned to look him in the eyes. She returned her gaze to the mountains and took a while before she answered. "No."

"Wanna talk about it?"

"No."

"Okay." Jake crossed his ankles.

The sun was down and the stars out before the silence was broken. Megan tossed her water bottle across the rooftop in a burst of anger. "I hate this."

Jake looked at her but said nothing.

With a wave of her hand, she continued, "I shouldn't have signed the last contract. I have more than enough money." She took a deep breath.

Jake watched her closely. She was trying desperately to control herself. He could see tears threaten to come, but this time she didn't let them.

"I shouldn't have. Something told me not to. Damn it."

"Then why did you?"

"I can't even go home for his damn funeral. Not that he would care. He'd understand. He's missed plenty of my important dates. Why the hell should I care about his dead body?" She shook her head. " 'Listen to your gut, Meg.' He once told me. 'Forget the head. Listen to your heart and your gut. They'll always lead you down the right path.' But did I? No!" She slammed her flat hand down on the arm of the chair. "I shouldn't have… I should have stayed in the States like my gut was telling me. No. One more tour. One more, he said. 'Just one, Meg. We need you to do this.' Damn him." She shook her head again. "Nah. I agreed. It wasn't his fault, the bastard. No. I shouldn't have. Why did I? Huh?" She turned to Jake as though he could provide the answer.

"Why did you?" Jake repeated, not knowing what she was talking about.

"Why do we do anything?"

"What?"

Megan sighed.

Suddenly she seemed to have given up her anger. She looked tired and depressed. Jake frowned. He understood that she was grieving, but this was odd to be switching so fast from anger to acceptance.

"I don't understand. Megan?"

"No. I guess you wouldn't."

"Because I'm a man?"

"Nope." Megan sprang from her chair and paced to the edge of the rooftop. She stood there for a long several seconds before returning to the chairs. "I've been accused of being an adrenalin junkie."

Jake smiled. *That would be an understatement.* "Are you?"

"Are you?"

"Hell no. I hate getting shot at." Jake scratched his chest then stood next to her. "Honestly. Why are you here?"

Megan chuckled. "Is that still bothering you?"

"I'm curious why a woman would want to go to a place where they're opressed and put her life on the line?" He took a step closer to her.

"I guess they're right, I'm an adrenaline junkie."

Jake shook his head. "There are others ways to get your adrenaline fix."

Megan looked into his eyes.

The brown of her eyes were almost black in the darkness, but the heat began to rise as they shared a moment. The intense stare caused an electrical reaction. He could feel it from his toes to the ends of his hair. He'd never felt anything like this before. Never.

"I guess… I'm damn good at what I do. There are a lot of things I do that I don't like, but then there are moments that I wouldn't trade for the world."

Jake couldn't break eye contact.

"Like now," Megan whispered and leaned toward him.

With a smile, he met her lips and pulled her into him. He took her head in his hands with an aggressiveness that surprised him. He made her mouth, his. As she returned the aggressive kiss, he could feel her hands tracing down his chest, rubbing, teasing, and making his skin tingle through his shirt. They circled his waist and she gave his butt a rough massage.

He wanted so much to move his hands from her head but knew if his hands strayed, they'd end up where neither of them wanted to be right now. It was testing his resolve. His body craved, no demanded, action. Pressure grew in his loins. Much more of this kiss and his resolve not to get involved with her would go completely over the side of the building.

Abruptly she broke the kiss and pushed him away. "I… This can't happen. God, I'm so weak sometimes."

Jake watched her move several steps away, shaking her head. "When can it happen?"

"Never."

"Even after I'm out of your crew?" Jake saw her nod. "Why?"

Megan turned to look at him. In the darkness, it was too far away to see into her eyes.

Jake waited.

"I, I just can't let it. There's too much at stake. And I, I swore that I'd never again…" Megan kicked at a rock on the roof. "Look, Cupcake…"

"Don't pull this Chief shit with me. Not now."

"It can't happen, Jake. It can't. And I won't let it," Megan said softly.

"I don't believe you." Jake moved a few steps closer so that he could actually look into her eyes. "Your lips, hands and body are saying the opposite."

"Yeah well, they don't control me."

"Maybe you should let them."

Megan shook her head and took a step away.

Jake could feel tension still building between them even as she moved away. His whole body ached for her.

At that moment, the door to the roof opened. The same man from the day of the Independence Day celebration stepped out. He hesitated, then seeing them, walked closer. "Megan?"

"Damn," Megan said softly under her breath. "Yeah?"

"We need to talk," the man said glancing at Jake, then looked directly at her.

Jake said nothing but his eyes panned from one to the other. The mysterious man was dressed like the rest of the White Pine crew, khaki pants, black t-shirt. Jake had only seen this guy on base once before. It was after that, that Megan and Gunner disappeared for over a day. She side-stepped his questions. Finally, he stopped asking. The man had authority. His bearing spoke of someone of importance. Not to mention Megan's acceptance of his authority.

"When?" Megan asked.

"Now."

Megan glanced at Jake then followed the man back to the door. She paused. With a glance back at him, she walked inside.

Jake stared at the closed door.

Who is he? What authority did he have? Why is she so infuriatingly stubborn? And why am I falling in love with her?

***

The next morning she was nowhere to be found. Nor was Gunner. Jake frowned after checking the crew chief assignment box. In it was a note from Megan.

"Cupcake, see the mission profile on my desk. Someone from Bob Timmerman's crew will fly you to do security at the runway construction site. You're in charge. Don't screw this up. The bigwigs are watching. Megan."

Jake crushed the note in his hand as he stood there for a few seconds then hurried to his room. He had over an hour before the crew was due in the meeting room. He needed to get himself together.

Shortly before the meeting, he headed down the hall toward Megan's office. He needed to find out if there was anything new happening at the runway. If not, this would be boring as usual. Usually he did a security pass then end up back near the helicopter to stand and talk with Megan and Kelly. Today would be like watching snot dry on a sidewalk.

As he rounded the corner near the front desk where the assignment boxes were, he saw Zarin busily working on something where they filed reports. She hung up the phone. He smiled at her as she looked at him surprised. "Hello, Zarin."

"Mr. McGrew," Zarin said in a higher than normal voice. Her eyes shifted and her hand fumbled with papers.

Jake's eyes took in the paperwork. It was one of Megan's reports. He recognized the handwriting. He continued on his way with a puzzled look. He had spoken to Zarin many times, yet that was the first time she appeared nervous. He shook his head.

He would never understand women. And to try to understand women from a foreign land was even worse. At least he could half way predict Megan's moods. Zarin had been raised differently, so he decided not to even try to understand her moods. *Women are just unpredictable.*

***

After returning that night from security detail and getting the paperwork done, he went in search of Megan. The lady pilot was still gone. So was Gunner. He went in search of Cowboy. He found him in the hanger checking out Death.

"What's going on?"

Cowboy glanced up. He stared into Jake's eyes for a second then went back to work.

"Where's Megan?" Jake waited but there was no answer forthcoming. "Is this another convert mission with Gunner?"

Cowboy stood up and faced him.

"I saw the three of you return the last time."

"You'll never learn," Cowboy whispered.

"Never learn what?"

He got in Jake's face. "To keep your mouth shut. When you need to know, you'll know. If you don't learn that soon, they'll wash you out."

Jake narrowed his eyes. "I care."

Cowboy's eyes flicked around the area, but no one was around that he could see. He sighed. "Yeah, I know."

"She said something?"

"No, but I know her." He squatted down, looking under the fuselage.

Jake hesitated, then squatted down too, acting as though he was helping him. "Is she in danger?"

"Like today is different from the others?"

"What?"

"Look, leave it go. And leave her go, pardner. Trust me, you don't want this."

***

The next day Jake noticed that Cowboy was gone in the afternoon. He flew out once more in the evening to return after dark.

The last time Jake met him at the hanger door. Their eyes locked.

Cowboy shook his head and moved around Jake into the hanger. "Corn!"

"Yeah?" The mechanic hurried out from the other side of a helicopter.

"Have Death prepped and ready to go at first light. Fully fueled. I'll be leaving 'fore the birds are awake." Cowboy turned to see Jake staring at him.

CHAPTER 10

At first light, Jake was sitting in the crew/cargo area of Death—his gun and pack near him, dressed in hot mission gear. His head snapped up as the door to the back of the chopper opened and Cowboy almost jumped ten feet in response. He smiled at the surprised pilot.

Cowboy hesitated for just a second then dropped his duffel bag next to Jake. "What ya'all doin' here?"

"Something's wrong."

Cowboy hesitated again, then sighed. "Yeah."

"Tell me."

Cowboy glanced around then motioned for Jake to follow him. As he did the pre-flight, he spoke softly. "She missed two rendezvous. Two."

"And?"

"There was only two scheduled." Cowboy glanced at Jake then continued with pre-flight.

"So this is unauthorized."

"Ya bet your ass, pardner." He smiled at Jake then glanced at the main building. "And I need to get outta here soon, afore the big bosses see me."

Jake glanced into the back of the Pave Hawk. "Ammo?"

"Fully loaded."

"Then let's get out of here."

Cowboy stopped Jake with a hand. "It might be your job."

Jake nodded.

Cowboy smiled again. "Hop in. Ever take a joy ride in your youth, Cupcake?"

"Nope."

"Well, just think of this as taking Daddy's car out without permission. When we get back, our asses'll be licked with a hickory switch, but it's usually worth it." Cowboy patted Jake on the back. "Let's just hope we come home with the prize."

***

The two men sat in silence all day. Jake sat with his legs over the side of the chopper, occasionally swinging them. His eyes continually panned the hillsides. It was boring and mind numbing.

Cowboy returned from a bush nearby and sat next to him. He checked his watch. "She's not goin' to make it. We need to be leavin'. Damn it, are we in for an ass chewin'." He sighed deeply.

Jake let out his breath in frustration too.

"I just don't know what to do." Cowboy ran a hand through his hair. "The first pickup was compromised. This is the secondary, but I can't come back here 'gain. Even today was too risky."

Jake glanced at him then returned his look back to the hills. "What's the contingency plan if she can't make the secondary rendezvous?"

"There isn't. She's on her own."

"Is this standard procedure?"

"Yeah. The bosses'll write her and Gunner off tonight. Within a week, there'll be no indication that she even worked for them." He stood up. With a last look into the deepening shadows of the mountains, he intoned softly, "Goodbye, Meg. God be with you where ever you are."

Jake stood up too. "Are you just writing her off too?"

"What'da ya want me ta do?"

"We have tomorrow off. We look for her."

"Where?" Cowboy asked.

"What was her assignment?"

"I don't know."

Jake could feel his blood coming up. "Cut the bullshit."

"I don't know. I dropped her and Gunner two valleys over." He pointed to the west. "That's all I know. The pick up was in the same valley. When I returned the next day, all I saw was locals swarmin' the hillside. I didn't even put down. I couldn't. Next morning, I showed up here."

"What was she to do?"

"I don't know."

"Guess."

Cowboy made a face. "Look pardner, I have no idea what she does. And I don't wanta know. She's the best pilot I know, but I don't delve into her other life."

"Her other life?"

"Ya just don't get it, do ya?"

"Get what?"

"She's a plant. Yes, she works for White Pine but she does more. Now do ya get it?"

"She's a CIA agent?"

"Boy, your Momma raised a slow one here. Yeah, she's a 'Player.' "

Jake nodded to himself. He should have figured, but he couldn't think about that now. She was in danger, if not already dead. His eyes panned the area and he thought about the missions he'd been on.

Most of them had been in valleys close to the drop off or pick up. This allowed for only a day's walk to the destination. That meant that whatever she was doing was probably in the valley between the two rendezvous. At least, it was a place to start looking. Jake returned his gaze to Cowboy as his thoughts simmered for a few seconds. "Will you fly back here tomorrow?"

Cowboy's eyes softened. "Ya'all got it bad." His eyes locked with Jake's then he gave a slight nod. "If I can get a chopper out again, yeah."

"Good." Jake grabbed a small pack from the back of Death. It contained MREs and other essential gear. As he swung it on, he grabbed the camouflage, floppy hat. "Meet me here, tomorrow night right before dusk."

"What are you...?"

"If this is compromised, go back to the first valley. They won't be expecting that." Jake grabbed his M-16. "If I'm not there, then watch the road. Have the military send out patrols on a regular basis. I'll travel down there."

"Jake..." Cowboy saw determination in his eyes. "Okay. I'll be here." He held out his hand.

With a quick nod and handshake, Jake took off at a trot toward the ridge that separated them from the other valley. He would use all of his training to find Megan. Jake had almost reached the edge of the clearing when he heard the helicopter take off. He paused once to watch it, then put his feet back into gear. Resting was not something he could afford right now.

Jake continued to trot then realized that the helicopter was still hovering in the meadow. He stopped and turned, wondering why Cowboy hadn't flown off. Shading his eyes so he could get a better look, he saw the pilot concentrating on a spot on the side of the meadow just a short distance from him. Jake turned his attention to the same area.

At first he saw nothing. Then he spotted movement. Within seconds, he saw a flash of reflected light aimed at the helicopter. Death settled back to the ground. Jake took off running toward the area where the light flashed. As he approached, he saw a smaller person emerge from the thick wooded area carrying a body.

"Damn," Jake cursed under his breath and pushed himself harder. He noticed Megan slowing down even as she got near the edge of the meadow. The load on her back dipped as she stumbled. With a glance back to the helicopter, he saw Cowboy standing near the cockpit, blades twirling.

Jake's eyes panned the area of the woods to make sure it was secured even as he ran faster. He saw no one in the vicinity. His eyes jumped back to his destination as he saw Megan stumble and fall, both bodies going down in a heap. Within seconds, he was at her side. "Chief?"

She struggled to her feet. "Cupcake?" Her voice was hoarse.

"Yeah." He pulled her up and steadied her. "Can you make it?"

She was bloody, dirty and exhausted. Her clothes were ripped and her lips cracked, but she nodded with a determined look in her eye.

Jake grabbed Gunner and swung him into a fireman's carry over top of his pack. He adjusted the weight on his shoulders and glanced at Megan.

She picked up the pack she had been carrying and motioned for Jake to go. Megan gave a quick glance toward the hillside that she had just come down.

"Company?" Jake asked as he walked, watching to make sure she was following.

"Don't know." It was barely whispered.

Jake glanced ahead to see Cowboy opening the back cargo door of Death then scrambling to the cockpit. The blades twirled faster as they got near. With a glance behind him, he saw Megan lagging behind. "Come on, Chief. Just a little farther."

A weary nod was the answer.

Jake moved faster and gently laid Gunner in the back of Death then ran back to Megan's side. She seemed hardly able to stay on her feet. He grabbed the pack from her and threw it into the chopper. As she stumbled again, he grabbed her collar. With a fast move, he swept her feet out from under her and carried her to the chopper.

After getting into the aircraft, he grabbed a helmet and plugged it in, telling Cowboy to go and swung the door shut. With a passing glance at Megan, lying on her back breathing hard, he began checking Gunner.

It looked like most of the blood had come from him. Jake ripped open his camouflage shirt to reveal a makeshift bandage on his chest. A closer look at the 'bandage' showed it to be Megan's black T-shirt. It was crusty on the edges and he left it alone. It didn't look like he was bleeding anymore, but Gunner was unconscious.

Jake adjusted Gunner's body so that he was lying flat with his feet elevated. He covered Gunner with an emergency blanket. As he turned his attention to Megan, a voice sounded in his ear.

"What's the verdict, Cupcake?"

Jake shook his head. "Gunner's in bad shape. Some sort of wound to the chest. Ghost bandaged it but it looks bad. I can't get a good look because it's crusted over. It's best to leave it as is. I'm checking on Ghost now." He leaned over Megan, shutting off the intercom. "Chief?"

Megan opened her eyes.

"Are you okay? Any wounds?"

She shook her head.

Jake reached into the cooler and grabbed a water bottle. He sat next to her and lifted her head, holding the bottle to her lips. "Take a drink, Chief. Come on."

The water splashed onto her lips and she became more alert. She eagerly took more into her mouth.

"Easy. Go slow, Megan." Jake spoke with a smile. "You're dehydrated. Take it slow." He keyed the intercom. "Cowboy, Ghost seems to be okay. Exhausted and dehydrated, but no wounds."

"Thank God. I'ma taken us directly to the military base for Gunner," Cowboy said then clicked off.

Jake smiled at Megan who was looking at him. "You need a better contingency plan. Always be prepared. We'll talk about this later when I can be the bitch I need to be." He winked.

"Okay, Mr. Boy Scout." Megan tried a smile then took another drink of water.

"How bad are Gunner's injuries?"

"Bad," Megan said after a swallow. "Gunshot to the side of the chest. One to the upper right shoulder." She glanced over at Gunner. "Tell Cowboy to light a fire. Death can go faster than this."

Jake smiled as he hit the intercom button. "Ghost says to light a fire, Cowboy."

"Tell that purty, little Darlin' back there to stop back seat driving," Cowboy said even as he increased speed.

Jake relayed the message and saw Megan's exhausted face form a half grin. She gave a sigh and closed her eyes. He gently pulled her onto him, so her head was cradled in his lap, as he continued to give her drinks of water. "Easy Chief. You're safe. Just relax."

Megan opened her eyes to look at him. "Thanks for the pick up, Cupcake."

Jake winked again. "It's my job. Never leave a man behind."

***

Before they received word about the two injured from the doctors at the military hospital, there were two people waiting with them. One was Massod. He took Cowboy aside and yelled at him. Jake had never seen the Afghan so mad. The other one was the mysterious man from the rooftop. He didn't speak.

Finally, the doctor walked into the waiting room. "Mr. Iniguez is in critical condition. He's still in surgery. We'll know more about his condition when the surgeons get done. However, he lost a great deal of blood. Both gunshot wounds did massive damage. Ms. Cartwright is stable. She'll be able to see visitors in a few minutes." He turned and left.

The mysterious man looked at Masood then turned to Cowboy and Jake. "Masood, I need to speak with you. Cowboy, head back to base. McGrew stay." He followed the doctor.

Jake glanced at Cowboy who stood staring at the mysterious guy's back.

Cowboy shook his head, catching Jake's eyes. With a look to be careful, Cowboy quickly left the room.

Following his exit, Jake narrowed his eyes. *What is going on?* He brought his gaze back to Masood, but the head of the base was staring out the window. Jake sat back and crossed his arms.

A few minutes later, the doctor stepped out and motioned to them.

Jake stood and followed Masood into Megan's emergency room. Standing off to the side was the mysterious man. Jake looked him in the eyes, but he was unreadable. Next his eyes panned to Megan. She met his glance then looked down at the floor.

He was puzzled, but decided to follow her orders for once and keep his mouth shut. This time her advice seemed fitting. He stood on the side of the room opposite the mysterious man and stuck his hands in his pockets.

After everyone was in the room, the doctor spoke, "We aren't keeping Ms. Cartwright. I wanted her to spend the night for observation, but she's refusing. However, I don't want her doing anything strenuous for the next few days. The dehydration and exposure will cause general weakness for a couple days. She's to take it easy. The flight surgeon will have to approve her status again."

Megan kept her eyes glued to the floor.

Jake glanced at her then at the doctor. The doctor had basically been addressing the mysterious man.

Megan looked up. "What about Gunner?"

The doctor shook his head. "Touch and go. He lost a lot of blood and is still in surgery. At this point, it's a wait and see game. If that's all…" When no one had other questions, he left the room.

Masood looked at Megan then spoke to the other guy. "There is a car waiting."

Megan scooted off the bed and smoothed the hospital scrubs top that the doctor had given her. She motioned for Jake to hand her the body armor sitting on a table near him.

"I got it."

She nodded at him then glared at the mysterious guy. "Let's go."

They stepped outside to find a van waiting. Masood climbed in first. The mysterious man motioned Megan to get in, then motioned for Jake.

With a slight hesitation, Jake climbed in to find Masood facing the front in one seat and Megan facing back. Jake sat down next to Megan facing Masood. The mysterious man climbed in, shut the door and sat next to Masood. The van drove off.

The ride was in silence as tension mounted. The mysterious man was staring at Megan, although his eyes were obscured by mirrored sunglasses that he put on as he exited the hospital. Largely they ignored him—as useless as yesterday's trash.

They were almost to the base when Megan finally broke the silence. "What?" She addressed the sun-glassed, mysterious man. He said nothing.

Jake got the impression that he looked at him, but the man's head hadn't moved.

"Were you successful?" the guy asked Megan.

"Don't you know?"

"Indications would suggest that you didn't accomplish your objective."

"Yeah well, shit happens."

"So, you failed."

"Yeah." Megan's anger increased. "Am I not allowed a failure every now and then?"

The man frowned.

"Look, you got a leak in the organization," Megan said. She crossed her arms. "The pickup was compromised. The target was alert and waiting. Someone knew we were going to be in those mountains. I'd like to know who."

"I'll look into it."

Megan huffed.

"I think you should be pulled."

"Why?" Megan spit out.

"Stress."

"Stress? When isn't it stressful?"

"You're under a lot of stress with recent events."

"You mean my Dad offing himself?"

"That would be one."

"So, he shot himself. It was his solution to a terminal problem. Gotta give him credit for taking control of the situation." Megan uncrossed her arms and folded them in her lap. They were still except for a finger tap.

Jake panned his eyes from her lap to the others in the car. He decided it was best to continue his silence.

"Are you saying you don't care?" the mysterious man asked.

"No. He was still my Dad, but I haven't seen the bastard in a couple of years. Not to mention shipping me off when I was young. It wasn't like we were confidantes or anything."

Jake was impressed with her bravado, although he knew the real depth of her love.

The mysterious man made it a point to let all know that he was looking at Jake.

Megan looked Jake in the eyes, then turned back to the mysterious man. "What about him?"

"Stress."

Megan faked a laugh. "With Jake? Please!"

Jake narrowed his eyes. It was obvious that he had been brought into the van for a reason and now he knew he would find out why.

"We have been watching you closely for sometime," the mysterious man said to Megan.

"So?"

"You appear to be losing perspective."

"Because I enjoy Jake's company? You've never cared about my friendship with Kelly."

"There's a difference."

"Really? So, I'm only allowed one male friend."

"You've been slow."

"I told you the last time, it'll be a mistake, but you didn't want to listen to me then." Megan leaned forward. "As I said, not everyone is suited for this. You know that."

"Yes, I know. But I think he should be the one to determine that." The mysterious man once more turned toward Jake.

Jake looked between the two. His eyes narrowed as he considered the conversation. Suddenly it struck him. *I'm being recruited. And I bet Megan was supposed to have done it.* His eyes rested on her, but she couldn't or wouldn't meet his gaze. He returned his gaze to the mysterious man.

"You've lived up to expectations, Mr. McGrew. We would like to offer you a more lucrative position in the White Pine family."

Jake said nothing.

"If you accept, next week you'll be sent for special training. If you decline, you'll be assigned a less critical role in White Pine."

"What's the whole deal, Mister... I didn't get your name."

"I didn't give it."

"Yes, I know," Jake said. He didn't like this guy. And it appeared from the feelings that Megan was broadcasting, she didn't like him either.

"Harding. William Harding." He stuck out his hand.

Jake looked at it but didn't return the gesture. "What's the whole scoop?"

"You're being invited to join us. You'll be assigned a crew in Iraq. We've followed your career with an eye to recruiting you for sometime. We've arranged it so that you won't be called back into active duty as the Pentagon is getting ready to do. So in essence, you'll be switching teams for your country. I believe that you would be a great asset helping us protect the interests of our nation."

"And this 'protecting' would include what sort of jobs?"

"Whatever needs to be done. For the most part, you would be doing exactly what the military trained you to do. We would capitalize on that training."

"I see," Jake said. "And when do you want my decision?"

"Whenever you decide."

"Then I'll need to think about it."

Harding smiled. "Of course. There are certain perks that come with the position."

The van rolled to a stop, but no one moved to get out.

"Certain perks that would allow us to rotate personnel into parallel positions." He nodded at Megan. "I'll be in touch, Mr. McGrew." He stepped out of the vehicle. There was another car parked next to the van which he stepped into, and it took off. After a few seconds, so did their van.

Jake turned to Megan. "What the hell was that all about?"

Megan let out her breath. She turned to Masood, ignoring Jake's question. "I hate him."

Fahim chuckled. "Yes, he makes everyone nervous. I just wish Washington would let us be. They always complicate things."

"Did he just pimp you to me?!"

"That's about the long and short of it, Cupcake."

"And you're okay with this?"

"Not at all, but I know when to pick my battles. Harding's not the person to battle right now." She blew out her breath as the van pulled into the White Pine compound. She exited the vehicle then twirled on Masood as he exited behind her. She lowered her voice. "Who knew where we were going?"

"You, me, Cowboy, Harding…" Masood paused thinking. "Gunner. The crew who readied the aircraft would know it was going out, but not the destination. I cannot think of anyone else." He paused. "Do you really think there's a spy?"

"Damn right," Megan said, watching the van roll toward the hanger where it usually parked.

Jake looked around. It was past curfew and there was no one about.

"Forget it." Megan walked toward the barracks. "I'll figure it out."

Jake caught up with her and glanced back to Masood, who headed toward the main base building. With a slight grunt, he got her attention. "Here." He handed her the body armor.

Megan took it as she stopped. She looked around then caught his eye. "Truthfully Jake, I was to recruit you using any means necessary."

"Why?"

Megan shrugged.

"When did you get these orders?"

"The assignment came before you showed up in Germany. I didn't read it until during the plane ride here. It was after we talked."

Jake's eyes narrowed. "Was it a game? Were you playing me all this time?" His heart was squeezing tighter and tighter—his gut twisted in knots. He didn't, no, couldn't believe it. He didn't want to.

Megan glanced at the ground then around the open courtyard. She looked at him and smiled. "I'm not that good, or I'd be in their 'whore squad.' No. I don't pimp myself even for the good of my country, Cupcake."

Jake smiled back. "Good. I'd hate to think I fell for a fake."

Megan blushed.

"Who's the leak?" Jake asked softly, almost a whisper.

Megan frowned. "I don't know, but this is the second time in Afghanistan that something funny has happened. That oil line was not... And it happened once in Iraq, but that could be a different..." She shook her head. "I think someone is trying to make me look bad." She grinned.

Jake frowned instead. "You mean get you killed?"

"Same thing in this business."

"So, how serious is Harding about recruiting me?"

"Very. They want you, badly. We're short on personnel right now. Very short. And they need people who can speak the language in Iraq. You fit their bill to a tee."

"But you think it would be a mistake for me to take the job?" Jake asked seriously.

"Jake..." Megan stopped, then as though she changed her mind, shook her head. "It's your decision. You're a big boy. I just... It takes a certain kind of person to do the things they want." She caught his deep, brooding blue eyes. "I'd hate to see such a good person turn into a stubborn, pigheaded bastard."

Jake said nothing. It seemed that she was being sincere at least.

Megan lightly touched his arm, just a brush. "Thanks for the help, Jake."

"My hero streak strikes again." He winked.

"Good thing." She started moving toward the building. "Now, if I can just get you to follow orders."

***

After working security at the runway the next day, Jake and the rest of the crew had two days off. He decided to hitch a ride to the military base to visit Gunner. The Chilean was still in critical condition, but the doctors expected him to live. However, according to Megan who gave them the news at the crew meeting the day before, Gunner would be leaving White Pine due to disability when he healed. As a matter of fact, as soon as he was off the critical list, he'd be shipped back to the States to finish his recovery.

Jake tried to find Megan to see if she wanted to go with him to visit Gunner, but she was nowhere to be found. Cowboy told him he had seen her first thing in her office on the phone, but after that he didn't see her again.

After visiting Gunner, Jake headed back to Chicken Street to buy another piece of jewelry. He was dropped off right outside the shop by one of the White Pine vehicles. He'd walk back to the compound.

This time he bought another Lapis Lazuli piece similar to the last one. He also purchased an orange/red necklace of Carnelian, worked in silver. The orange colored gems were oblong beads threaded with a silver chain. Two of the Carnelian stones were elegantly encased in silver, and the centerpiece of the necklace was a large, lighter, almost translucent, orange gem.

Again the shop clerk seemed to be especially proud of the Lapis Lazuli piece as he wrapped each necklace in a red silk cloth in similar fashion as last time. He pointed out to Jake a small silver bracelet with several small Lapis Lazuli stones imbedded in silver. It was elegant yet not imposing. It spoke of strength with a touch of feminism.

Jake shook his head at first. He had enough now to send something to everyone, but as he reached the door of the shop, he stopped. His eyes flew back to the bracelet. He seemed to be drawn to the silver bracelet for some reason. He had no idea why, but buying it felt right. So with a smile, he nodded and pointed at the piece.

The shop clerk laughed, but quickly wrapped it up.

Wondering why he succumbed to buying it, he stood a few feet from the door checking out the area. Now that he had this much jewelry stuffed into his pants pockets, he needed to make sure that he didn't fall prey to local hoodlums. As he did his security check, he vaguely thought he heard shouting. He cocked his head, and sure enough there was shouting from a side street not far away.

His eyes panned the streets to see several of the ever-present street urchins heading his way. Suddenly the four boys stopped and glanced back toward the side street. Within seconds and like a wisp of fog, the boys disappeared from sight.

Jake frowned, but decided to follow the wise example of the street kids. If they feared the shouting enough to miss getting candy, there was probably a good reason why he too should 'disappear.' He stepped back into the recess of the shop doorway. A glance inside showed that the store clerk had disappeared too. He wished desperately that he understood the language.

Jake peeked out of his hiding place to see a turbaned man burst from the side street, then race down the street toward him. He frowned, this was the same guy from the coffee house and here in the jewelry store. His gut yelled to stop this guy.

The turbaned man turned to look behind him as he ran. It seemed from the shouting, that the guy had put some distance between him and his pursuers. He carried a small bundle in his hands and switched his hold on it, carrying it more like a football now.

Jake waited until the man was almost even with him, then stepped out. He lifted his hands to stop the guy, but the turbaned man's speed just increased as he refocused on running. Not having the time or ability to stop the collision, the guy ran headlong into Jake, even as Jake tried to step out of his way. They both fell to the ground in a heap.

A curse escaped the man's mouth. An English curse word. Familiar.

Jake, on the top, took a closer look at the man. His eyes focused on the face, this time at extremely close range. He couldn't keep the shocked look off of his face. The big brown eyes were beginning to focus. "Megan?"

"Damn," Megan said again as she tried pushing Jake off her.

"What are you...?"

"Shut up. And lower your voice," Megan said glancing around. "Get off me."

Jake quickly jumped up, pulling her up too.

Megan, dressed as a man, looked behind her with a grimace. The shouting was getting louder. "Crap." She turned to Jake and pressed the bundle into his stomach. "Don't ask questions," she whispered. "Take it to base. Hurry."

"Chief?" Jake grabbed the bundle with a puzzled look.

"Do it. Now." She didn't wait, but took off across the street, pretending to still carry the bundle.

Jake followed her with still stunned eyes. Out of the corner of his eye, two other turbaned men exited the side street. With a quick step, he moved back into the recess of the shop and hid the bundle.

He watched as they pointed down the street at a slower moving Megan. It was obvious she was waiting for them to see her. She was providing a diversion. They followed, yelling, and Jake saw her once more pick up speed and disappear around another corner.

He looked at the bundle. With a slight shrug, he slowly walked back to base holding the bundle as he had seen Megan carrying it, cradling it like a football—alert and on guard.

Whatever it was, she had risked her life in more than one way to get it. Besides stealing it, he was sure, if she was caught and discovered, they would beat her to death. Jake shook his head. *Why do I always get involved with these 'different kind' of women? For once, I'd like to have a normal relationship.*

***

Jake sat in Megan's office an hour later. He had his arms crossed and looked pissed off. Megan hesitated as she crossed the threshold, but continued into the room. She was dressed in her normal khaki pants and black shirt. Silently, she moved behind the desk. She pulled out her chair to find that Jake had 'hidden' the bundle on it. She transferred the bundle to the desk and sat down.

She smiled. "Thanks for the help."

He didn't do anything. He didn't smile. He didn't nod. He didn't blink.

Megan sighed. "I guess you'd like an explanation."

Jake uncrossed his arms.

"Close the door."

Jake leaned back and swung the door closed. He returned his stare at her.

With a swallow, Megan began to unbundled the package. She could tell that he hadn't taken it apart since it was still wrapped as she had stolen it. "It's not what you're thinking."

He merely motioned with his hand to explain.

"Before the Russians left, they were excavating large parts of the country. In one archeological dig, they came across a huge find of gold, ivory, and things that dated back two thousand years to old Silk Road Bactrian times and earlier. It was an impressive find. The value of the works was, well, invaluable. When the Taliban took over, these valuable pieces of Afghanistan history disappeared. Scholars feared that they had melted down the gold or sold it piecemeal, or worse destroyed it, like the Bamiyan Buddhas."

Jake's mad face softened to a more neutral look.

Megan stopped unwrapping the package as she spoke. "Do you know the story of the Bamiyan Buddhas?"

"No."

"Well, in the Bamiyan Valley…" She waved her hand in a westerly direction. "Centuries ago two huge Buddhas were carved into the cliffs. Then in 2001, the Taliban went on a rampage destroying images 'offensive to Islam.' The world tried to convince them not to destroy the statues. But they did it anyway. It sparked an outage around the world among archaeologists and historians. Now all that exists are the two coves where the Buddhas once stood. Anyway, during that time and still going on today is the selling of Afghanistan artifacts. There is a huge trade in Pakistan. Anyone with money can buy a piece of ancient Afghanistan.

"When the Taliban took over, many loyal Afghans hid or, in any way possible, tried to preserve national treasures. For example, some workers at the National Film Institute built a false wall to conceal the room where the negatives of scores of movies were kept. Many were documentaries on the antiquities that the Taliban were destroying. In some cases, pictures of those things are all that is left for the world to see. In the National Gallery of Art, some painters actually went to the building and began a series of deceptions. They painted in watercolor over offensive parts of the oil paintings. After the Taliban fell, they wiped the water paints off." Megan leaned back in her chair. She stared at the bundle on her desk as she spoke. Finally, she looked up at Jake.

"And what does that have to do with this?" he asked, pointing at the bundle.

"Those Bactrian artifacts I mentioned were one of the things that were feared destroyed or melted down for the gold. Several days ago, I got a tip from a source that part of the collection was still in tact, but that it was being shipped to Pakistan to be sold to the highest bidder in order to finance al Qaeda. I managed to find out where and when." She leaned forward and unwrapped the last layer.

A jumble of items lay in a pile: ivory figurines, coins, and a couple of clay figures. The one that caught the eye was a shiny, gold necklace in the middle.

Megan reached out, gently extracted the small necklace from the pile and handed it to Jake. "This is part of Afghanistan history. What you hold is worth hundreds of thousands, if not millions of dollars."

Jake stared at the small gold discs and what looked like maybe leaves stamped out of gold. All were held together with finely hammered, golden links. It fit in the palm of his hand. After studying it, he looked up at Megan.

She righted the remaining items in the bundle. "This is an ivory statue that I would guess is from about the same time period. This clay mask-like looking thing is probably older." She gently laid them on the desk. "Here's a small piece from maybe the same type of necklace that you hold in your hand." It was another small disc of gold. "And there are maybe twelve or fifteen ancient coins here too." Megan leaned back.

Jake's eyes panned the items. Then he gently laid the gold necklace back with the other items. "What are you going to do with them? And, did you steal them?"

Megan gave him a wry grin. "You bet I stole them. Damn right. The al Qaeda guys have no right to them, least of all to be financing more terrorist acts." She leaned forward, picked up the phone and dialed an extension. "Could you come to my office? Thanks."

"What are you going to do with them?"

"Wait," Megan said, her smile softening as she covered the items with a single fold of the cloth.

Within minutes, there was a knock on her door. Jake leaned back and opened it.

Fahim walked in with a puzzled look. "Yes?"

Megan smiled. "Close the door, Jake." She waited until Jake had done so. "Have I got a surprise for you, Fahim."

Fahim smiled back as he took the other chair in the room. "Yes?"

Megan uncovered the items with a flourish.

Fahim's eyes took in the artifacts then he moved closer. His face went from puzzled to shocked to astonished in seconds as he recognized the items on the desk. He slowly looked up at Megan. "Is that...?"

"Yep. A uh, source, clued me into a situation and I, with Jake's help, managed to secure these items. They won't be smuggled out of the country as planned." Megan glanced at Jake who was smiling as he watched Fahim take in the artifacts.

Lifting his face to look at Megan, Fahim had tears in his eyes. "I thought that... We feared they were lost forever." He reached out and reverently touched the gold necklace. "This is..." He lapsed into Pashtu for the rest of his sentence.

Megan nodded with a huge grin on her face. "You're welcome, Fahim. Can I ask you a favor?"

"Anything. Anything at all." Fahim's eyes riveted on the pieces.

"Can you make sure that these artifacts make it back to their appropriate places?"

"Absolutely." He tenderly began to bundle them up. "This is a great day in Afghanistan history. We will never forget your contribution—"

"Stop, Fahim," Megan interrupted him. "You know you can never tell where you found them. My name can't be connected. Secrecy. Remember? Say they were left at the gate or something."

"But how can we properly thank you?" Fahim once more had tears in his eyes.

"Your reaction is thanks enough, and so is getting them back where they belong, so the world can enjoy them too."

Fahim bowed to her. "Consider it done." His face was lighting up the room as he began to leave.

"One more thing, Fahim," Megan said before he reached the door.

"Yes?"

"Rumor has it that there might be treasures in the presidential palace buried in a vault long forgotten." Megan winked. "Perhaps you could investigate and contact the right people to look into this?"

Fahim chuckled. "I will. I will. Do you think it is the rest of the Bactrian treasure?"

Megan shrugged. "My source didn't know either, but I would bet that it must be something of importance. What do you think?"

Fahim bowed and left with a bounce to his step, as Jake closed the door behind him.

Megan looked at Jake. "Are you still mad at me?"

Jake smiled. "A man?"

A shrug greeted him. "As I said awhile ago, I can blend in as a man if I dress right."

"What about your voice?"

Megan swallowed hard. She smiled at Jake as she spoke, her voice dropping an octave. Although it sounded like she had a very sore throat, it was so different from her natural voice that it could easily pass as a man's voice. "I can't talk for long speeches like this, but I can hold conversations if need be."

"That's incredible."

Megan shrugged. She swallowed again. Her voice returned to normal. "It just takes practice."

"Do you play 'dress up' often?"

"No. It's too dangerous."

"Yeah, I bet. And those other two times I saw you?" Jake leaned back in his chair.

"I was…" Megan hesitated. "Tracking down leads for other reasons."

"Like?"

Megan shook her head.

"So, just how many languages do you speak?"

"Four. Pashtu, Dari, Arabic, and French. I know a bit of Russian and Kurdish but I wouldn't say I speak either."

"Who taught you that?" Jake motioned with his hand to her neck and voice.

"My Dad." Megan looked down at the desk then suddenly stood up. "I'd appreciate it if you forgot this afternoon. My life depends on secrecy."

Jake stood with her. "You did a good thing here."

She could feel her cheeks turning hot and red.

Jake winked. "So beautiful." He walked out the door.

CHAPTER 11

Later that night, Jake stepped out onto the roof to find Megan again by herself looking at the mountains. He grabbed a chair and sat down by her without asking. He poured a drink out of his bottle and handed it to her, again without asking,

Megan took it without speaking and slugged it back, then handed the glass to Jake. He refused. Megan turned it several times in her hands then returned to looking at the mountains. Neither spoke for a long time.

"Today was his funeral," Megan said softly, hardly above a whisper. "I got a message from Todd."

"What was he like?" Jake asked, settling deeper into the chair.

"My Dad?" Megan asked rhetorically. She shrugged. "I don't know. Strong. Independent. A pig-headed bastard."

Jake poured himself another and held the bottle out to pour her one too.

She hesitated then held out the glass. She sniffled as she held the shot glass aloft. "Here's to you Dad. I hope you found happiness." She slugged it back, then glanced at Jake who didn't join the toast. She looked puzzled.

Jake tilted his head at her. "Your Dad. Your toast." He reached out and poured her another shot. "To his daughter." Jake lifted the glass and waited until Megan joined him. Together they toasted.

"He was a good guy. He tried hard, but I think a ten-year old daughter mystified him—a weenie for a son and a daughter that defied everyone." Megan smiled, looking into her empty glass. "He always called Todd 'his little girl.' "

Jake looked at her, incredulously.

"I'm not kidding. I think he was trying to get Todd to toughen up. He's eight years older than me. With me, Dad was clueless. I was the boy he wanted, wrapped in a girl's body." Megan chuckled. "When I was growing up, he didn't know whether to discipline me for my behavior or praise me for being my own person and thinking for myself. He settled for somewhere in between." She lapsed into silence.

Jake watched her. It was obvious that she needed to talk. He was glad that he had joined her. He hesitated at first to climb the stairs. He hated it when women cried, feeling useless, never knew what to do or say. "Your dad sounded like a fine man."

"Yeah. He was. Taught me a bunch of stuff that would have been useless except in my line of work. He saved my life numerous times with his warnings playing in my mind. Snotty, old bastard."

Jake smiled.

"He tried hard when he was around, which wasn't that often. When he wasn't around, he had people looking out for me. I got used to having someone watching my every move. Even that proved useful, the smart bastard."

Jake poured himself another and again offered her another. She held out the glass for a refill.

"He tried to be around for me, which is hard, working for the company that we do. He was many times so far under that he couldn't even send a note on my birthday. I always received a card, he hired someone to do that, but I knew the difference." Megan slugged the drink back then set the shot glass on the rooftop.

"What about your mom?"

"She died when I was nine. Car accident. I was with her. It was scary. She was still alive after the accident. All she said to me was 'Stay alive.' I climbed out of the car and ran to get help. When I returned she was dead. Dad couldn't come home right away. Todd had turned eighteen so he got custody of me. I hated it. We fought like the Cold War. We have never gotten along. Dad came home some weeks later. At ten, I was shipped off to my first boarding school. Got kicked out and went to another. I got kicked out of around six of them over all. Finally Dad threatened me, said I would amount to nothing."

"He actually said that?"

Megan nodded. "He didn't know how to father. He was never around. He treated us more like employees. But I buckled down to prove him wrong. Which, of course, was exactly what he knew I would do. He tried to spend as much time with me as possible. Even took me to West Germany once before the Wall fell." Megan looked at Jake and smiled. "My first spy case."

"How old were you?"

"Sixteen."

Jake's jaw almost dropped.

"Yeah. He was meeting a contact, so he sent me to a café to hang out. I saw a drop happen before my eyes. I knew what it was because Dad liked to share things with me. Probably his big downfall as a spy. Anyway, I knew that the two guys were Russian. I heard them talking and recognized some of the words. Dad spoke flawless Russian. I figured out that it was important, but Dad was nowhere. So I nonchalantly picked the guy's pocket. Turned out, it was an extremely important piece of information."

"At sixteen?"

"Yeah. The Company recruited me out of high school. They sent me to college with an eye to working for them afterwards. Dad was both proud and saddened at the same time. He knew the life I was getting ready to lead, yet I could tell he was proud of me for finding my own way." Megan lapsed into silence as she stared into her hands loosely crossed on her lap. Finally after a long silence she looked up at Jake. "What about you? Your life? I only know the basics from your file."

"Not nearly as exciting as yours."

"Don't feel bad about that. My life wasn't that great. It sounds exciting, but it was mostly lonely."

Jake nodded, watching, for once, as emotions played on her face.

"When I was little I used to want a normal life. You know, a mom and dad that went to work and came home for supper. Holidays spent together. A real family."

"If your Dad was always gone and you were in a boarding school, where did you spend holidays?"

"If Dad happened to be free, with him. I've lived for short periods all over the world, but usually I stayed at school. Occasionally, I would spend time with Todd and his assortment of girlfriends or who ever. That never lasted long. As I said, we never got along. Mostly, I stayed at school. There was always one teacher who took pity on me or a classmate's family."

"Sounds sad."

Megan nodded, not looking up. "Yeah, but it taught me to rely on myself and how to really value friendships. I don't make friends easily but when I do, it's deep."

"Like Kelly?"

"Yeah. He's funny. We're total opposites, yet from the first day, I knew he'd be a great friend."

"Anything romantic ever happen with him?"

"No. He loves his wife. And I've never had those types of feelings for him. I'd give my life for him, but I don't want to sleep with him." Megan smiled at Jake. "Purely platonic." She stared into his eyes. "You never answered my questions about your life."

"What's to tell?" Jake said. "I grew up in the All-American family. Five sisters and me. Four older, one younger. I excelled at sports. Went to college and joined the Army. Got picked for Ranger school. Excelled. Retired. Here I am." He smiled. "Not much to tell, really."

"What's it like living with that many siblings?" Megan leaned back relaxed in the chair.

Jake shrugged. He normally didn't think about things like this. He gazed into the distance. "I don't know. I got yelled at a lot for leaving the toilet seat up."

Megan chuckled.

"It was tough dodging hormones. If one sister wasn't pissy at me during her period, another one was. Guess I got used to dealing with difficult women." He shrugged. "I know more than most men about feminine hygiene products. Dad taught me how to keep my head down during the worst parts of the month, but it did foster in me a better understanding of women, I guess. Still didn't help in other aspects." He looked over to see Megan staring at him.

"Any one special woman?"

"No. I seem to have bad luck in that respect," Jake said staring into her brown, doe eyes. "I never found the right one. You?"

"Yeah right. Too busy. Oh, I'm not inexperienced. Lost my virginity at seventeen." She chuckled. "Still, I can't settle down. And most guys, although they don't like to admit it, are looking to settle down and breed. I can't see myself cooking and cleaning." She snorted a laugh. "I have to be honest. I can't cook. I'd starve any kids I had if it weren't for take out and ready made meals."

"Seriously? I thought all women could cook," Jake spoke teasingly.

"I guess Dad did okay raising me. I mean, I didn't end up in jail or dead. Yet."

Jake offered another drink, which she accepted. "So when your contract is up, what are you going to do?"

"I don't know. I guess try to stay Stateside. I mean, I have enough time in grade to pull it off. But the agency is so low on people who speak the languages and know the areas, that I might not have a choice. And now that Dad is gone, I've no reason to stay in the States. Still, it would be nice not to have to be on guard every second of every day."

Jake watched her closely. She looked like she wanted to talk or maybe the alcohol was making her tongue loose. He drank with her again.

"You?" Megan raised her eyes to meet his again. "Have you decided?"

Jake merely shook his head.

"No, you aren't, or no you haven't decided yet?"

"Haven't decided. If what they say is true, and I heard rumors before I even left Iraq that I'd get called back, I'll be heading back there anyway. So, I guess my real decision is in what capacity do I return?" Jake took a deep breath and looked out over the mountains.

"Both have their bad points," Megan said, stating the obvious.

"Yeah. And both have their good. I just need to let my mind work on it." Jake looked at her. "How long do you think he'll give me before he puts on pressure?"

Megan stared into his eyes. "Knowing Bill, don't be surprised if he contacts you tomorrow or every day until you give him an answer. He can be quite a prick."

Jake smiled. "Is it a prerequisite to be pushy to be CIA?"

"No." Megan smiled back. "But it helps."

***

Two days later Megan was flying for the first time again. They were helping transport military personnel to a small base in the mountains. This was a base near the Afghanistan/Pakistan border. The military needed extra troop transport vehicles since two of their Chinooks were down. Megan was flying Death with Cowboy, while Pucky and Stick were flying Pestilence with full troop capacity.

Bill's crew was also on the same mission. His pilots were flying the other two Chinooks. The third White Pine crew was flying two Black Hawks for cover. And along with them were four Army Chinooks and two other Black Hawks flying cover. It was rumored that al Qaeda didn't want the transfer of personnel, at least not this many on this day for some reason.

Megan thought it was a bunch of bunk, but they were flying fully loaded for a fight. In her Pave Hawk was Cupcake and Tiny, each manning a door gun and two others for back-up.

The day dawned bright, and they were in the air before the sun rose. Within minutes, the Chinooks were loaded with GIs and the whole group set off for the northeast. The convoy was less than five minutes out when one of White Pine's Black Hawks called that they were having problems with an engine and heading back to base.

Megan frowned at Cowboy. "Sounds suspicious."

"Could be a coincidence," Cowboy intoned, but the look on his face said otherwise.

"Do you believe in coincidences?"

"Not with you, Darlin'," Cowboy said with a huge smile. He noticed Megan chewing her lip. "What?"

She shook her head.

"Spit it out, Girl."

"One of my sources said that al Qaeda is unhappy with White Pine because they believe one of the personnel stole valuable merchandise from them."

Cowboy narrowed his eyes. "And?"

"I wouldn't rule out sabotage." Megan paused. "Last night I checked on the choppers. My gut was telling me that someone had been in the hanger, but I couldn't find proof of anything. This has me worried."

"Why wait until now? Why not just sabotage on the ground?" Cowboy shook his head. "I don't know."

Megan shrugged.

They flew in silence for a few more minutes. Suddenly, they heard cursing over the radio. "That sounds like Cruiser," Megan said. Cruiser was the co-pilot of the other White Pine Black Hawk. "Call 'em," she ordered Cowboy. As she did so, she fell out of formation and took a visual look.

A piece flew off of the tail rotor. The nose dipped then immediately came back up. The other Black Hawk slowed. Fast. And began spinning.

Cowboy hit the button. "XXO this is Famine. Come in—"

"Mayday… Mayday… Mayday… We lost our tail rotor… We are going down… Famine, we are going down…"

That was obvious. They could see the helicopter spinning its way to the ground. Megan flew in that direction even as Cowboy was calling out to the rest of the helicopters, which had of course already heard. There was pandemonium on the radio.

The damaged helicopter crashed hard into the ground.

"Survivors?" asked a military Black Hawk pilot.

Megan shook her head as she began landing.

"We don't know," Cowboy said.

Megan hit the intercom to the back. "Okay boys, you heard too. Tiny stay on a gun. Everyone else check to see if anyone survived," she said as she landed nearby. "Ask the military to keep one Black Hawk with us for a minute."

Cowboy complied. The others in the convoy slowed, but kept going. One military Black Hawk did wide circles as support. They could hear him calling back to base to dispatch any other helicopter available.

Megan turned to Cowboy. "I'm shutting down to take a closer look at the engines and tail rotor." She began to turn everything off.

As the other crewmen scrambled to the crashed helicopter, Megan jumped out of the cockpit and hurried to the tail rotor, which was just slowing down. She hurriedly inspected it. Soon Cowboy was helping. One on each side.

Megan glanced twice to the crashed helicopter to see that at least two men survived. Jake was directing the men in carrying survivors back to their helicopter. She was still looking at the end of the tail rotors when Jake ran up to her.

"Two dead. Two in critical, I don't want to move them if we don't have to. Two minor." His blue eyes bored into hers.

"Monitor the injured. Retrieve the bodies. The military's trying to get us help."

Jake patted her on the shoulder and moved off. He was already directing Bosser and Fisher to bring the bodies back to the helicopter.

Suddenly Tiny stuck his head out the open door. "Ghost!"

Megan looked to see him motioning for her. She looked at Cowboy on the other side of the tail rotor. "I didn't check this end."

"I'll get it. Go."

Megan ran back to Tiny. "Yeah?"

"Chicken Hawk…" He pointed up at the military Black Hawk circling them. "Reports four trucks approaching rapidly on the road. ETE about four minutes." He pointed down the road past where the Black Hawk had crashed. "Military wants to know what you're doing?"

"Damn." Megan looked over at Jake then spoke to Tiny. "Make room for the rest of the wounded. Stay on the radio. Tell them I'm fishing." She ran to the crash site. Her face screwed up in anger. It was every helicopter pilot's worse fear. "Cupcake, company approaching. Four minutes maybe. Move the wounded as best you can. Move it!" She ran back to the helicopter.

"Nuthin'," Cowboy informed her.

Megan chewed her lips and let her eyes rake the helicopter. "You check the oil lines. I'll do the engine. Hurry. Company. Four minutes if we're lucky."

"Shit. Even less. We gotta get airborne."

But Megan had already gone. She was climbing up the outside of the chopper. Cowboy checked the oil lines and fuel lines again. Nothing. He tried the linkages. Basically he was doing a preflight in a fraction of the normal time.

"Cowboy!" Megan yelled from the engine area on top of the Pave Hawk near the rotors. A glance to the downed Black Hawk showed that they were moving the last of the two injured. She looked down to see Cowboy waiting for her.

"Get me something heavy and metal. Fast." Megan looked up the road but no sign of company yet. She narrowed her eyes; in the distance she could see what looked like maybe a dust cloud. She looked down to see Cowboy searching. Then she turned her attention to the small black box attached to the non-rotating swash plate near the control tubes and main column that controlled the rotors on top of the helicopter. It was easy to miss on the pre-flight since it was the same color as the plate, and mighty hard to see unless you were looking for it. She studied it even as she heard gunshots. Her head flashed up, but still the trucks were at a distance. Yet.

***

Cowboy was frantically searching as Jake stepped up to him. "Problem?"

"Something heavy and metal. Ghost needs it on top of the chopper."

"Why?"

Cowboy shrugged still looking. "My guess is she found something."

Jake joined the frantic search.

"Hurry!" Came a yell from the top of the helicopter.

Jake stepped back to look up at her. "What?"

"I found a… a…. something attached to the engine. I need to knock it off. Find something, anything I can use to knock it off. Hurry. I can see the trucks approaching." She pointed down the road.

Jake frowned, climbing the helicopter. As he got near Megan, she pointed. Sure enough there was a small box attached to the metal holding the rotors in their casing. Lop off one rotor and the whole thing would fly like a box of rocks.

She glanced again at the approaching trucks.

Jake un-slung his rifle and with the butt, began hitting the box. The first couple of hits it stayed tight. On the fifth hit it broke loose just a bit. He hit it harder, knowing they were running out of time.

"Again. Harder," Megan coached. She looked over the side. "Cowboy be ready to fire up Death when we jump off. Redline her."

Jake continued to beat on the small metal box. It was coming loose but not fast enough. Both of them glanced to see that the trucks were now within firing range. And at the same time, Tiny opened fired.

Jake continued to beat on it. "Get inside. Fly. We need you to get us out of here. Go." He beat on it again.

"But…"

"Damn it. Go. You're our best hope. Go." Jake yelled at her, as he beat on the slowly loosening box. A bullet whizzed past them.

"Keep that box if you can," Megan said as she slid off the helicopter, literally sliding all the way down. She hopped into the cockpit and finished getting ready.

Cowboy frowned, looking behind him at the trucks now circling the two downed helicopters. Someone in back had armed the other gun and now they were firing from both sides. Not to mention, the military Black Hawk flying overhead was also firing at the trucks.

Both Megan and Cowboy ignored the warnings and questions of the pilot in Chicken Hawk.

Megan waited with her thumb on the start button. "Come on, Jake," she whispered.

"He down." Came from the intercom. Fisher's voice.

Megan hit the start button and the panel lit up. She gave it full power immediately, which was hard on the engine, but they needed to get out of here. Still, it would take about two minutes before they could even try to get airborne and that was pushing it.

As she watched, dials fluttered to life and the blades began spinning, she noticed Jake running back from the downed Black Hawk. A bright light came from the cockpit of the crashed chopper, but she didn't have time to speculate on it. She thumbed the intercom. "Is Cupcake in?"

"He in," Fisher confirmed.

As soon as the dial hit the right place, she lifted off, backing away at the same time from the location of the trucks and downed helicopter.

"Here we come Chicken Hawk," Cowboy said, so that the other Black Hawk would know they were going airborne.

But they were overly heavy. With the armament and crew, plus the wounded and dead from the other helicopter, she was over capacity. The higher altitude and heat didn't help either. She chewed her lip as she could feel the helicopter groaning.

An explosion blew from the direction of the crashed helicopter, adding to the stress.

The helicopter seemed to hesitate for a few seconds under the added weight then quickly responded. After several seconds, Megan slowed to catch her breath.

"What happened down there?" the pilot in Chicken Hawk asked.

"Sabotage," Cowboy answered him. "We found something attached to the swash plate. I bet the others had similar things."

Cursing was heard from the military Black Hawk. "Wounded?"

"We got four wounded, two are critical. And two dead," Cowboy informed him. He looked at Megan. "Who?"

Megan shrugged. She glanced back toward the crash. The four trucks emptied of men rushing to the wreck. "Damn it."

"We saved the personnel, Meg. That's a point in our favor," Cowboy said then hit the button for the radio. "We're heading to base with wounded, Chicken Hawk."

"Do you need an escort, Death?"

"Negative," Cowboy responded. "Head back and make sure the others are okay. Tell the White Pine crews after they land to check rotors, transmissions, tail rotors and engines, hell, have 'em check everything as a precaution. Death out."

Megan turned the chopper toward home. "All those electronics. Damn it." She shook her head. "What was the explosion?"

"I dunno. What else could we do, Darlin'?"

"Nothing. Damn it anyway." She clicked the intercom button. "Cupcake?"

"Yeah?"

"Did you keep the box?"

"Got it right here. Looks to be some sort of remote control device or something. I damaged it pretty good getting it off."

"That's okay. You did good." She frowned. "Did any of you happen to retrieve any of the GPS stuff or other electronics?"

There was a chuckle on the intercom—Jake's. "Ghost, let's just say they won't be using any of that from the Black Hawk."

"What?"

"Standard operating procedure. Destroy it, if it's down. As you were starting up, I threw a thermite grenade in it. Boom." There was a huge smile on Jake's face, Megan could tell from his voice.

She chuckled. "I knew there was a reason I kept you around."

Now general laughter sounded from the back.

"How are the wounded?"

"We're doing what we can Ghost," Jake said. "The two critical ones, I don't know... Hand me that, Tiny. Thanks... We're limited here with what we can do for them Ghost. The other two have semi-minor injuries, they'll survive."

"Do your best, Cupcake." She clicked off the intercom and looked at Cowboy. "We got problems, Kelly." She could feel something through the seat of her pants.

"What?" He looked around outside then at the gauges. Finally, his eyes got a strange look. "There's a wobble."

Megan nodded. "Cupcake must've damaged a control tube in getting the device off."

Cowboy frowned. "What to do?"

She once more chewed her lips. "I'm flying tree top. That way if we have to put down, we won't fall as far." She shook her head. With a sigh, she hit the intercom button as she headed to ground level. "Okay boys, listen up. We got a problem. There's a shimmy in the rotor system. I think we can make it back. But just in case, we're going to be flying as close to the ground as possible, flying along the road. I want someone manning those guns at all times. I mean cocked and ready to fire. Cupcake, make sure everyone is strapped in, including the wounded, as best you can."

Cowboy shook his head as he panned the road.

"This is more than dangerous, guys. If anyone sees anything suspicious, speak up." Megan clicked off. She turned to her co-pilot. "Pray, Cowboy."

"Darlin', we ain't got a shot in hell of making it along this road. You know this goes right into the heart of al Qaeda country."

"It's our only shot."

"Yeah, I know. Luck be a lady tonight."

"Kiss her for me, Cowboy. A nice, big smack right on the lips," Megan said concentrating on everything. This was extremely dangerous. With all the bends in the roads and the winding through the mountains, they didn't know what lay ahead. Once they cleared the foothills, it'd get easier. But even a frightened bird flying off the ground could cause major problems. Not to mention bad guys being in an opportunistic place taking pot shots at them.

"Bend up ahead," Cowboy said, pointing.

Megan nodded and rose into the air a little to fly over the bend instead of around it. Then she immediately went back to car level about four feet off the ground.

"How's she feeling?"

"Shaky," Megan said. This was crazy. If it weren't for the wounded and fearing for their lives if she put down, she'd ditch the aircraft. "How far do we have?"

"Too far."

"She'll hold together," Megan said softly. "She'll hold together."

***

Jake tended the wounded with Fisher. Tiny was manning one gun, Bosser the other. Jake did everything he was trained to do, but he knew that unless they got help soon, the pilot of the crashed helicopter would die. Tippy was a good man, and Jake didn't want to see him go, but he didn't tell Megan that. She had enough pressure as it was. It would take all her skill to get them out of this alive.

He sat down next to Tippy when he felt the helicopter rattle. He looked up at Fisher whose eyes widened in fear. Jake smiled. "Trust the Ghost."

"I do. Most well. It is…" He waved his hand to the top of the helicopter. "I do not trust."

Jake smiled, but inside he felt that same way. He could feel them swaying one way and then the other as she negotiated turns. Then they would momentarily rise, then fall back down, as they cleared bends in the road. It felt like an amusement ride. Only, this wasn't amusing.

He laid his head back against the headrest and took a deep breath. This was not a good day to die. He knew they'd get back. Megan was flying. She'd get them home safe. He opened his eyes to see Fisher once more staring at him. Jake smiled. He winked and got comfortable. There was nothing else he could do. Their lives and safety were in the hands of a woman pilot. And that's just where he wanted it.

***

"Crap," Megan said softly. They had been flying for some time in silence. Megan was concentrating on the road, Cowboy was doing everything else, navigating, checking radar, and adjusting gauges.

"What?"

"She got shakier. We're losing something."

"We're almost past the mountains, if we can get clear of the foothills we can radio for help."

"Not until we are well beyond the mountains."

Cowboy frowned at her.

"Contacts tell me that al Qaeda has been monitoring radio communications. If we call out too soon, our guys will never get to us in time."

Cowboy cursed loudly.

"I'll push her as far as possible before calling," Megan said then thumbed the intercom on. "Guys? How're the wounded?"

Cupcake's voice came on. "Not good. Tippy's in shock. He's no longer responsive. And Snake isn't much better. The other two will make it." There was a pause. "Ghost, you're doing good."

Megan gave a half second smile. "Thanks, Cupcake. We'll be leaving the foothills soon. After that it's a straight shot home. Hold'em together back there." She shut off the intercom.

It was about ten minutes later, and they had just cleared the mountains when Tiny's voice came on. "Ghost, we got company. Left side. Nine o'clock."

Cowboy immediately looked out his side of the helicopter. "Damn. Trucks. Can't see how many. Heading our way fast on an intercept course."

Megan cursed softly. "Tiny, get me a count." She clicked off. "Not that it matters. It won't take much to bring us down."

"Maybe five. It's hard to tell in the dust," Tiny answered.

Megan chewed her lip. "How close Tiny?"

"Half mile, maybe."

Cowboy stared at Megan then glanced back out the windshield. When he looked back, Megan was smiling. "There's a shitty grin on your face, Darlin'. I don't think I'ma gonna like this one."

Megan chuckled. She slowed down, then turned to face the approaching trucks. "Cowboy, arm missiles."

"Shit fire, woman, I totally forgot 'em," Cowboy said with a smile appearing on his face. It was mere seconds. "Armed."

Megan hovered and waited. It wasn't the fuel she was worried about it. It was holding this damn wiggling contraption steady. "How many did you arm?"

"All of them."

"Good deal," she said glancing at her co-pilot. "Wait until they start firing at us. I want to be able to spit on them."

Cowboy keyed the intercom. "Hells bells boys, we gonna have a little weenie roast out front here. Hold on ta ya pants." He let out a yee-haw.

Both of their eyes were riveted on the quickly approaching trucks.

"Wait for it," Megan said softly.

Cowboy grinned.

Suddenly the trucks stopped. Quickly, they began backing up.

"Chickens," Cowboy stated.

Megan smiled. "Do it."

"Don't mess with the best," Cowboy said and he sent one then another missile toward the group of trucks. Both struck the trucks head on. The Stingers were heat seekers and the engine block was a perfect target.

"Again."

Cowboy fired another. This one hit too.

Megan chuckled as she turned the helicopter homeward again. She clicked on the intercom. "Fly fast and carry a big stick."

Laughter from the guys in back was heard over the intercom.

She turned to Cowboy. "Give me another five miles then call for help."

Cowboy nodded.

"Hold on, baby. Hold on," Megan pleaded with the helicopter.

***

Megan sat in the cockpit, her head resting back. She didn't move, she didn't even have her eyes open. She just sat there.

"Are you okay, Chief?"

Megan finally opened her eyes. She turned her head slightly and pulled the scarf off her face then took off her helmet. She held it in her lap. Only then did she sigh. "Yeah."

Jake smiled at her. He glanced at Cowboy who looked like he had wet his pants. "Congrats guys. You got us here in one piece."

Megan nodded and closed her eyes again.

Cowboy sat up, releasing his seatbelt harness. "How are the wounded?"

"Same as before. The Army is transporting them to the hospital," Jake said standing outside the cockpit door.

They had called for help shortly after clearing the mountains because the wobble became worse. Within minutes, several more trucks were following them. The trucks hung back, due to the 'sting' of the helicopter, but they paced the helicopter across the plains as they approached Kabul, apparently hoping that the helicopter would crash. The military radioed back that they were sending out the last running Black Hawk to help them.

Megan made a decision to keep flying instead of transferring the wounded to the military helicopter. She didn't know if once she landed she'd be able to take off again. The other Black Hawk flew nearby but at a higher altitude, just in case. It also caused the trucks to abandon the chase. As long as she had control over the Pave Hawk, she wanted to bring it home. So she flew directly to the military base, which luckily happened to be on this side of the city.

It had been tense. The closer they got to the civilized area the worse the aircraft flew. Still she pushed it. After landing just inside the fenced-in military base, she shut down. The wounded were transferred to the military helicopter and it took off immediately.

Jake exited the back to see the two pilots sitting in the cockpit, laying their heads back in relief. At first, he'd been worried that they'd been hurt, but after opening the cockpit door, he realized they were just relaxing after the harrowing experience.

"Sure you're okay?" Jake asked both.

Megan merely nodded.

Cowboy turned to look into the back of the helicopter to see that the rest of the crew was out and resting on the ground nearby. He held up a finger to wait. "White Pine Tower, this is Death."

"Go ahead, Death. We've been monitoring your communications. We have land transport on its way to you. It'll be about half an hour until it gets there. How are the wounded?"

Cowboy relayed the facts as Jake looked closer at Megan.

"Megan?" Jake asked softly, he glanced back but no one was listening. "What's wrong?"

Megan sighed and lifted her head wearily. "You need to thank God for looking out for us today. We shouldn't have made it."

Jake frowned.

"She broke right as I shut down. Did you hear the big clunk?"

Jake nodded.

"Something fell off. Take a look."

Jake backed up and looked. There was a tube hanging down near the main column about eight inches from the top. Three of the rotor blades were horizontal, the fourth was at an angle. He took a closer look at the tube, it was broken in two. He swallowed hard.

"Yeah," Megan said exiting the cockpit. She stepped up to Jake's side. "We got lucky. Damn lucky."

Jake shook his head as he noticed the other guys were also now looking up at the rotors. Shocked expressions showed on their faces. He suddenly grinned. "Three cheers for the Ghost and Cowboy."

The others yahooed and whooped.

Cowboy smiled as he rounded the front of the helicopter. He held up his hand to Megan who high fived him. "I swear Darlin', you play with fire and beat the devil at his own game."

Jake smiled at Megan who was chuckling.

***

An hour after getting back to base, a knock on the door sounded. Megan rounded the desk, opening it.

Jake. "You wanted me?" he said with a wry grin.

Megan frowned. "Come in." She closed the door behind him and noticed the smile fled his face when he saw the person sitting near the desk.

William Harding.

"Sit." Megan said as she headed back around the desk. Both of them had been studying the small, black box Jake had beaten off the top of the helicopter.

Jake took the other seat in the room.

"You've heard that the other White Pine helicopter, the first one that had trouble, barely made it to the ground outside of Kabul, right?" Megan asked Jake. He nodded. "It too had one of these on its transmission." She pointed at the box. "Like you said, it's some sort of remote device. This one should have gone off as you were beating on it. There was a small amount of explosive in it, probably meant to damage the rotating swash plate, causing us to crash instantly."

"Why didn't it go off?"

"Faulty wiring," Bill Harding spoke.

"Lucky for us, who ever put it together is an amateur." She smiled at Jake. "Still, it might have worked."

Jake looked at her then Harding. "Why?"

Megan sat back and stared at Harding.

He cleared his throat. "My sources say it was in retaliation for stealing Afghanistan artifacts from the al Qaeda group. They knew it was a White Pine employee from the helicopter crew, just not which one. One other box was found on Megan's Chinook. It was also mis-wired. That one malfunctioned and did no damage."

"And, so?" Jake asked him.

"Just be aware," Harding said with a piercing gaze. After his statement, no one spoke, but he continued to look at Jake. "Your decision?"

"Not yet." Jake shook his head.

"I need to know soon," Harding replied.

"And when I know, I'll let you know."

Harding stood and looked at Megan. "Talk to him." He walked out the door shutting it behind him.

Jake turned to Megan.

She ran a hand over her face. "That was way too close today." She held out a shaky hand in front as her.

***

The next night after curfew, Megan was standing in her office, hands on hips, pissed off. "Why now?"

"Because we have a tip that he'll be in the village during tribal quarrel disputes. Since it's so close to last time and we don't have a team operational, they won't suspect that we'll try again," Harding insisted. He sat behind the desk with an open file on top. It showed the picture of a man, the local warlord, and information about him.

"Well, they would be right; we don't have a team operational. Gunner's just barely alive."

Harding nodded with a slight smile.

"I hate it when you smile," Megan said with a quiet sigh.

Harding pulled another file from his briefcase. He pushed it across the desk.

Megan sighed out loud this time, picked up the file and sat down. Opening it, she saw immediately it was the military operational jacket of one Jacob L. McGrew. She looked up at Harding then returned to reading. After quickly skimming the report, she saw what Harding wanted her to see. "Damn."

"You leave in four hours."

"No."

"You have no choice."

"Yes, I do. You can't just buddy us up like that without spending time on the range. Damn it, Bill, we're talking lives here. I can't take a guy out without working out the bugs."

"This is easy enough that you could do it alone. I'm sending McGrew to help. You're not back up to speed, despite what the doctors say. I know you; you pushed the flight surgeon to certify ahead of time. Again. Combined with the near miss of yesterday, you're still weak. Besides, this will give him a taste of what might be expected." Harding crossed his arms as he leaned back.

Megan narrowed her eyes. "And who knows about this?"

"You, me, McGrew, and you'll have to inform Cowboy." Harding for once seemed nervous as he wiped his lips with his hand. "I've looked into your claim of a leak. I have reason to agree with you, besides the sabotage on the helicopters. My sources are checking things out. As soon as I know who it is, he'll be taken care of."

Megan shook her head as she tossed the file back on the desk. "We'll have to be dropped a distance away from the valley. That means a longer time in country."

Harding nodded. "Supplies are already being loaded on the aircraft. Gunner's pack with supplies is also on board. All that's required are personnel and your pack."

"Damn it."

"You've already said that."

"Full secrecy until we return. Make something up about our absence."

Harding agreed.

"I'll wake them in three hours," Megan said as she stood, motioning for Harding to move out from behind her desk. "Hand me the mission file."

He left the file lying on the desk.

Her heart constricted as she went over the information. She would, in less than four hours, be revealing to Jake one of the biggest secrets of her life. She didn't know how he would respond to the news. And if he responded badly, she knew her heart would break in pieces.

Because it was just at that instant she realized she loved the ex-Ranger. And now she would have to tell him something that might make him hate her. She sighed. Such was her life.

Three hours later while it was still dark, Cowboy was headed to the hanger to pre-flight Famine. Megan hesitated, then softly knocked on Jake's door. Without waiting for an answer, she entered the room to find him just waking up.

"Again?" Jake asked with a smile as he rubbed his eyes.

"Quietly. I need your help."

Jake was instantly awake and alert. He glanced at the alarm clock then looked at her with a puzzled look. "Yeah?"

"We've got a job. Meet me at the hanger in ten. Hot mission gear." She patted Jake on his naked shoulder. "Sorry to interrupt your dreams again."

Jake caught her hand and kissed it. "Don't be sorry."

"You say that now."

CHAPTER 12

Jake sat in the back of the Black Hawk watching Megan go through a pack that looked suspiciously like the one Gunner used on their last mission when he got shot. They were already airborne with Cowboy flying alone in the cockpit. He purposely fixed his face to neutral before speaking. Their helmets were plugged in, but the intercom was switched to the crew compartment only. "Do I get to know what's going on, Chief?"

Megan nodded as she dug into the duffel. Finally, she seemed to find what she needed and tossed it to Jake. "Do you know what that is?"

Jake caught the long tube. After looking at Megan for a second, he looked down at his hands. He turned the thing over, then looked back at her. "It's a Leupold spotting scope."

"Very good. I've read that you know how to use one."

Jake did the eye narrow thing again. "I've been trained."

Megan shook her head. "You worked for a while as the spotter on a team."

Jake said nothing but continued to stare into her brown eyes.

"I need a new spotter."

Jake's mouth almost dropped open but he caught it in time. "Masood's relative?"

Megan nodded.

"This last time with Gunner?"

Another nod. "We're after the same target."

"And if I refuse?"

"I'll do it on my own."

"You aren't back to full strength yet."

"True, but it should be a fairly easy mission."

Jake leaned back against the side of the helicopter. "Harding put you up to this."

"He assigned the mission, yes."

"You know it's risky, taking a team out that's not blended."

"His response was that you're along merely to help me out. An insult to me but again, I know when to pick my battles. He also said it would give you a taste of the kind of jobs that they'll expect of you."

Jake grunted. "So whether I go or not, you're still putting it on the line?"

"That's why I get paid the big bucks."

Jake looked down at the instrument in his hands. He hefted and looked through it. It was an expensive scope—one of the best. He brought it down to look at Megan. The look on her face was neutral, a look he had yet to see on her. "I would never have pictured you a sniper."

"One of the best, Cupcake, or the Agency wouldn't put me in such positions." Megan pulled a long item out of her pack and unwrapped it. It was her rifle.

Jake whistled. "Impressive. A Tango 51. Match Grade. McMillan McHale stock. Guaranteed .25 MOA. With a..." He leaned forward. "A Leupold MK4 M3 10x scope. Very expensive. Around thirty five hundred dollars." Then suddenly his mind flashed back to Iraq and the last mission he had been on there, the information and intelligence gathering trip. He narrowed his eyes at the lady sitting across from him. "Don't tell me..."

"What?"

"In Iraq. Did you kill Saddam Hussein's high official, the day before we met?"

Megan hesitated, looking Jake in the eyes.

"You did, didn't you?"

Megan still didn't speak, but her eyes told volumes.

Jake looked out the side window of the Black Hawk before returning his gaze to Megan. His blue eyes were hard. "Answer me."

"You already know the answer," Megan said. There was an odd look to her eyes. One he'd never seen before. "It's my job."

Jake stared into her eyes. He would never have suspected her of being a sniper. Worse, she was a cold blooded killer, an assassin for his government, a government that didn't do assassinations anymore, or so he had thought.

"Here. You'll have to use Gunner's ghillie suit and clothes. You guys are about the same size. Leave your clothes on the aircraft. We'll dress back into them when Cowboy picks us up." Megan was already undressing.

Jake watched her peel off her flight suit to reveal another outfit, camo and black.

She sat down and looked at him. "Okay. So, I'm not the nice person you thought I was, but I'm not a monster either. I do a service for my country, a service that not many people have the stomach for or want to hear about." She looked down at her hands then back up at him, her big brown eyes staring—pleading with him to understand.

Jake finally sighed. *Why can't I fall in love with a normal woman?* He shook his head. "You drive me insane woman." With that, he undressed to his skivvies, then redressed in Gunner's old clothes. He tried on the ghillie suit then took it off and shoved it back into the duffle bag. He sat and smiled at her. She had kept her eyes glued to his body the entire time. She was hooked too. He knew that Megan just didn't want to admit it. Of course, neither did he, at least out loud.

***

They crawled the last hundred yards on their bellies. Both had small backpacks and were in ghillie suits, including full-face mask. The ghillies were designed with short tags of material that matched the surrounding environment so that their outlines were broken up. The pattern of their crawling was short movements followed by a minute or two of lying still, eyes panning the area. Always on alert.

Finally, after what seemed like hours, they made it to the ridge overlooking the small village. In the town were twenty-five houses made of mud, all with flat roofs. The terraced landscape made it so they were at different levels, almost on top of the other.

Across the small valley, men and boys were tending sheep. Several youngsters were playing on the hills in front of the houses as women mashed grain on the doorsteps.

A peaceful village minding it's own business.

Jake took time to concentrate on the surrounding area. During the ride to the drop off that morning, they had discussed the layout of the village via maps. All of the information collected was studied quickly. They had little time to do this. It was decided to use this ridge line because it not only provided the clearest shot at the central area of the village where the meeting was to take place, but it also allowed the farthest possible distance from the village. At six hundred and fifty yards, no one in the village would even hear the crack of the rifle.

Another thing that had been decided was to change the pick up point. Megan said she trusted no one now. So she and Jake picked a new rendezvous plus two alternatives. All new. They informed Cowboy of them as he landed. Cowboy wasn't happy, but he agreed that it was for the best.

Jake tapped Megan on the arm and pointed off to the side of their ridge. There was a sheep herd on their side. Megan frowned but nodded. They were in no danger from the herd. Megan had had sheep walk right around her before. As long as the herdsman didn't stumble upon them, they were safe in their ghillie suits. The sun was just dipping down as herds began to descend to the village.

They waited until the sun was gone before slipping off their packs to eat for the second time. Jake passed a canteen to Megan as she passed a thick slice of bread to him. They ate in silence.

"You take the first sleep," Megan whispered.

Jake scooted around making a better indent in the ground. He finished off the bread and smiled at Megan. "Pleasant dreams, Chief."

Megan snorted. "I've always hated camping."

Jake closed his eyes with a smile on his face.

***

Megan sighted through the scope attached to her rifle. She ran the village again. People were just heading out at sunrise to get sheep up the slopes where there was a little green vegetation. A tap on her shoulder caused her to look at her companion and the canteen he held out to her.

She took it with a smile. As she drank, he grabbed her pack and brought out another wrapped food. He handed it to her with a soft kiss to the cheek.

"Good morning."

"I got a cramp in my calf and a face full of dirt. Some good."

Jake smiled at her attempt to make light of the situation. He grabbed his scope and sat up. As he got comfortable in the upper position, he extended the mono-pod on the scope and settled it in place. He glanced down at the still prone Megan.

She placed the canteen back into the pack. Then gathered up the other stuff and shoved it into packs too. After the shot, they would slowly make their way off the ridge, back to their base camp to pick up what was there. They had another day in the mountains before pick up, and it would probably take them close to that long to make the new destination.

They waited another two hours before there was any important movement in the village. A group of men were working their way down the side of a sharp incline.

Megan took a breath and put the shell case into the gun. With a slow and steady movement, she got the gun ready for firing. This was done with no sound.

Jake watched the group through the scope. He also took in the wind as it blew the men's robes and the vegetation near them. "The wind's picked up a bit."

"Yeah," Megan whispered back. "Where did that second sheep herd get off to?"

Jake panned the hillside to find both herds. "One is eleven o'clock. The other is lower, around ten."

"Yeah okay, got'em," Megan said then focused her scope on the village again.

"More company," Jake informed. "Check out the trail from near the eleven o'clock herd."

"Who the hell is that?"

It was a much smaller group of four men—all heavily armed—even the one in the middle that looked elderly and thinner than the rest.

"Damn it," Megan said softly.

"What?"

"It's bin Laden. The thin guy in the middle." Megan laid her head on her gun.

"This is the chance of a life time."

"Not again. Not again," Megan whispered even softer.

"What?" Jake asked back. They were whispering, not that it mattered. They could have shouted and no one would have heard them.

"I've been in this position before, Osama bin Laden in my sights." Megan stared at him through her sights. Just a quick finger twitch and he'd be dead. So close, yet so far away.

"And?"

"It was before the Madrid bombing."

"Before?" Jake asked. "Are you saying you could've prevented it?"

"The operation probably would've been carried out anyway. But yes, I guess that is a possibility," Megan said. "Damn you, Harding. You knew this."

"What?"

"Check out the reception bin Laden's getting. This was a planned event."

"If Harding knew he was going to be here, why not tell you to strike him?"

"That's not the way this game is played, Cupcake. For some reason, Harding and the boys in Washington want the warlord dead. Not bin Laden."

"I don't get it."

"Me either but my guess is…"

Jake looked down at her. "Yeah? Go on."

Megan sighed. "We can't 'off' him. We, as in the United States. If we do, the whole Muslim world will come down on us. He's viewed, unfortunately, by most of the Islamic world as a sort of Robinhood. They don't think of him as a terrorist. If we kill him, every Muslim country will cause us problems, but if one of their own kills him, then we're not the bad guys."

Jake was silent for a moment then looked down at Megan. "That's why you made it seem that bin Ladin was responsible for the killing of Masood's tribal leader?"

"Yep."

Jake shook his head, frowning. "This is wrong."

"Yep."

"Are you still going to shoot?"

"Yep," Megan said settling in. "I'll wait until they sit down and get cozy. If my shot is blocked, I'll take it when they leave during the ceremonial goodbye."

"Damn," Jake said. He got resettled into position. "Wind's from the north. I make it about two to three knots."

Megan nodded at the information. She was actually calculating the wind too. She adjusted her sights up a click. As the men settled into position in the village, she wiggled one last time. Jake gave her range and windage readings. She took slow and even breaths. With the mil dot settled on the target's chest, she put everything out of her mind except the target. "Ready."

Jake slowed his breathing as he concentrated on the sight picture through his spotting scope. "Send it."

***

All day they traveled pushing themselves, first Jake leading, then Megan. As the evening approached, so did ominous storm clouds. This hadn't been on the satellite information Megan pulled up at base.

Now, they huddled under a single camouflaged tarp. The storm was ferocious. Wind and rain. Lightening. There was no way Cowboy was making the pickup tonight. The best they could hope for was the next night.

It wouldn't be that hard. Food would last until tomorrow afternoon. They could stretch it further if it looked like the storm was sticking. Water was being collected from the rainstorm and would be added to the canteen. It was just a matter of waiting it out.

Jake's arms were behind his head, eyes closed, laying, listening to rain pelt the tarp. It reminded him of a night in Fort Bening, Georgia when he was in training. Temperatures were about the same. He almost smiled at the memories until he remembered where he was. Jake opened his eyes to look at the lady sitting next to him. He studied her.

Megan was staring out at the meadow. The dappled light made it hard to get a read on her face.

"Does it ever bother you?"

Megan jumped slightly. "What?"

"The assassination thing. Does it ever bother you?"

Megan shrugged. "What about you? You've killed. Does it bother you?"

Jake looked straight up at the tarp. *Did it?* His gut twisted. "Yeah, it does. Sometimes. You?"

Megan merely nodded in the affirmative.

"How many?"

"What?" Megan turned to look at him.

"How many have you assassinated?"

"Why?"

Jake thought about it. He knew several snipers in the Rangers and he had never asked them. His team, when he was a spotter, had never been assigned a killing. He'd taken out inanimate objects, trucks, planes, even a satellite dish. Still, he knew of several that had been called on to exercise their training to its fullest potential at military targets. It never bothered him about his buddies. *Why does it bother me about her?* His eyes met hers. "I don't know."

Megan looked down at the ground. "Maybe too many. I can handle some of them easily enough. Some of the people I've killed were monsters and that's easy to justify, but there are some that I don't understand."

"Like Masood's relative?"

She shrugged. "I understand the reason, I guess, but..." She drifted off. It was a few seconds before she spoke. "In answer to your question, yeah. Each and every one of them bothers me. Sometimes late at night or in my dreams, I see them." Megan flicked dirt off of her pant leg. "Sometimes it's hard."

The rain continued unrelenting as the two fell silent. The darkness came quickly under the storm but neither moved to eat. The ground was soggy under the tarp and everything felt wet.

"Look at it this way, maybe we could build an ark," Jake said with a grin at her, breaking the silence and tension.

Megan laughed. She laughed holding her sides until she cried.

Jake eventually joined in.

The wind picked up, plummeting the temperature. Megan pulled her outer coat and emergency blanket around her. Hugging her legs, she rocked slightly.

Jake looked up from his lounged position. He wasn't cold yet, his silver, thin, emergency blanket still in his pack. With a quick move, he grabbed the pack from under his head. "Megan."

She lifted her eyes.

Jake patted the ground next to him. "Temps are dropping. We're wet and we don't want to get cold." He scooted out from his place, laid his foil blanket on the ground then resumed his place. "Climb on. We'll cover up with yours and conserve body heat."

Megan narrowed her eyes. "No."

"Seriously, Chief. No hanky-panky. You aren't completely well. I'm pumping out heat here and you're already two shades of cold. Survival mode." Jake held out his left arm for her to cuddle in close. His right hand he held up as if in court. "I swear."

Megan frowned. "So help me..."

Jake grinned, still waiting. "Come on. Harding will drum me out, if you catch your death of cold."

Megan relented and was soon cuddled up in his warm embrace. She shivered and involuntarily, snuggled closer.

"See."

"You make a good furnace."

Jake chuckled. "I could make your furnace burn."

"Knock it off. I told you that can't happen."

"I know what you said." He pulled her in tighter with his arm. "Just relax. You take the first sleep." It took everything in his being to stop his normal reaction to having a woman in his arms, especially this beautiful woman. He gave her arm a gentle caress.

Megan closed her eyes and shivered again.

Jake smiled. This time he knew it wasn't from the cold.

***

Megan sat contemplating the situation. It was after daybreak but the storm clouds were still hanging on. *Could Cowboy make it in today? If the clouds gave up more rain this morning and the storm didn't regenerate, maybe. Or should we walk to the road and hope for a friendly pickup?* She frowned.

No. We'll give Cowboy one try at a pickup. Worst case, we'll start walking and at intervals call out via a beeper radio for Cowboy, if he's in the area. She almost smiled. The radio was small and concealed in her outer jacket collar, a precaution that no one knew about except Cowboy. It was to be used as a last resort only.

Jake's movement next to her caused her to look down at the sleeping man. He wouldn't be asleep for long, he was probably entering his last stage of REM sleep because he was getting restless. Something he would need to work on if he worked for the Agency. All good agents, those that survived any length of time, learned the trick of waking without telltale signs. Her Dad had taught her that at the age of eleven.

Still, she doubted if he would actually sign up. She was surprised that he had gone for working at White Pine. When they had proposed it and asked her opinion, she had told them he'd refuse, but he obviously had a reason for joining the organization. Maybe he would surprise her and join the Agency.

She sighed. *It didn't matter. This is my last rotation. If, if I continue on the job, I'm not leaving the States, so help me God. And I have the pull and seniority to make that demand.*

Her eyes panned the area near them. There was no movement of anything, even animals. A natural quiet settled over the area as the day began to assert itself still under dark, stormy clouds.

"Morning, Chief."

Megan glanced down to see a set of blue eyes looking up at her. "Yeah."

"Anything?" He glanced around without getting up, his head lying near her thigh.

Megan shook her head. "All's quiet on the meadow front."

He sat up part way. "How's the cloud front?"

"Heavy."

As he scratched his chest, he sat all the way up. "At least the storm provided us with plenty of water." He glanced around the immediate area. With a quick move, he stepped out from under the tarp and headed to a huge rock that they were using as a bathroom.

Megan grinned after he rounded the rock. She watched his waking with glee. It was always fun to watch men wake up.

"Something funny I should know about, Chief?" Jake asked as he sat back down.

Megan blushed as she handed him the canteen. "Nope."

Jake chuckled. "Sure." After drinking, he handed her one of the last food packs. "Here."

Megan broke it in half and handed it back, then broke the half in her hand in half again. "We'd better conserve. If this doesn't break, we'll have to hoof it out. Frankly, I'd rather have extra food for the march. Besides, I'm on a diet."

Jake chuckled again, took the half and put it away in the pack. He then took the part that Megan held out for him. Together they ate in silence. After they finished, Jake turned to her. "So, what's the game plan?"

"What do you think?"

"Doesn't matter. You're in charge." Jake gave her a wry grin.

"Now you start to obey me."

His grin got bigger.

"Still, I want your opinion."

"But you've already decided haven't you?"

"So?"

Jake nodded. "Okay." He glanced around the whole visible valley. "I say we stick it out one more night. If Cowboy can't make it in, we head toward one of the main roads. The military patrols it occasionally. Or we may get lucky and hitch a ride." Jake rested his eyes on Megan. "Well, did I pass the test?"

Megan smirked. "Smart ass."

***

The day drug out only as it can when you're waiting for something, like Christmas morning to open presents. They were cold, tired and hungry. They talked only in short spurts, not knowing how far the sound would travel.

It was mid-afternoon when their eyes met. Simultaneously they smiled at each other. They were sitting side by side under the tarp. Off and on all day the storm had dumped on them. Right now there was a break in the wet. And even though they were under the tarp, both were soaked to their skins.

Jake reached out and took her hand in his. "I know a way to pass the time."

"I bet you do," Megan replied without retracting her hand.

"No one would ever know."

Megan said nothing but her pulse was elevated and she knew she was getting wet in all the right places, which had nothing to do with the rain.

"A chance of a lifetime."

Megan glanced down as he began to gently rub her hand. The gentle massage was causing explosions in parts of her body, explosions she couldn't ignore. She squirmed a bit and glanced out into the meadow.

Jake reached with his other hand and brought her face back to look at him. He held her chin. "I felt the same in Iraq. Let it happen. Right now."

Megan knew she had lost as she looked into those piercing blue eyes. Even the voices that usually yelled at her in her head were strangely quiet.

Jake leaned forward and lightly brushed her lips with his.

Megan responded by gripping his head and exploring his mouth. He replied in kind and the explosions in her body went off like fireworks. The fire blazed hot in her as he gently laid her on the ground, the mud under her providing a surprisingly soft surface.

A dirty finger traced her jaw as the kiss lengthened. Megan's own dirty hands were enjoying themselves in his light brown hair, massaging and groping. She brought both hands down onto his chest and his hands helped take off his body armor. It fell to the side with a squish in the mud. Her hands started unbuttoning his shirt, to find another barrier of t-shirt.

Jake had her coat already unbuttoned as they greedily lip locked each other.

She started pulling his shirt up, rubbing his chest en route. As he fumbled with her body armor, she quickly and efficiently released the Velcro straps on one side to help him. Within seconds, her body armor followed his onto the muddy mess next to the silver blanket.

They broke the kiss long enough for both to take off their black T-shirts. As they did, Megan stared into his blue globes. Before her shirt was all the way off, his hands were exploring her chest through her black bra.

Megan arched her chest toward him as he twirled her erect nipples between his finger and thumb. A moan escaped her lips involuntarily. She gripped his head and pulled him back into a mouth-exploring kiss.

Jake's right hand pushed the bra off of her breasts and exposed them to the air. He broke the kiss long enough to glance down.

Megan smiled as his eyes took in her tighter than a virgin's nipples. They were dark pink and topped her small breasts like a crown.

Jake grinned back. "Beautiful."

"I'm glad you like."

His head moved down and took the right nipple into his mouth.

Megan groaned at the slightly painful, playful nip he gave it. His teeth putting pressure on the sensitive end making her lay her head back in pleasure. She did so miss this.

Her hands weren't still either. She slid her hands down his chest, rippling over the washboard abs and over his pants. As she gave the turgid organ a rub, he massaged her left breast with his hands and let up on her right nipple with his mouth. His tongue flicked at the now extremely sensitive nib.

A soft squish caught her attention, but Jake had moved his body so that she had a better angle to grope his growing erection. Another moan escaped her lips as his left hand started to descend to her lower region. His fingertips circled lightly on her hard stomach, making her wiggle in pleasure.

A loud click snapped her back to reality.

Jake's hands froze.

Megan's eyes focused on a gun barrel two inches from her face.

CHAPTER 13

Seconds became hours.

In her hand, Jake's erection softened as though a floodgate had opened. Her attention switched from the black, endless hole of the gun barrel, she recognized it as a AK-47, to the one pressed into the back of Jake's head.

Megan's eyes flashed to Jake's. The blue was deep as though they had dropped into his stomach. A look of 'fuck' filled his face as he was pulled off of her, their eyes still locked. Her own heart suddenly beat again, at six times its normal speed.

As she followed Jake's body with her head, a gun barrel pressed into her nose, grabbing her attention instantly. With fingers and hands outstretched, she lay staring into the eyes of the strange man standing over her—her mind numb. Frozen.

Sounds off to the side jumped started her brain. Impact sounds. Flesh pounded. Guffs of air forcefully expelled. Grunts. Flesh hit again. A loud intake of air. Seconds of silence. Laughing.

Jake.

The beating seemed to last forever as she stared into the black eyes of the man over her. His smile changed from a warning to a sneer. As the beating off to the side continued, his smile increased. His eyes roamed her naked chest. The gun barrel lowered to between her breasts. The dark haired man's eyes changed again, this time to lust as his eyes studied her nipples.

A shout, in a dialect she didn't understand, pulled his eyes up and away even as he shoved the gun barrel harder into her chest, causing her to take shallow breaths. Her ears also detected that there were at least five or six guys standing around, and Jake's beating had stopped with the shout.

The voice got louder as it hesitated near where Jake was lying moaning. Then it continued giving instructions, as it got closer to her.

Megan swiveled her eyes up and to the left to see a new man standing over her. He ignored her half dressed state but stared into her eyes. A motion from him moved the gun toting man off. Another motion indicated that she should sit up.

Megan did, slowly. As she moved, she glanced toward Jake. Her eyes hardened as she took in his condition. Jake lay in a ball, moaning. Eyes closed. Hands hidden in his genital area. Three AK-47's pointed at him.

"Up."

Megan slowly stood.

This guy appeared to be in charge. He bent down and grabbed her outer coat then threw it to her. He rattled off more in his language. Another man came and pointed his AK-47 at her. The head guy bent down and began going through their packs.

Everything was examined then tossed onto the ground. Jake's pack was finished with the scope examined in more detail. This the head guy tossed to one of the men standing over Jake, who tucked it into the folds of his clothes.

Megan almost grimaced when the head guy picked up her pack. The first thing taken out was her rifle. She kept her face as neutral as possible. *Shit! I love that rifle. I finally got it just how I...*

The head guy growled and immediately headed to Jake's side. Grabbing Jake by the hair, he pulled him into an upright position. He shook Jake several times before McGrew opened his eyes to look at him. The leader growled in Jake's face for several minutes then stuck Megan's gun into his face still talking in a dialect. He switched to English. "You gun?"

When Jake refused to answer, the leader tossed him to the ground. In a swift motion, he slammed her gun butt into Jake's stomach eliciting a loud guff from the ex-military man. As the leader swung the gun to hit Jake in the face, one of the others yelled at him and pointed at Megan.

'*Crap. Here it comes. I'm dead.*' She finished buttoning her coat.

The leader twisted to look at her then with a swift step headed to Megan's side. He grabbed her by the coat collar and brought her up to his face, growling something in his language.

Megan shook her head that she didn't understand.

The leader tossed her to the ground.

Megan stayed down, looking up at him but not looking him in the eyes. Any protest by her would elicit a beating far worse than Jake's. Women were considered worthless and had no rights.

The leader growled in his language again as the rest of Megan's pack was searched. Nothing else of value was there except for the gillie suits and the rest of her ammo. He pointed once again at her.

The second gunman grabbed Megan by the hair and coat, hauling her to her feet. Roughly her pockets were searched. When nothing was found, the leader swung. The punch knocked Megan back to the ground.

Megan saw bright lights and shapes but hung onto consciousness. Her face now lay half submerged in the mud as the men over her began a discussion.

When she opened her eyes, she looked immediately toward Jake. He also lay half submerged in mud, but his eyes were riveted on her. The area around his eyes softened just a bit as her eyes focused on him. She looked up and around, but everyone was ignoring her. With a slight grin, she gave him a nod.

At that moment, Jake was grabbed and stood up. His hands were roughly tied behind his back. Twice the men, who were securing him, punched him, causing him to double over and almost fall. A black hood was placed over his head as he gave a quick glance back at Megan from his doubled over position.

Megan was yanked up by her hair. Her hands were tied so tight behind her back that she could feel the circulation being cut off. She wiggled her hands a bit and a gun butt slammed into her back, knocking her down. Two more hits landed on her head and back before a shout stopped the beating.

She was stood again and a hood was put over her head. As it descended, she took a deep breath. It was now or never.

"Keep your head, Cupcake."

No sooner had the words left her mouth, the beating continued as she knew it would—one more to her face. She felt her lip split. She was just recovering from that one when a loud crack sounded in her ear.

***

When Megan woke again, she was laying in a room of some sort. This wasn't the first time she had become conscious, just the first time without the hood. Her eyes panned the area immediately in front of her. It was either an earth house or cave. She blinked her eyes trying to focus them. Taking a shallow breath, she took inventory of her body.

Her wrists were still bound behind her back, and she couldn't feel her hands. Her feet felt like they were unbound, and she managed to wiggle each slightly. Everywhere else hurt. Her back throbbed, as did her head. She scrunched up her face. There was something dried on the side of her face. Probably blood.

She moved her head and the walls began to pulsate. *Not good. A concussion at least.* She closed her eyes to stop the nausea. It helped only a little.

Her hearing detected no sound at all. It was dead quiet. She opened her eyes and tried her mouth, a metallic taste. Blood. Then she smelled something she couldn't identify. She sniffed again. *I know this smell. What is it? Think. Earthy…stinky…* She scrunched up her face. She knew what it was.

Dung. Animal shit.

She opened her eyes again for another look at her surroundings. Sure enough, it looked like a stable. She was near some sort of pile of animal waste.

ABBY HOLDEN

Scrunching up her face again, she tried to ignore the thoughts of what she might be laying in.

She moved in a snake like motion. It also moved her perspective so that she faced another direction. Yep, this was a stable of sorts, maybe a place to tie up a horse or donkey.

Lifting her head, she got a better look. Definitely a stable. It looked like she was in a small holding area. A bag of grain with Arabic writing sat against the wall. Two shovels leaned in the corner. And that pile of manure.

Another snake like movement gave her a look outside. She could see the sky. Instinctively she analyzed it. Clouds were rolling in as another storm front threatened. This huge front definitely was going to stall in the mountains. And rain. She knew it would drop tons of rain.

Sounds of footfalls quickly approaching caught her attention. They were coming from the right, over her shoulder. A hand grabbed her by the hair and yanked her head up. With a sneer, the man clutched her coat, yanking her to her feet.

Megan swayed badly. The whole stable area swirled in circles around her. She blinked, desperately trying to stay conscious.

The man cut her bindings and pushed her toward the opening in the wood fence.

Megan promptly fell flat on her face.

Again he roughly jerked her up, and this time he kept a pinching grip on her arm. He dragged her along with him.

Megan worked on getting her eyes to focus and to move her feet in some sort of walking motion. Mostly she just stumbled. Only his grip and forward motion kept her moving.

The first part of the trip was just a blur of colors. None of it registered in her brain. By the time she was focusing and making sense of her surroundings, the man opened a rough wooden door. Megan focused on the interior of the room.

Seated at a table were three men, all dressed in local garb, expect one. He was dressed in a camouflage outfit and wore sunglasses. Her captor dragged her in front of them as he spoke. It was Dari but her brain wasn't making sense of it. He stood by her side until she gained a semblance of balance.

She brought her hands together and touched each one gently. Her eyes panned down to look at them. They were a light brown and quickly becoming painful as blood flowed back into them.

"What is your name?" It was asked in English.

Megan's head snapped up to the three men.

The silence drug out. One of the locals spoke again. "Your name. Give it to us."

Megan licked her lips. She opened her mouth to speak when a moan caught her attention. Her eyes swiveled to the side of the room to find Jake

166

crumpled in a corner, barely conscious. But his eyes were open and he seemed to be focusing on her. She panned her eyes back to the men.

"Mary…" Her voice cracked from lack of use then she continued, "Mary Poppins."

The two men nodded but the one in sunglasses smiled. He spoke softly to the other two in the dialect she didn't know. They grimaced and the one spoke again.

"Do not lie to us. What is your name?"

"Mary Poppins," Megan said louder.

A small discussion then commenced between the three.

While this was going on, Megan looked around the room quickly then focused on Jake. He was actually smiling. She gave him a slight grin back.

A man stepped up and kicked Jake in the back.

"Bite me," Jake whispered.

Megan almost smiled again but returned her attention to the table and the three men.

"What were you doing in the valley?"

"Obviously, we were screwing."

The two other men put their heads together. The sun-glassed man smiled again.

"Why were you there?"

"We heard it was a good place to neck." Megan shrugged her shoulders. "By the way, thanks for interrupting the action. I finally find a guy that isn't a jerk and you go and stop him mid-grope…"

A rifle butt hit her in the small of her back, tossing her forward onto the floor. She caught herself with her hands then immediately fell to her face as her hands hurt worse than her back. Before she had a chance to think, she was yanked back upright.

Megan took a deep breath. "You're just jealous."

The sun-glassed guy laughed out loud as the rifle butt descended again. Once more she was brought to a standing position. This time she was slightly bent, holding her side. *Must've cracked a rib.* She blinked back tears, grimacing.

"Who is that man?" the local pointed at Jake.

"Bart Simpson."

"Is he a member of the United States CIA?"

"I dunno know." Megan grimaced in pain as she moved slightly. Her vision swirled a little.

"What are you doing in this country?"

"I heard the waters were good for my health."

The two locals glanced at each other in puzzlement. Again the sun-glassed man smiled. He leaned over again and whispered to the other two. They nodded in agreement and spoke in the local dialect.

Megan was quickly hustled out of the room by two men each with a grip on her arms that caused her hands to tingle. She was moved swiftly down the hall and tossed into a room. The door slammed shut.

Megan lay on the ground taking short breaths. She was close to passing out again. The small rug in the room gave her something to focus on as she willed her swirling vision to go away. The door opening and the sounds accompanying it barely registered in her mind, then the slamming of the door. She hardly heard the slight grunt in pain from behind her.

"Chief?"

Megan opened her mouth but nothing came out.

"Chief?" His voice had taken a more urgent tone.

A slight shuffling noise followed several grunts and groans.

Megan willed her eyes to focus on the edge of the rug. Black and red. Typical Persian rug pattern. Worn. *Worth a mint, I bet.*

Suddenly Jake crawled into her field of vision. His blue eyes looking into hers as he laid his head on the rug in front of her. "Chief, talk to me."

"Can't focus," Megan whispered.

Jake frowned then grimaced in pain. "You've taken some mighty hard hits to the head, Mary Poppins."

Megan gave him a slight smile. "Practically perfect in every way," she quoted. It had been her favorite movie as a kid.

Jake smiled back but the swollen lips and bruised cheek made it more of a lopsided grin. "I wish I had a spoonful of sugar."

"Figures. What good are you then?"

"I give a good grope."

Megan chuckled. "You give an excellent grope."

"You weren't doing bad yourself, Lady."

"Talk about coitus interruptus."

"Yeah. What do you think?"

"We're in a shit load of trouble, Cupcake."

"Who are they?"

"al Qaeda."

"Are you sure?"

"Yeah. The guy in the sunglasses is on the American hit list from Homeland Security, Ali Albunimda or something like that." Megan closed her eyes. "I'm dead." She whispered to herself.

"What? What did you say?" Jake asked, his hands gently exploring her head.

"I'm dead."

Jake's hands paused momentarily as he stared into her eyes. "Why do you think that? You're a woman."

"Precisely."

"At the rate they're going, we're both dead."

"Yeah." Megan groaned as Jake's hands began to examine her again. "Stop. That hurts."

"Chief, your head doesn't look good."

"Yeah." Megan locked eyes with Jake. "If you get a chance to escape, go."

Jake merely shook his head.

"That's an order."

"So fire me."

Megan huffed and moved slightly to get into a more comfortable position. The room swayed only a little. Jake lay next to her and gently swept the matted hair out of her eyes as they lay side by side.

"I'm sorry."

Megan made a face. "For what?"

"Disrupting our concentration."

"Forget it. I just wish they'd have waited until we'd finished. I haven't been laid in a long time." She smiled at Jake's astonished look. "I wanted you really bad." Her eyes twinkled. "Wanna try again?"

Jake suddenly laughed. Then stopped and held his head. "Oh God, that hurts."

"Yeah." Megan closed her eyes again.

It wasn't much longer and Jake was shaking her to consciousness. "Footsteps."

"Round two," Megan said as the door swung open.

Jake was yanked to his feet and dragged out of the room. The door slammed shut, but the latch didn't sound like it was thrown on the door.

Megan struggled to sit. The room again began to dance, but she crawled painfully to the door. She lay down and put her ear to the gap under the door. There were no sounds. With energy she got from where she didn't know, she cautiously opened the door.

The hall was deserted. She stuck her head out and looked both ways. No one. Gingerly she pulled herself to her feet, swallowing down the pain throbbing in every part of her body. She shuffled and swayed down the hall, bouncing from wall to wall.

Several doors down was an open doorway. Peaking out, she noticed it opened to the area where the animals were obviously kept, and farm equipment. She also recognized the stall she had been kept in. Her eyes rose to the sky involuntarily.

The storm was hanging on as she had predicted, and from the light it would seem to be about mid-day, which meant that they had probably been held over night. She looked around the valley. *Familiar. Yes. This is the village where I killed that guy. And there's the ridge to the valley where...*

Cowboy.

Her stomach twisted. The pick up had been compromised. And the only person who knew about it had been Cowboy. She had never considered him the leak. Yet it fit. Every mission that had been loused up, Cowboy had flown or been a part of. Her mind registered the betrayal, but her heart pleaded with her. *Cowboy's a friend. Friends don't do that. He wouldn't. But there's no other explanation. He knew. Only he knew. I trusted him.*

Tears stung her eyes as she pushed herself off the doorpost. She glanced once more at the open doorway and the ridge. She hesitated a second. She should leave, but couldn't. Jake was taking the beating meant for her. She gave one last look at the sky and the ominous storm clouds before softly shuffling back to the room.

She lay down and tried to not think about Cowboy. It hurt more than anything else.

***

Megan sat against the wall, much later the door opened. She didn't even move except to look up to see two men drop Jake's body into the room. They glanced at her, but retreated and closed the door behind them. Again there was no sound of the door being locked.

She frowned as she crawled over to the moaning body. Her heart stopped when she saw the damage that had been inflicted on him. His face was bloodied almost beyond recognition. His bare chest already showed bruises forming along with several swollen areas.

Megan reached behind him and as fast as possible untied his hands. He grunted at her when his hands came free. She moved him into what looked like a more comfortable position and with her fingers wiped at the blood on his face. She cleared his eyes and nose first. Then using her coat, cleaned the rest as best she could.

"Thanks," Jake whispered.

"How are you?"

"How do you think?"

"I meant, are you mobile?"

"Possibly."

Megan leaned down and whispered in his ear. "They're not locking the door. Four doors down on the right is the exit to the fields and animal paddocks. The storm's stalled on the mountain and it looks like a doozie."

Jake's eyes caught hers as she backed away from him. "Why didn't you go?"

"Never leave a man behind."

"That's my line." Jake's face changed into what was probably a smile. "They're only taking a break, you know."

Megan nodded. "Yeah. And when they start on me, they won't stop." At his puzzled look, she grimaced but continued, "I'm a woman."

He grimaced. "They tried to get me to make a video."

"And?"

He motioned to his face. They sat in silence for a few minutes.

"Cupcake?"

"Yeah?"

"Remember that old lady when the kid had the bomb attached…"

"Yeah?"

"The father of the kid beat her to death before we even left the area. And she was his mother. They don't give a shit about women."

Jake cursed softly under his breath.

"If you get the chance, take it. Don't come back for me. I'm already dead," Megan said softly.

Jake's blue eyes were devoid of emotion.

"It's part of the job description when you take it," Megan said leaning against the wall again. She saw his disbelieving look. "No, really."

"But this is a stupid reason…"

Megan interrupted him. "Promise me you'll take the first chance. Promise."

"No. Can't do it."

Her heart twisted again. "You have too. I need you to make it back to base and do a dance on Cowboy for me."

"Cowboy?"

Megan studied the blood splashes on her boots. "Who else could have compromised the pickup?"

"But…"

"Yeah," Megan barely whispered. "Revenge, Cupcake. And you need to be the instrument that deals it out. For me. Promise me."

"I'll get your revenge." There was an odd tone to his voice. "Trust me."

Megan nodded, still staring at her boots.

Jake moved to lay his head on her thigh. "I'm sorry."

Megan didn't answer as one tear fell on her cheek. The betrayal hurt the worst.

They sat that way for a few more minutes.

"Hey, just so you know…" Jake said as he moved to a more upright position with lots of grunts and moans. "That kid with the bomb, when we almost bought it in Famine…"

"Yeah?"

"I checked out his head wound, just like you ordered." A frown curved one side of his mouth down; the other side was too swollen. "The doc said that the big area was a massive blood clot and that disturbing it might cause him to bleed to death, instantly." Jake took a deep breath. "I didn't see the metal until you yelled at me. The doctor was in shock when I pulled the cloth away."

"In that case, sorry I yelled at you."

"No. I deserved it. I just wanted you to know."

"Thanks. Speaking of that…" Megan looked up into his eyes as the door opened. "I haven't felt like this before, about a man…"

Both of them were yanked to their feet, but their eyes stayed locked. Jake's blue took on a sad look as he was hustled first out of the room. He struggled to an extent; mostly it looked like he was trying to keep sight of her as long as possible.

Megan didn't even struggle. With her head down, she let them pull and drag her out of the door and down the hall. Soon she was stood against the wall in the same room as before.

"Which CIA plant at White Pine stole the treasure? And why did you kill the leader here?" Ali Albunimda stood before Jake.

Megan lifted her head to watch.

Albunimda grabbed Jake by the hair and pulled down on his head, ramming Jake's face into his thigh. Blood spurted all over his pants as Jake's nose mushed.

Megan grimaced. Her lover was taking the beating that she should be getting. And she knew he was doing it to protect her. Being a man, they assumed that he was the CIA agent. What they thought she was, she had no idea.

"Where is the gold? Tell us and when we retrieve it, we will release you."

Jake lifted his watering eyes, another effect of the nose impact, to meet Albunimda's eyes. "Fuck you."

Instantly, Albunimda hit Jake so quickly with four punches to the stomach that they were a blur. A quick motion brought Jake back up off the floor. Two more punches landed on Jake's back, right at kidney level. This time Jake fell on his side. Albunimda landed a kick to the ribs. Another motion and once again Jake was stood up, this time held by two other men.

"You can last a long time with this kind of beating, American. It is extremely painful and you will beg for me to put a bullet in your head. Answer the questions, and I will put you out of your misery."

"Eat my shorts, asshole."

Ali swung and took Jake off his feet again.

"Stop!"

Everyone turned to look at Megan, including Jake from the floor.

She shrugged away from the man holding her and stumbled to stand in front of Ali Albunimda. She stole a quick glance at his watch to see that it was nearing early evening. A break maybe, if she played this right.

"He has no idea about anything Ali Albunimda."

Albunimda took a step back with shock on his face.

"Yes, I know you. I'm briefed on all of the al Qaeda in the area. I also know that you're a frequent guest of bin Laden and various warlords in Pakistan." Megan was now staring into the eyes of the terrorist.

He swung on her, but she blocked the punch.

"What? The idea of a woman CIA agent gets you right in the old gonads, huh?" The silence in the room was deafening.

"Chief?" came whispered from the floor.

"He's a piece of shit no name." She pointed at Jake. "A drone worker if you understand the analogy. You were educated in New York right, you pig-shit, towel head?" Megan adjusted her weight on her feet. This would get ugly real fast, and she was counting on that.

Sure enough, several punches flew her way. She blocked most of them, but one landed on the side of her head as she blocked a different one. She landed on the floor, inches from Jake's face.

Megan blinked several times then winked at him. Two men hauled her to her feet.

Ali Albunimda was breathing hard in anger. Then a light seemed to go off in his head. "You are the Ghost? It is true, a woman pilot. It is you that was dressed as a man. I gave no credence to the rumor."

Megan wiped the blood dripping down her face. "Your Momma raised a slow one in you." She swiped at more blood pouring down her face as she swayed again. "Ain't no fast ones here. Did all of you eat pig dung for breakfast or what?"

A red flush flooded his face.

Megan laughed. "I hate all you men. What? A woman can't do as good a job as a man? Yes, I stole that treasure. It didn't belong to you, it belongs to the Afghanistan people, asshole. I'll be damned if I'm going to let a pig-eating terrorist organization use it to kill more innocent people in the name of your religion. Bullshit. Just 'cause you got a dick doesn't mean you're better or smarter than me. I would guess that half of the women in this country are smarter than the lot of you."

"What are you..." Jake began as he was yanked off the floor. "Don't go this way, Chief..." Was all he got out before the door slammed closed behind him.

Megan's eyes rested momentarily on the door then came back to Albunimda.

A smile greeted her.

She spit a mouthful of blood to the floor then smiled back. "Is this going to be professional or are you going to get nasty?"

CHAPTER 14

Jake slowly and painfully pulled himself to an upright position. Every inch of his body competed for his attention. But his heart hurt the worst. He would trade anything to be getting the beating he knew Megan was receiving. And he also knew that he would probably not see her alive again.

Resting his head on his knees that he drew up toward his chest to alleviate some of his stomach pain, he contemplated his options. He should already be moving toward the door that Megan told him about. With everyone watching the beating and probably participating in it—he didn't even want to think of the possibility that they were raping her—it would be his best shot at escape.

Yet, he sat there.

It seemed like forever before he heard footsteps heading down the hall. Jake had moved back to a laying position since this gave him the best rest possible, which he knew he needed. Footsteps and a dragging sound, then the door flew open and two men walked in. Between them was Megan, limp and seemingly unconscious. They dropped her to the floor, and with just a passing glance at him curled in a ball, they left the room.

Jake listened and just like Megan said, there wasn't any sound of a lock. Of course, there was probably a guard now. He got up on his hands and knees and crawled over to the still body. The first thing he did was to feel for a pulse. It was there but very weak. He gave out a sigh.

As he rolled her onto her back, a moan escaped her clenched lips. Jake cradled her head in his hands, whispering, "Meg. Megan come on, talk to me. Wake up."

Jake was surprised that her face had not been beaten. Her lips was split and swollen from earlier. One eye was swelling with a large reddish area that he knew would turn into a massive black eye, if she survived. But other than that, her face was still intact.

She opened her eyes.

Jake could tell she was having trouble focusing by how she kept blinking. He tried to smile for her. Not that she could probably tell he was smiling; his own face was smooshed like yesterday's potatoes. "Chief?"

"Why are you here?" she managed to squeak out.

"Waiting for you."

"Go. I'm dying."

"Not on my watch."

"Go. Prayers."

"What?"

"They're at prayers. The storm is raging. Best chance."

Jake considered. This was a good time to escape. With everyone participating in the religious ceremony, there would probably be no guards. If the storm was bad enough, they might not even chase them right away. His attention came back to the lady in his arms.

"Can you walk?"

"No." Megan groaned. "Broke my leg."

Jake glanced down her body and sure enough her right leg lay at an odd angle. He grimaced.

"Just go."

"I won't leave you."

Megan opened both eyes. Tears filled them. "I have internal injuries. Please go. I don't want you dead."

Jake placed his head on her forehead as tears threatened to spill out of his eyes. His breath became ragged as he tried to contain his emotions. He was mouth breathing since his nose was crusted and blocked by dried blood.

"Jake…" Megan moaned again.

"Yeah?" he whispered, his voice cracking.

"Please go. Live. You took my heart, now get away from here."

Jake lifted his head and looked into her eyes. "If I leave you, I'm leaving my heart."

Megan smiled. "Follow orders, Cupcake. Last time."

Jake watched as her eyes got a vacant look then rolled up into her head. His hand flashed to her neck. There was still a pulse. He stared at the door for a long second then looked back down at his lady. "No, Chief. Together or not at all."

Jake gently laid her head on the ground and quietly made his way to the door. He opened it cautiously. With a quick look, he saw that as she said, there was no one there. Maybe they thought the two of them were too hurt to escape, or more likely they knew that the chance of getting down the mountain during this storm was next to nil.

A grin burned in his heart. *Next to nil was still a chance.*

He backtracked to the unconscious body. With a massive grunt, he managed to get her into his arms. She should have weighed a lot to his sore and bruised arms, but she seemed more like a feather.

Determination burned in him. It was all he had left.

***

Megan opened her eyes briefly as consciousness returned. The first thing she realized was that she was wet and cold—no longer in as much pain, but cold.

A slight movement over her caused pain to lace again through her back and abdomen. She blinked and focused on the area above her. A body. She was laying in some sort of crack with a body over her.

Jake.

She groaned louder as pain laced up her leg.

He jerked awake. "Meg?"

"Yeah." She managed to get out. "Why?"

"Why what?"

"Why didn't you leave? Knew you couldn't follow orders." She closed her eyes again.

"We did leave."

Megan took several seconds to process that thought through the pain. "What?"

"Look around, Chief."

"Can't. Hurts too much."

"We're about half way down the other side of the ridge. I found a small recess between two rocks. I need to rest. I figure it's about midnight or so." Jake moved with a groan to a slightly more comfortable position over top of her on two ledges of rock. "How do you feel?"

"Cold."

"Good. It's helping with the pain." Jake felt her head gently. "I set your leg."

"Yeah. It doesn't hurt quite as bad. Now it's only a major pain."

"That's the spirit."

"Shut up," Megan said, with a slight grin, knowing from his voice that he had been amused by her attempt at humor. She grimaced in pain and felt his arms tighten around her. A drop splashed on her face as she felt him move. She moaned at his movement.

"Sorry."

"Is it still raining?"

"Yeah."

"How come I don't feel it?"

"I'm sheltering you."

"My hero." It was said with a touch of sarcasm. "You should have left me, Special Forces hero. I'll only slow you down." She held back the grunt of pain as her leg cramped. Cramp was the wrong word for what her leg just did. It felt like someone had shoved gravel into her leg and was trying to turn it into sand. Her leg was on fire as though a volcano spewed out of her thigh. The large quads and hamstring contracted at the same time, grinding bone against bone.

"What's wrong? Talk to me."

"Cramp." She got out softly between clenched teeth. "Jake?"

"Yeah, Chief?"

"Do me a favor." Her teeth were still clenched tightly, her words strained and tight.

"What?"

"Kill me."

"What?"

"Kill me. Put me out… of my misery. I can't do this. I'm… not that strong, Jake. The pain. Just kill me."

Megan felt him lay his head on hers.

"Can't."

"Why not?"

"I love you."

"Then if …you really do… kill me."

"Can't."

"Why?"

"I won't let you die. I promise. I won't let you die."

"Cupcake…you ain't…got much choice…in the matter." She opened one eye to see him staring at her from his one open and one half-open eye. His face was mushed and turning colors. "I'm dying. Nothing…you can do… Make…easier on me."

Jake shook his head. "You aren't going to die."

"Wanna bet?"

Jake's lip twisted in what was probably a smile but with his swollen lips it was hard to tell. "You're on. What's the bet?"

"I die…you…dance on Cowboy's…face."

"And if you live and I win?" An amused tone was in his voice.

"Name it…'cause…ain't happening."

"Sleep with me."

Megan tried a chuckle, but it came out more of a cry of pain. She nodded. "Done…I think…you'd …a great lover."

"I am."

"Lucky…me."

Jake leaned forward and kissed her with his cracked, swollen lips.

She gave a huff of pain after he pulled away from her; the leg was more than dominating her thoughts. All she saw was red. "Oh yeah..." She managed to get out. "Now you... foreplay."

Jake grunted out a chuckle. "What can I say? I'm that kind of a guy."

She shook her head. "If... not kill me... What's...game plan?"

Jake sighed softly. "Keep moving."

"Where...we?"

"Straight down over the ridge. Several miles. I ran out of energy and had to rest."

Megan struggled not to cry out in pain. Her head and stomach were now competing for attention from her leg.

"Meg?"

"Oh God...hurts," Megan whispered as she screwed up her face in pain.

"What? Where?"

"Every...where. What...was I thinking?"

"Meg?"

Megan opened her eyes again looking straight up at Jake. "Are...heading to...secondary rendezvous?"

Jake nodded. "We'll make it."

A smile cracked her lips. "Liar."

Jake opened his mouth but she shook her head.

"You got...chance without me...Go."

"Stop talking like that. I'm not leaving you, so just shut up. We'll get out of this together."

"One way...or other?" Megan asked with a slight grin.

Jake nodded back. "Stubborn, old coot."

Megan's smile got bigger. "Sure...Mr...Optimist." Her hands moved to feel her upper body. Her outer coat was still on. She patted the collar. Still intact. A larger smile formed on her face.

"What are you doing?"

"If...one of ours...mini-transmitter...sewed collar...my jacket." She arched as a lightning bolt of pain struck her leg from the bottom of her foot. "It only...beep... but if... Cowboy... around... he'll hear... He knows... Oh God... Jake!" She grabbed his arm as the pain got worse. She stifled a scream.

She barely felt the soft, gentle hands grip either side of her head, or the whispered, "I'm sorry, but you are going to live, my love." A kiss touched her lips.

Her head was twisted and blissful darkness swept over her.

***

Jake held her head, his forehead resting on hers. His eyes closed in heart aching pain as he had knocked her out. He felt for a pulse and it was there—weak and fast. He knew she was in shock, not to mention probably bleeding internally. He felt the tremors of her broken leg as he lay on top of her, shielding her from the downpour with his body. The last muscle spasm actually pulled the broken bones together. He heard the femur ends grinding and snapping.

The splint he'd made was simple—two branches bound by his belt, meant only to keep her leg straight. If he had the ability to stretch the leg, to hold the broken bones apart, the pain would be less, but he didn't have any way of doing that.

The best he could do was to knock her out. Besides, he knew she wouldn't be able to handle the movement of him carrying her. He knew that the jostling as he carried her would cause her even more pain.

Jake let go of her head and gently placed it back down. He took a breath. He was more than tired. He had numerous injuries, probably internal ones too. He shook his head of water and reaching out to a small shallow in the rock next to him, scooped up a small amount and took a drink.

Before moving her, he felt around her collar. *Damn. An emergency beeper radio. Very high tech. Very James Bond.*

Jake smiled through cracked and swollen lips. "You aren't cashing in, Little Lady. Not on my watch, even if I have to carry you kicking and screaming all the way down the mountain. I'll win that bet, so help me God."

With that, he pushed himself up with sore hands and arms. As gently as he could, he scooped her up into his arms and got her settled in a comfortable position. He shook his head again of the water raining on him.

Down.

Go down.

With a grim determination, he put one foot in front of the other. His mind was numb from the pain in his body and heart.

***

Megan's leg contracted again in his arms. He took another step then paused to lean on the hillside path he was following. Jake let out his breath, and took another deep one.

This was taking way too long.

Jake looked out at the bleak, almost nonexistent sunrise. The rain was still coming down in torrents. Shaking his head to clear the cold water, his eyes spied something dark only a few feet away tucked into the hillside.

Narrowing his eyes, he looked harder at it in the twilight of the rainy morning. A cave. Hefting her again in his arms, he stumbled toward it. The last hour or so he had been moving on pure adrenalin, not knowing or caring where he was walking, just as long as it was down. He needed to rest, preferably out of the rain.

He stepped into the semi-dry opening and gently laid his warm burden on the ground. Jake gave out a sigh of relief then stumbled to look around the small cave.

It was more of an indent, no animals, and small, only about six feet in depth and width. But it was dry—the wind blowing the rain in the opposite direction.

Jake stumbled back to Megan's side and checked her neck for a pulse. He knew that she was in grave danger. Her broken femur was grinding away as the broken ends rubbed together. And he worried about the blood vessels. If they were torn and she was bleeding into her leg or hip…

He shook his head. *Can't think that way. She'll make it.* He looked around again. If only he had someway to relieve the pressure of bone on bone, but there was nothing here.

As gently as he could, he laid her straight, elevated her feet on a small rock and lay down next to her. He pulled her into him and held on, trying to impart body heat, or as was the real case, to get body heat from her. She was hot, most likely a fever.

His eyes dimmed as he thought about the storm. It was here to stay for awhile. He figured all day. Maybe, just maybe, it would clear tonight, and if he could make it to the rendezvous, maybe Cowboy would be there.

He opened his eyes at the thought. *Cowboy won't be there. He's the leak. He knows we've been captured and probably dead.*

Jake thought about that. He shook his head. His gut couldn't get around the fact that Cowboy was the traitor. He would try for the pickup. It was on the way down anyway.

It wasn't like the al Qaeda guys were following them. The wind and rain would wash away any trace within minutes of their passing. He doubted even bloodhounds would be able to track them after this storm.

His last cognitive thought before he drifted off into numb sleep was about Megan. He would carry her through hell if need be.

***

A groan got his attention. He looked down at the body he was still carrying. Yes, she was coming around. This was not good. He gently but quickly laid her on the ground. He barely got her legs straight when she groaned into consciousness.

Jake moved to her head and tried for a smile. His face hurt worse than anything he'd experienced before. He hoped at least his eyes showed a smile, although deep inside he was worried, seriously worried about his wounded lover. "Hey. How're you doing?"

Megan looked up. He could tell she wasn't totally with it. Her eyes had a glazed look.

"Meg?"

"Jake." A whisper.

"Yeah. How are you doing?"

Megan smiled sickly. "Peachy. You?"

"More Applely for me," Jake said, trying to relieve the tension.

"Cold."

"What?"

"I'm cold."

Jake frowned. She had at least a 103 fever. It had kept him warm during his sleep and walk. He tried harder for a smile. "How's the leg?"

"Which one?"

"The right leg."

"Still broke. Thanks."

"For?"

"Resetting it again. The pain's almost gone."

Jake nodded even as his heart sank into his boots. She was in massive shock, her body starting to shut down. This was not good. He forced his smile to stay. "I told you, you aren't dying."

"My one time I'm wrong and you have to see it." Megan's eyes began to glaze over again. "Jake."

"Yeah?"

"Tell me a secret," Megan whispered.

"What?"

"You know about my secret life. Here, I'll tell you another secret, I'm scared of heights."

Jake chuckled. "I never would have guessed."

"Yeah. I hide it well. You?" Megan's eyes were closed and her voice got softer and softer.

He swallowed hard, knowing that she was slipping away. "Uh…"

"Come on. Won't tell anyone. Good at keeping secrets."

"Okay." He felt a slight flush rising to his face even though he knew that the blush would never show through the bruises and dried blood. "I, uh, I like bubble baths."

"No shit?"

"Yeah."

"Special Forces Hero likes to soak in a bubbly bath," Megan tried teasing. "Jake, I never said this before to anyone… I love you."

Jake's eyes filled with tears. "Yeah. I know. Just hang in there. We're almost to the rendezvous."

Megan mumbled something.

Jake reached out and felt for a pulse. Still there, but her neck was hotter than ever before. He lifted an eyelid but her eyes were glazed over and vacant.

"Tell Cowboy to light a fire under Famine, but to watch the collective. She's been sticking." Megan's voice drifted off then she was unconscious again.

"Just hold on," Jake said and with a deep breath. He looked around the area. He was only about a mile from the rendezvous.

The rain had stopped but the clouds were hanging tight. It was late afternoon, but he couldn't get a more precise time than that. The ground was slippery with mud. He had only to cut across a small valley to get to the other side, then get to a small grove of trees to be at the rendezvous. In reality, if any rescue showed up, even at this distance, he could probably flag them down. But he wanted to be near cover. If they had to stay the night, he wanted concealment.

Jake glanced behind him and up the mountain. He knew that the al Qaeda guys were probably on the hunt for them. And it wouldn't be long before they might pick up the trail, now that the rain wasn't washing their footprints away.

Still, he hoped that he had put enough distance between them. He glanced down at Megan again.

"Chief, if they find us... I won't let them hurt you again." He leaned over, gave her a kiss on the lips, then stood up.

Once more he got her settled into the crook of his arms and started walking. His eyes riveted on the other side of the valley, the trees, and his destination.

***

After getting Megan settled under a small tree near the edge of the small grove, Jake checked the area. There was no movement anywhere. He let out a soft sigh of relief. He could rest for a while.

He'd wait the night. *If no one comes by morning, and they probably won't, I'll start the walk out of the mountains.* He didn't have a hope in hell that either of them would make it, particularly Megan, but he would try.

Jake wiped the sweat off his forehead and realized that he had a fever too. Not surprising. He probably had internal injuries as well. He glanced down at Megan then settled his butt into the dirt near the base of the small tree and leaned back.

***

Jake woke with a start. Something wasn't right. His gut screamed at him. He always trusted his gut. His eyes panned the meadow area. Nothing. The sun was lower in the sky.

He berated himself for falling asleep then looked back at Megan. She had a sheen of sweat on her face, it was draining of color and whiter than ever. He cursed softly to himself as he caught movement out of the corner of his eye.

Slowly, he swiveled his head back to look at the meadow. He swept the far hillside again and this time found the movement on the hillside. Narrowing his eyes, he finally figured out what it was. A deer had just darted over the ridge.

A deer running scared.

Jake became more alert. Something had pushed the deer over the ridge. He waited but nothing showed itself. Slowly, he relaxed. Probably it was a natural predator.

He flexed his muscles to get them ready for the pain that would hit as soon as he moved. Then he painfully leaned over Megan's side. He felt for a pulse.

It was racing. And her skin was hot and clammy.

Damn.

He squatted down by her and sighed. He was fighting a losing battle. As much as he hated to admit that Megan had been right, she was dying. And there was nothing he could do for her. That tore at him the worst. He'd have to leave her body somewhere so when he came back he could find it. His heart was breaking.

With tears in his eyes, he went into survival mode, stripping her of the outer coat. Then he searched her pockets for anything of value that he could use. There was nothing.

He felt around the collar of the coat again but decided to leave it in tact in case something happened. The beeper was still well concealed. He put his face into the coat in desperation, hiding his grief.

He didn't want her to die. He had finally found someone he truly loved and loved him back, and now he had lost her. With a plop, he sat down on the ground and looked at Megan, tears streaming from his swollen eyes.

Jake grabbed her hand then leaned over and kissed her. "I'm sorry, Chief. I failed."

With a burst of anger, he tossed the coat away, grabbed Megan and pulled her onto his lap. He held her tightly to his chest, rocking and whispering to her. He poured out his soul sitting there, telling her things he could never otherwise admit.

A gunshot snapped his head up.

Jake quickly laid her down and moved cautiously past the tree. His eyes immediately moved to the ridge.

Two men were firing at another deer from the ridge. They were pointing at the carcass that had fallen farther down the mountainside. They were too far away to recognize, but he had a strong suspicion that they were with the group that had captured them. He watched them as they slowly topped the ridge, then after checking the area, headed to the fallen deer.

Jake cursed again and glanced back at Megan. There was no way, unless the guys left, that he was getting out of here carrying her. He might be able to scoot away by himself. He hurried to Megan's side, looking down at her. He started crying again.

"Guess it's time," his voice broke, "...to follow your orders... one last time, Chief." Jake squatted down by Megan and grabbed her head. He held it. *I can do this. It's for the best. She wants this. I can do it. I can do it.* But in his heart he knew this moment would haunt him the rest of his days.

Tears streamed out of his eyes. *I have to do this. It's the only way.* Anger suddenly burned in him. *I'll kill the leak, just like this Meg. I'll kill him too.* His training started to kick in. *Survival. Live. Anyway you can.* He adjusted his grip. *Survive for Megan. Do it for her. I love you.*

Jake took a deep breath, hardening his heart to what he had to do. He took another deep breath and tensed his muscles. He squeezed his eyes shut as he took his third deep breath.

A whirling noise sounded in the distance.

Jake opened his eyes, his ears straining to hear what had to be his imagination.

Whirling.

Jake released her head and sprang to the edge of the woods. He cocked his head again. Yes, there was the distinctive sound of a helicopter. His eyes panned the far hillside, but the al Qaeda guys apparently couldn't hear it yet. Jake turned back to look at Megan.

The coat. The transmitter.

He sprinted to the coat and literally tore the collar open. His eyes swung back to the meadow and the other guys on the side. Even as his hands worked the material away from the small device, he kept an eye on the al Qaeda guys. *If I can just get the helicopter's attention before the other guys see or hear...*

He saw their heads snap up and look at the ridge near him.

Jake looked down at his hands. *Concentrate on what you're doing.* He quickly had the small transmitter out of the collar and gave it a quick look; he started to assemble it. He'd seen an article on one of these in an instruction book during training. He barely remembered it, but his training came back instantly. Even if he hadn't seen the article, he could probably guess how to assemble it. As he got the pieces in order, he glanced at Megan.

Pale. No sweat.

"Stay with me, Chief. Help's on the way."

Jake tapped out an SOS on the small device, then the word 'Ghost.' He did it again even as the whirling sound of a Black Hawk became distinct.

He moved to the edge of the trees and watched as the helicopter topped the ridge and hovered. His eyes panned the opposite hill and saw the al Qaeda guys running toward his side of the valley.

Famine hovered.

Jake looked at it again as he tapped out the message again. He didn't want to run out and flag the chopper down because if he missed, the guys would be sure to see him. And it had been drilled into him in training; never expose yourself to the enemy unless rescue is waiting.

Still, Famine hovered.

Jake tossed the transmitter aside and grabbed Megan. *Screw normal procedure.* He was taking the chance of letting the enemy see him. As he reached the edge of the woods, the helicopter did a bob, then turned and headed away from the ridge top.

"No!" Jake yelled. He stopped at the edge of the woods, not quite clearing it. He put Megan down and grabbed the transmitter.

In that glance, he had seen that Cowboy was flying Famine. He tapped out the same message. "Come on Cowboy. Pick it up."

S-O-S G-H-O-S-T

S-O-S G-II-O-S-T

The helicopter disappeared from view and the whirling of the helicopter faded from hearing.

Jake sat down with a plop in the mud. He tried one more time.

S-O-S G-H-O-S-T

All of the fight went out of Jake. There was nothing left to do but put Megan out of her misery and high tail it out of here. He clenched his fists in anger.

With a broken heart, Jake bent over Megan again. This time he gripped her head and kissed her lips.

"I'm sorry, Chief."

He kissed her again and began tensing his muscles.

The whirling noise sounded again.

Jake's eyes sprung upward.

Famine was back.

Jake shoved the transmitter into his pocket, picked her up and stepped out from the woods. He heard shouts behind him from the other side of the small valley, but his eyes were on Famine.

The helicopter hovered on the ridge top as though waiting for some sign.

Jake began running toward the chopper.

Famine lifted up briefly then swung down and swooped toward them as Jake cleared the trees.

Jake smiled his first genuine smile in a long time.

A bullet hit near him, but he ignored it. He continued to run toward the quickly approaching chopper, his eyes taking in the fact that Cowboy was flying, alone.

Famine landed and Cowboy jumped out and opened the back door.

Jake could see him watching the fast approaching al Qaeda. Bullets hit around him and the chopper, but they were wild as the guys firing were running too.

Cowboy hopped back into the cockpit. The blades began to rotate faster, preparing for take off.

Jake expended one last burst of speed as he neared the aircraft. He reached it just as his energy ran out.

Literally tossing Megan inside, he jumped in and pounded on the wall separating him from the cockpit. He lay down next to Megan, breathing harder than he had ever done. His breath came in gasps as he tried to suck air into his mouth. The helicopter went airborne, without a second to lose.

Several bullets hit the helicopter. One passed so close to Jake's head that he heard the whiz. He stayed on the floor of the Black Hawk. Once the flight leveled out after erratic maneuvers to escape the bullets, he sat up and looked at Megan.

Somewhere in the running or jumping onto the chopper, he had moved her leg. It was once again at an odd angle. He straightened it out then got her comfortable. He reached into the first aid kit and pulled out the emergency blanket. Not that it would do any good but it felt right. He could do no more for her, so he sat back, taking a deep breath of relief.

A blinking light caught his eye. He reached up with a groan and grabbed the handset. "Yeah?"

"Hey. Uh… How uh… Meg looks bad."

Jake nodded, even though Cowboy couldn't see him. "Yeah."

"You okay, Cupcake?"

"No. We need a hospital. Like yesterday."

"Yeah, I gathered that pardner. Hold on. I'm goin' as fast as I can," Cowboy said.

"Thanks," Jake said as he slumped back down.

"For?"

"The pick up."

"That's my job."

Jake grimaced. Megan's suspicions were still running around his mind. Half of him thought that Cowboy was the leak and the other half was pleading to him that he wasn't. Just his presence here spoke of the fact that he wasn't. But. "Flying alone?"

"Had to. You guys were written off the other day. I hope you can give me a good reference, 'cause I was already fired. I kinda stole Famine from White

Pine," Cowboy said with a smile in his voice. "When Meg wakes up, I'll need her okey-dokey too."

Jake swung his eyes to her. Her color was tinged with gray. "If," he said, not keying the handset. Jake laid his head back and relaxed. Relief washed over him. His job was done. Now, if they got to the hospital in time, Megan might live.

"Hey Cupcake. Cupcake? Ya'all still with me?"

"Yeah." Jake blew out his breath.

"What tree did you hit?"

"Huh?"

"Your face. Man, someone did a number on you. What the hell happened pardner?"

"al Qaeda happened."

"Shit."

"Yeah." Jake grimaced. He wanted so much to confront Cowboy, but he knew he had to wait until they reached the hospital for Megan. His anger was like a volcano, so near the surface just waiting for a chance to explode.

Jake laid his head back and closed his eyes. He started to relax, which caused him to get drowsy; he felt the helicopter swivel to the side then float back the other way. Jake's eyes snapped open. He raised the hand set to his head. "What's up?"

There was no answer.

"Cowboy?"

"Minute." Came the answer. Then several muffled curse words. "We got a problem, Cupcake."

"Damn," Jake said keying the handset. "What?"

"Those al Qaeda boys shoot damn good."

"What?" Jake turned to look into the cockpit.

"One of them there bullets musta hit something vital. I'm getting' a rattle in the tail rotor. It's makin' the pedals spongy."

"And?" The aircraft slowed considerable and dropped lower to the ground. "Why are you slowing?"

"Can't push the steed."

Jake glanced at Megan. "Look Cowboy, you push this son of a bitch. Megan's dying. I don't care if you burn out the whole damn helicopter, just get us to the hospital."

"I'll try but…"

"But what?"

"If I lose the tail rotor, well, there ain't gonna be help for Megan then, 'cause pardner no one cares 'bout us," Cowboy said even as he increased speed a bit.

Jake cursed loudly. "Do your best."

"That I am."

They flew in silence for a few more minutes then the helicopter began to get unstable. Jake crawled over to Megan and strapped her in as best he could. He grabbed one of the helmets and pushed it on her head to protect her. Then he crawled back to where he had been and buckled himself in. He grabbed another helmet and put it on.

Jake heard cursing from Cowboy as he plugged in the helmet. "Anything I can do?"

"Pray."

Jake looked out the open door to the area where they were quickly descending. He noticed several houses a short distance away. His face scrunched up in puzzlement. These looked familiar. "Cowboy, where are we?"

Cowboy didn't answer as he fought the helicopter for control.

Suddenly, Jake recognized the valley. This was near where they had stopped the kidnapping of that Warlord's son. *What was his name? The village owed White Pine. Megan had said that.* "Cowboy, can you control it enough to land without crashing?"

"That's what I'm fuckin' trying to do."

Jake smiled. "Land as near to the village as possible. It's near the valley where we stopped the kidnapping."

"Can't guarantee that, but I'll give it…" Cowboy's voice drifted off as he again fought the almost spinning helicopter. "Just lost the tail rotor. Hold on. We goin' down."

The helicopter spun down.

Jake held on.

The ground rushed up at them, even as he heard Cowboy doing some creative swearing. The aircraft thudded into the wet field which used to contain poppies, then tilted to the side, blades digging into wet dirt, but it stopped moving.

Seconds seemed to stretch as Jake waited.

"Cupcake?"

"Still here. You okay?" he said, already unbuckling himself. He'd received a tremendous knock but the helmet had saved his head. Over all, he was unhurt by the crash.

"Yeah, sort of. Meg?"

Jake crawled over to her. He immediately felt for a pulse. "Still with us." He tore off her helmet and then his. As he slid out of the helicopter, he saw Cowboy trying to exit too. It looked like he was in pain as he shoved something into his pocket. He unbuckled Megan and hefted her once more in his sore, aching arms.

By the time Jake got completely out of the chopper, Cowboy was standing next to him. Cowboy had a stream of blood running down his head and he was holding his arm with his other one. He shook his head as he looked at Megan.

"Can you walk?" Jake asked even as he began moving toward the village.

"Yeah. I think." Cowboy pulled out a thermite grenade and after pulling the pin, tossed it into the cockpit. He hurried up to be near Jake. After a minute, there was an explosion. Neither of them flinched.

"Good. Do you know the language?"

Cowboy shook his head. "Megan did. Not me."

"Shit," Jake said. His eyes moved ahead to see that there were several men running toward them, each had a rifle. "Let's hope they still like us."

Cowboy walked beside the ex-military man. Soon the Afghans were within shouting distance. Two raised their rifles and pointed at the Americans. They yelled. The two groups stopped only feet apart.

Jake shook his head. "We helped you. We're from White Pine, we need help." He glanced down at Megan then back up. "Cowboy, put your arms up in surrender."

"Can't."

"Why?"

"I re-injured my shoulder in the crash."

"Re-injured?" Jake asked still eyeing the rifles and the yelling men.

"Long story."

Jake turned his attention back to the natives. He tried a smile. "Help us. Please. Help."

One of the slower running men stopped next to the older man obviously in charge of this group. Jake looked him in the eyes. It was the guy they had saved from being kidnapped, Abdul Jameel Daud. His mind jumped back to the moment that he was staring into the injured man's eyes. He tried the words that Megan had told him to tell Daud in the helicopter. They came out wrong even to his ears.

Abdul squinted at Jake with a cocked head. He stepped forward past the guns. "You. You help me."

Jake nodded. "Yes. We need help. Help us."

The Afghan turned and rattled off something to the other men. The rifles slowly lowered. Duad turned back to Jake. He held out his arms as though he didn't know what could be done.

"Do you have a car? To drive us back to Kabul."

"Kabul?" Abdul asked.

"Cowboy act as though you are driving." He adjusted Megan in his arms again, groaning softly in pain.

Cowboy complied with only one arm.

Abdul frowned and turned to the older gentlemen. They seemed to have similar facial features. Jake bet that they were father and son, or at least relatives. They argued for several minutes. Finally, the guy in charge said something to Jake.

Jake looked at the son for a translation.

The father nodded yes and motioned to one of the other guys who moved closer to Jake, suspiciously and slowly. He held out his arms for Megan.

Abdul pointed at Megan. "He help you. You hurt…" He motioned to his face. He then pointed at the guy, made a carrying motion and pointed back toward the village. Abdul made the sign for driving a car, then pointed at himself, then at the mountain separating them from the city.

Jake nodded in understanding and handed Megan to the other guy. They moved as quickly as possible to the village. One of the guys ran ahead and had a beat up truck waiting. Megan was laid in the back of the pickup. Jake crawled in next to her. A villager helped Cowboy in as Abdul and the one that carried Megan hopped in front.

The engine roared and they took off like a bee for the road. But it wasn't really a road. It was more like a wanna-be path, bumpy and full of ruts. Jake bounced next to Megan and closed his eyes.

"Cupcake…" Cowboy tapped him on the shoulder. "Hey, Cupcake, can I do anything?"

Jake sat up and nodded. When Cowboy moved closer to hear over the wind, Jake clenched his fist and smashed it into his face.

"What the fuck?" Cowboy sat up. Now his nose was bleeding and he had a split lip.

"You're lucky I'm injured or you'd have a broken jaw. When I'm better, I might beat you to death. So when we get back to civilization, I suggest you run fast and hard. And keep running," Jake said. "I haven't decided yet if I'll pursue you. If Megan dies, you can count on it."

Cowboy stared, dumbstruck. His hand was touching his lip. "What the… Some way to thank me for saving your ass."

"Save our ass?" Jake's anger got the best of him. "You betrayed our ass."

Cowboy's face got even more puzzled then a light seemed to go off. "Whoa, pardner! Back it up one step. I didn't compromise the rendezvous." He shook his head. He grabbed Jake's shirt and pulled him closer. "Listen and listen good, asshole. After I dropped the two of you off, I got back to the base. As I was heading toward the apartments, a sniper hit me in the shoulder."

Cowboy tore his shirt open and showed Jake the bandaged wound which had started bleeding again. The white bandage was soaked with blood.

"They also attacked the base with mortars. We lost ten people including Tiny and Bosser." Cowboy grimaced in pain. "At the hospital, I couldn't get Harding's attention, so I told Zarin, who visited me, to find him. She came back an hour later and said he was busy, what was the message, she would deliver it to him. I told her about the change in pick up. She left. The next day right after the scheduled pick up, I inquired about you guys. Turns out Harding sent another crew to the old rendezvous, the ones arranged by him. I finally got a hold of him and he told me that he had gotten a message minutes before that you two had been captured. I told him about Zarin." Cowboy took a deep breath.

Jake stared. It fit. He had seen Zarin reading some papers with Megan's handwriting and talking to someone on the phone right before the other loused up mission. He narrowed his one eye in thought; the other was swollen shut.

"Harding investigated. Turns out she was the leak. He told me that she's been taken care of, whatever that means, along with a couple of other people working in White Pine, including Kit the mechanic. He sabotaged the aircraft the other day. All four of them. And that bad oil line, when we first got here, was a deliberate attempt on our lives, too, but when Megan made him fly with us, he had to go back and affect a quick fix. Didn't work. Harding told me that. Turns out, Kit is married to Zarin. They're connected to al Qaeda somehow; Harding wasn't real specific with me. So as I sat in the hospital, I told Harding about the alternate pick ups. He shook his head. 'They're dead,' was all he said. I argued with him and he fired me on the spot. When I could walk, I stole Famine and headed out to try to find you guys. It was a long shot but something told me..." Cowboy stopped and hugged his side in pain.

Jake held out his hand. "I believe you. Sorry."

"Shit," Cowboy said, with a smile. "Iffan a person can't take a little love tap every now and again." Cowboy touched his lip and nose then shook Jake's hand. His eyes panned to the pale Megan. "Is she that bad?"

"She's dying."

"Damn."

"Yeah." Jake lay down next to her and pulled her into him for body heat and covered them up with the emergency blanket. "She won't make this trip."

Cowboy patted Jake on the shoulder. "She's a fighter."

"She already gave up."

Cowboy frowned, then once more patted Jake's shoulder. "Don't ya'll give up on her, pardner."

Jake nodded, giving her a hug. He laid his head down next to her head and closed his eyes. It was the last thing he remembered.

***

Jake jerked awake. He was lying in a bed. Bandages were holding him together. And his stomach hurt. His head hurt. Hell, everywhere hurt. He opened his eyes and saw that he was in the hospital. As he moved to sit up, he groaned in pain and immediately decided he wouldn't try that again for a while.

A female face appeared over his head. "Good morning, Mr. McGrew. How are we today?"

Jake opened his eyes and looked at her. She was an American. He couldn't remember any female nurses at the Army base hospital in Afghanistan. He glanced around. "I hurt. Where am I?"

"Landstuhl Army Hospital."

"In Germany?"

"Yes." She stuck an instrument into his ear then pulled it away. She felt for a pulse next. "All back to normal. How do you feel?"

"Like shit. How's Megan?"

"Who?"

"Megan Cartwright. She would have come in with me. She was gravely injured. How is she?" Jake asked. He continued to look around confused.

The nurse shook her head. "You came in alone. You were air lifted from Kabul to us. There was no one else on the aircraft. I need to know how your stomach feels. Does it hurt? Your surgery went well, and the doctor will be in soon."

"Surgery?" Jake asked. "What day is it?"

"Friday the eighteenth."

"Friday? Are you sure?"

"Yes, I'm sure." A smile lit her face.

"What day did I come in here?"

"Yesterday."

"Surgery?"

"Yes, Mr. McGrew. You were stabilized at the military base in Kabul then transferred as I just told you. You'll be here at least two weeks, if not more. At some point, they plan on doing reconstructive surgery on your face. The doctor will talk to you about that. Please rest." She turned and walked out.

Jake tried to absorb the information. He remembered falling asleep in the truck with Megan, then nothing. He did have a few vague images of doctors, but nothing substantial. Jake shook his head.

He was missing three days that he couldn't account for. Cowboy had picked them up on Monday afternoon. He figured the drive back to civilization took the rest of the day. Then nothing. Thursday he'd been flown into Germany. *What the hell had happened?*

CHAPTER 15

Three months later Jake stepped out of a yellow, rented Mustang and quietly closed the door. He looked around.

The house he had driven up to was at the end of a road. It was small, yet impressive, with three sides facing the ocean. The other houses were either on canals or also had back yards near the ocean, but this house was situated right at the end of the cul-de-sac. And the other houses were quite a distance from it.

The gates on the drive were standing open and he had slowly driven in to park right in front of the white house with light yellow trim. The bungalow was surrounded by trees native to the Florida Keys.

The house was in a middle Key, one of the biggest and therefore also one of the quieter Florida Keys. And this part was even more quiet, especially since tourist season was still months away.

He glanced at the house again. Then taking a deep breath, walked up to the house and rang the bell.

The front door was open, but the screen was closed. He peeked inside to see what had to be a sort of sitting room—two sofas, a chair and a small fireplace. Tastefully decorated. More masculine than feminine. The art on the walls was tasteful and subdued. Nothing flashy in this room. Very conservative.

And there was no answer to the ring. He rang again and waited. Still no answer. As he stood there in the quiet, he heard a whining noise. Barely audible.

Wheeeeeeeeeeeee.

Jake scrunched up his face. *What is that?* He cocked his head to listen and sure enough he heard it again. It sounded like it was coming from the back yard. He tried the screen door, but it was locked. With a little bit of apprehension, he left the porch and rounded the house. He picked his way through the shrubbery and finally made it to the back yard.

Jake stopped at the corner of the yard. His eyes panned the area trying to find out where the whine was coming from. Immediately he saw the source of the noise.

A radio-controlled helicopter was flying around the back yard. It went in and out of trees then out over the water. Jake smiled and stuck his hands into the pockets of his Bermuda shorts.

The small helicopter dipped then hovered over the water. With blinding speed, it flew back and buzzed the shore, then flew straight up. As it gained altitude it did a flip and flew inverted, then flipped back over and did a loop-d-loop. It shot back out over the water. It sputtered once, then the helicopter was quickly brought back to shore. It landed gracefully on a small covered patio several yards off the back of the house.

Jake stepped out from the side of the house to see, sitting in a lounge chair, the pilot of the radio aircraft.

Megan.

She fiddled with the radio in her hand, her crutches lying on the ground next to the chair. Her right leg, still in a brace, was laid out in front of her on the lounge chair.

Jake's heart beat faster. *God, she looks good. No, she looks even more gorgeous than ever.* He stared, wanting to soak her in before she knew he was there.

"Don't just stand there, Cupcake," Megan called over her shoulder. "Shake a leg."

Jake chuckled. He slowly advanced toward her, hands still in his pockets. He didn't say anything until he was standing next to her chair. "Chief."

Megan looked up, gave him a slight smile and motioned to the chair next to her. "Sit, if you want."

Jake sat. "You look good."

A smile cracked her lips as she pulled the helicopter next to her and began fiddling with it. "Yeah, same to you. Looks like the plastic surgery went well. They repaired your face pretty good. I was wondering about that."

Jake watched her work on the mini-helicopter. Finally, she refueled the little Bird and started it up. Once more she sent it airborne.

Jake smiled and relaxed. This was nice, sitting here with her with no one watching. He scooted the chair into a more comfortable position, watching her fly. She seemed as good with the miniature version as she did with the full-scale version.

"Want to try it?" Megan asked, concentrating on the craft.

"No. Thanks," Jake said. "You're pretty good."

Megan quickly brought it in for a hover. She turned to Jake and smiled. "Thanks. It just takes practice."

Their eyes locked with an intense stare. Megan broke the look. "Are you sure you don't want to try it?"

"Yeah, no thanks." He smiled.

She quickly brought the still running helicopter next to her then shut it down. Megan laid the transmitter on the table next to her and turned her attention to Jake.

"How's the leg?"

Megan shrugged. "Two surgeries. Maybe another coming up. It depends on how it heals. I have physical therapy every day. I'll probably limp for life." She looked out over the ocean then back at him. "Thanks."

"Is it getting any easier?" Jake's smile increased as he remembered the other times they had similar conversations.

"Not at all." Megan smiled back. "Really, you saved my life. I owe you."

Jake shook his head. "You've saved mine before with your skills. We're even."

Megan nodded, accepting the thanks.

"However..." Jake began then stopped. "Why did you disappear?"

Megan looked down at her hands. After studying them for a few seconds, she finally looked up at him. "SOP, standard operating procedure. When an operative is gravely injured, the operative is whisked away to a non-disclosed location for the operative's safety. After he or she has recovered... well, then come the debriefings."

"Cowboy was in Italy. I was in Germany. You were somewhere else. Is that SOP?"

Megan nodded.

"No one would tell me anything, even if you were alive. SOP?"

Megan nodded again.

"That's bullshit."

Megan just smiled, but it quickly faded. "Yeah. How did you find me?"

Now it was Jake's turn to grin. "I tracked down Cowboy. He mentioned you said one time that your Dad used to own a house in the Keys. Took a little bit of work to find it, but I did."

Megan didn't change her expression.

Jake got more serious. "Then after I got to Florida, I got a visitor."

"Harding." It wasn't a question.

"Harding." Jake nodded. "He apparently has been following me or having me followed or something. He asked what I was doing here. He didn't buy the 'on vacation' spiel. I asked him point blank if you were here at the house."

"And?"

"He wouldn't answer me at first. He wanted to know my reason and intentions."

Megan scooted nervously in her chair. "What did you say?"

"That I intended to find you and if you weren't here, I'd track you down sometime in the future, but rest assured I would find you. No matter how hard you tried to hide from me."

"I'm not hiding."

"Yes you are, don't lie to me. You're a crappy liar. Even Cowboy couldn't find you or find out anything about you, except for that one note you sent him."

"I'm not hiding."

"Then tell me what you call it?"

Megan looked down at her hands and cleared her throat. "It's called trying to make a decision." She looked at Jake, but he didn't say anything. "I have to decide if I'm staying in or getting out."

"And your decision?"

Megan shook her head. "I haven't made it yet."

"So why not communicate with Cowboy or me?"

Megan shrugged. "It's the way I am. Live with it."

Jake leaned forward on his chair bringing him closer to Megan. "What about what happened in the mountains?"

"When?"

Jake sighed. "What happened between us?"

Megan shrugged.

"Do you still feel the same way?"

"I don't know."

Jake leaned back, smiling. "Crappy liar."

Megan didn't answer.

"How did you know I was here?" Jake pointed at the corner of the house.

Megan smiled. "I'm a spy, Cupcake. It's what I do for a living. My gate is monitored." She pointed to a covered item that at first glance looked like a gas grill. It was a monitor. "Besides, Harding told me you were in the area. I figured you'd come, so I opened the gates for you."

"And?"

"What do you want from me, Jake?"

"You owe me."

Megan scrunched up her face in question. "Owe you? You just said we were even."

Jake shook his head and smiled a wry grin. "Our bet."

"Bet?" Megan asked, momentarily puzzled then her eyes widened. "Crap."

"Thought I forget about that one, huh?"

Megan shook her head. "A bet made in that sort of situation is null and void."

"Bullshit."

Megan sighed. "Yeah. Okay. You got me."

"Besides," Jake said, reaching into his pocket. He pulled out a small, red silken wrapped package. He hefted it once then handed it to her. "I got you this."

Megan looked at it suspiciously. "What is it?"

"Just open it."

Megan slowly unwrapped it. As the bundle unrolled, she gasped at the beautiful, blue-beaded bracelet. Her eyes softened and she looked at Jake. "What's this for? It's beautiful."

"It reminded me of you. I bought it the day I knocked you down on the street dressed as a man. Put it on."

"Why?"

"Why did I buy it for you?" He waited to see her nod as she tried on the bracelet. It looked lovely on her as he suspected it would. "I don't know. I guess even then I knew I loved you." Jake saw a strange look flash on her face. He leaned back and stared at the uncomfortable lady sitting next to him. He bet if she didn't have the brace she would have sprinted away from him. "Why are you running?"

"Running?"

"From me. Us."

"I'm not running—"

"Yes, you are. Fast and hard."

Megan picked up her crutches and with a grunt stood up. She hobbled to the edge of the patio and looked out over the ocean. The water lapped in soft, gentle waves. The sea gulls screamed in the distance.

Jake stood and stepped in front of her, looking down into her eyes.

She glanced away.

"You're scared."

"Am not."

"Are too." Jake lowered his voice. "Am I that scary, Chief?"

"It's not you." Megan sighed.

"I know."

"Damn it, Jake. You are the most..."

Jake grabbed her and laid a kiss on her lips. When he let her come up for air, he gave her a huge smile. "I'm the most what?"

"Damn you."

"You owe me one night."

"Damn you."

"You already said that." The smile was almost breaking Jake's face.

"Shut up." She stared out at the ocean.

Jake reached out and tipped her head up to look at him. "Well?"

"Well, what?"

"What's your decision?"

"I told you..."

"Not about your job. About us." Jake still held her chin.

She pushed his hand away and then went back to holding the crutches. She looked back out at the ocean to his side. Her eyes slid back to his.

Jake smiled again, seeing the look in her eyes. "That's what I thought."

"I have to warn you, I'm not easy to be with."

"I already know that."

"I uh… I uh… I'm not that good with relationships…"

"Stubborn old coot," Jake said softly as he leaned in to give her a gentle and smooth kiss.

Megan grabbed his head, holding the crutches with her armpits. She kissed him with a passion that he hadn't felt from a woman in ages.

Jake reached behind her and pulled her into him, then took control of the kissing. He wanted to explore every cell, to know every part of her body, then start over again.

Gently, he pulled the crutches out and tossed them to the ground, all the while still kissing her. His hands traced her face then through her hair. In a sudden move, he stopped kissing her, reached down and swept her off her feet. He cradled her in his arms.

"What the fu…"

"Shhh," Jake said with a smile. "I carried you this way for over a day while I was injured. I think I can manage to get you into the house without dropping you." He gave her another kiss as he began walking toward the back porch.

He stopped once he reached the door. He looked Megan in the eyes. "The first time I met you, you saved me. You rescued me from a desperate situation. I'm returning the favor. I'm going to turn your 'desperate situation' into a reason for both of us to find love. Is that okay with you, Chief?" He softened the last word as he had been lately.

Megan smiled as she reached for the door handle. Swinging the door open, she looked at Jake. "I can't wait to see what sort of reaction I'll get out of you this time, Cupcake."

Dedication

Inspiration for stories can come from anywhere. This one came from a photograph that was part of a PowerPoint presentation to my writer's group by a Major in the Army who had just returned from Afghanistan. I don't remember his name but thank you anyway.

I'd also like to thank William 'Mud' MacIntire and Mark Doellman, both former military, who were indispensable in helping me with information on helicopters and keeping the helicopters 'real.' Thanks to Ray Ellis, Cheryl L. Maude, and Ruth Seydlitz, my writer's critique group, for keeping me 'real.'

And, as always, thanks to my family.